Sit, Stay, Slay

Sit, Stay, Slay

Linda O. Johnston

LARGE PRINT

This large print edition published in 2005 by
RB Large Print
A division of Recorded Books
A Haights Cross Communications Company
270 Skipjack Road
Prince Frederick, MD 20678

Published by arrangement with Penguin Putnam, Inc.

This book is a work of fiction. Names, characters, places and incidents either are
products of the author's imagination or are used fictitiously. Any resemblance to
actual events or locales or persons, living or dead, is entirely coincidental.

Publisher's Cataloging In Publication Data
(Prepared by Donohue Group, Inc.)

Johnston, Linda O.
  Sit, stay, slay / Linda O. Johnston.

  p. (large print) ; cm.

  ISBN: 1-4193-3400-X

1. Pet sitting—Fiction. 2. Large type books. 3. Mystery fiction. I. Title.

PS3610.O356 S58 2005b
813/.6

Printed in the United States of America

**This Large Print Book carries the
Seal of Approval of N.A.V.H.**

CHAPTER 1

I stood across the two-lane, twisting street staring at my house.

Up in the part of the Hollywood Hills overlooking the San Fernando Valley, it was a sprawling chateau behind iron gates that gave passersby a tantalizing glimpse of decadent luxury.

Lord, how I loved that place!

The lump in my throat might as well have been some of the expensive fertilized soil my gardeners used on the lushly tropical grounds; it tasted like shit, and I could hardly swallow around it. The new people were moving in that day.

My unwelcome renters. Well, no. The rent they were to shell out was very welcome. With it I could pay the hefty mortgage so the house could stay in my name. For now.

A tug at my arm nearly made me jump. "Lexie, no."

My voice reminded me of the house: It was like someone else's. I'd always projected self-confidence in my tone. It gave me an edge over less-assured litigators.

Now, I had no confidence at all.

How could I? I was jobless, careerless, and nearly broke.

But Lexie, my tricolor Cavalier King Charles spaniel, didn't understand that. Standing so near the place she'd ruled as top dog for the two years she'd owned me, she tugged on her leash, telling me she wanted to go inside for a biscuit.

"Okay," I said. It was time for us both to get used to the reality of our new lives.

I pushed the button on the control in my hand, and we walked through the front gate as it opened.

"Hi," I said as someone approached us from the house. My house.

It was Charlotte LaVerne, one of my tenants. An alumnus of one of TV's reality shows, she'd been a bachelorette, an idol, or a survivor, I wasn't sure which, but her face had been plastered on every tabloid in town. There must have been money in it, whatever she'd done, because she hadn't blinked when I'd named the rent I wanted. Or when I told her she'd need to pay for the gardeners if she wanted the grounds to remain pretty and pruned.

Her housemate or fiancé or stud—her business, not mine—was a hunk-and-a-half named Yul Silva, who probably saved all his speaking for acting auditions, since I hadn't heard him utter more than three words strung together at a time.

Charlotte, all five-foot-ten of her, had a long, black braid down her back and the whitest, toothiest smile I'd ever seen. Her blue jeans were snug, her frilly shirt bared her midriff. She considered herself best

2

of friends with everyone in the world, including me. "Oh, hi, Kendra," she bubbled, making a beeline for me as if she intended to give me a hug.

Lexie lunged at her.

Cavaliers love people. Sure, they're territorial and protective and all that. They're *dogs*. But they're lovable dogs who crave being adored. When Lexie lunges, it's because she thinks someone else is stealing her sole prerogative as the center of attention.

Charlotte gasped and moved back, nearly tripping. And no wonder—she wore strappy sandals on three inch heels, as if she needed the extra height. This was her moving day, yet she was dressed as if a camera crew were about to swing a van into the driveway. Lord, I hoped not. I'd had more than enough media meddling.

I was in jeans, too. Comfortable ones. And a pair of white walking shoes. The plain black short-sleeved T-shirt I wore covered every inch it should. I grabbed for Charlotte, steadying her, while at the same time using my other arm to tighten Lexie's leash. "Lexie," I scolded, "bad dog." She sat immediately and looked at me as if I had slapped her upside the head. I wanted to kneel and comfort her, but that was a good way to lose a tenant before she'd even moved in. "Sorry, Charlotte."

"No harm done." But she slanted hard blue eyes toward Lexie. "She isn't ever loose in the yard, is she?"

Of course she was, *was* being the operative word.

While Charlotte and her *Playgirl* centerfold were in residence, I'd have to curb Lexie.

"I'll keep her with me, don't worry."

"Hmmm," Charlotte said. And then she flashed her white teeth at me again. "Well, the movers are set to arrive any minute with my things."

My cue. "Anything I can do to help?" *No, no, no,* I prayed.

"No thanks. Yul's on his way, and the movers will do the rest."

To let this woman and her pet hunk take over my home . . .

How could I even pretend to be best friends with someone who hated dogs?

"Well, good luck," I said vaguely, leading Lexie down the driveway to the back of my estate, to what was to have been the maid's quarters, if I'd had a maid. At least I hadn't had to include maid services in the lease, for though I didn't know what I was going to do to support Lexie and myself for now, becoming a housekeeper, especially to Charlotte and her beefcake, was as appealing as driving a garbage truck.

The silver BMW parked beside the garage was nine years old—and mine. I put the gate control inside, then patted it reassuringly on the hood. Before, I'd been waiting for the right time to replace it, but since it had been the prize I'd awarded myself for winning my first big case, sentiment had won over practicality. Now, that was a good thing. Its Blue Book value wasn't bad for a car its age, but not high enough for me to sell. The proceeds would have been a drop in the very deep bucket of my debts resolved by cents on the dollar in my newly discharged bankruptcy. With all the hearings, proceedings, and negotiations, I'd managed to keep the car. And the house.

But little else. Certainly not my pride.

Even so, we would survive, Lexie and I. Although just then, as we mounted the steep steps to our one-bedroom apartment over the garage, I wasn't sure how.

I heard the moving truck pull up to the driveway and pushed down a slat of my front room's mini-blinds to look out.

In another minute, once Charlotte had flicked the security button to open the gate again, the van would pull in, trapping the Beamer where it was. Trapping *me*.

"C'mon, Lexie," I said, grabbing her leash and my large purse. "We're going out."

Her fluffy white and black tail wagged, and she grinned as I opened the apartment door. Tricolor Cavaliers are mostly black and white, with red trim here and there. They have expressive red eyebrows, and I swear she raised them as I opened the door.

A minute later, the Beamer leapt through the gate, us in it, just in time. I watched through the rearview mirror as the truck usurped the rest of the driveway.

"Close one," I said. Lexie, sniffing out the passenger

5

window that I'd cracked open for her, was too busy to respond.

I turned downhill, away from Mulholland Drive, with no destination in mind. The story of my life just then . . .

Nope, I'd promised myself I wouldn't get maudlin, no matter what.

I didn't consciously head there, but I wasn't particularly surprised when, a short while later, I found myself in front of the Doggy Indulgence Day Resort, on Ventura Boulevard, on the Valley side of the hill.

"Don't get too excited, Lexie," I told my dog, who was frantically scrambling on my lap to let me know she wanted out of the car. She knew where we were. "We're just going to say hello, then leave."

We caught Darryl Nestler cleaning an accident left by one of his charges as he knelt on the otherwise shining pine-look linoleum floor. He drew his lanky body up to standing and smiled behind his wire-framed glasses. "Kendra, good to see you." He stooped again and gave Lexie a pat. "You, too, girl."

Darryl was maybe half a foot taller than my five-five, with clean-cut short brown hair, and all-American faded blue jeans. One of his usual Henley-style green knit shirts hugged his skinny shoulders, sporting a Doggy Indulgence Day Resort logo on the breast.

"You leaving Lexie here today?" he asked.

I looked down at the dog in question. She sat beside me, a small, alert bundle of well-brushed fur, looking at the other animals in the large room with rapt attention. Lexie knew better than to bark at the beagles growling over a ball or lunge at the schnauzers sleeping on the doggy daybed. I'd taught her manners, but I knew she wanted to run with the pack.

"No, she won't be hanging out here for a while." I didn't need to tell him I couldn't afford his prices now. Maybe not ever again.

"Oh," he said. "Sorry to hear that." He offered to let Lexie come anyway, but the idea of getting something for nothing, even when I knew it was meant with the best of intentions, still smacked of charity to me. And I hadn't sunk that far. Yet. "Everything okay?"

"Sure, except that I've been displaced from my house by a Hollywood wannabe and her glamour boy."

He grinned. "Your new tenants?"

"Yeah. And she doesn't even like dogs."

"Tough break," he said sympathetically. In the best sense, Darryl's eyes reminded me of a dog's. They were brown, glistening, and very, very sincere. Darryl was different from the men I met in my profession. Despite being the alpha male here, leader of the pack of pups in his charge, he was a kind human being. He didn't act all mean and macho, like he had to assert his masculinity at least once an hour.

7

Which was probably why he wasn't married. I didn't think he was gay—not that it mattered to me—because he'd jokingly asked me to fix him up with one of my girlfriends once.

It was also why I'd allowed myself to confide in him now and then, when I'd felt so miserable that I thought I'd burst if I couldn't talk to someone.

As a result, Darryl was one of the few people who'd been treated to a selective digest of my story without being involved in its sickening plot.

The entire city of Los Angeles had heard more than they ever wanted to, thanks to the obsessed media.

"Well, I hope the new tenants work out," Darryl finished. He glanced down at his watch. "Oh, damn."

"Everything okay, Darryl?"

"What? Oh, yeah. Sorry, Kendra. I've just got to . . ." He didn't complete his comment but headed toward one of the attendants, a college student who worked at the spa on the days she didn't have classes. "Julie, what about you?" he asked. "Any chance you could help me out here?"

"I just can't, Darryl. I'm sorry, but I've got exams coming up. I live near campus and I need to stay there."

"Right. Fine." He didn't look at all as if it were fine. "Damn," he muttered under his breath. His mouth was a narrow line of anger.

"What's wrong?" I asked him.

"Not a damn thing," he snapped. I blinked at

him. Darryl never snapped. "Sorry, Kendra." He walked away, toward his office.

I drew in my breath, inhaling the familiar aroma of urine overlaid with a cleaner that was *supposed* to neutralize urine. Darryl had a lot of dogs whose training was imperfect. He was patient with them. At his rates, he could afford to be.

But even at his rates, he had a full house. The front room was large, with different doggy zones, from a sitting area with human furniture to a fenced-in pen containing the best canine toys. A couple of his other employees fussed over the numerous clientele, petting them, fawning over them, and stepping in to quell the frequent growl-filled quarrel. Things looked under control.

But something was obviously eating at him. And after all he'd done for me, the least I could do was find out what it was.

Since I'd be here a few minutes longer, I released Lexie from her leash. With a grateful look, she loped toward her favorite corner, right up onto the ragged sofa where a couple of other dogs raised sleepy heads to see who'd disturbed them. Run with the pack? Heck, what she wanted now was to sack out with them.

In Darryl's office, I sat on the plush chair in front of his cluttered desk. He was already seated behind it and looked as pleased about my presence as the other dogs on Lexie's sofa had been about hers.

"My turn," I said. "I can be a good listener,

too, if I can't keep your attention focused on my problems." I raised my eyebrows hopefully.

He laughed. "Nope, I've got my own problem today. Not as juicy as yours, but I need to deal with it."

"What's wrong?"

"Actually, it's one of my clients. He's got the problem, and he's offered a big bonus if I can help him out. Plus, it's a matter of honor, since I kind of promised to fix things for him. But all the dog-sitters I know are booked up or out of town. He needs someone starting tomorrow, someone who'll stay at his place and take care of his Akita and his house. And . . ." Darryl broke off and eyed me speculatively. "Tell me again about your new tenants."

I didn't follow the segue, but I bit, describing Charlotte—the reality TV graduate, and her too-zealous embracing of everyone around her—and her muscle-bound boyfriend Yul. It sounded silly as I told it, and yet, seeing them in my house . . . it was painful, damn it.

"It'll be hard for a while, won't it, seeing them take over your house?" Darryl always had been adept at reading my thoughts and reflecting them back in a way that showed he understood.

"You got it." I stayed flip, despite the ache I felt deep down. "I love that place, Darryl. I had to sell off most of my good furniture, everything of value, but it's still mine."

"And the bank's?" He didn't wait for my irritated

nod. "Are you moved into the space over the garage?"

He made it sound as if I'd decided to live in some unfinished attic, not a reasonably nice one-bedroom apartment. I'd get used to it. This particular apartment overlooked not only my house, but also the swimming pool I'd used for workouts every day. Both would be off-limits to me now, per the lease.

And Charlotte had oohed and aahed over the surrounding garden area, about how she couldn't wait to throw one of her big bashes there. I'd get to watch from my perch over the garage. Not that I'd want to join in with Charlotte's Hollywood hopefuls.

"Yes, we're moved in," I said as brightly as I could muster.

"How is Lexie with the tenants?"

"She's fine. It's the tenants who are the pits." I sighed. "I may have to put up a fence for Lexie to have room to run."

"You know, Kendra, this new client of mine has a nice house in the flats of the Valley. A full yard that's fenced, and his Akita has the run of it. Name of Odin. I don't think you've met Odin, since he's only come in a few times while you were . . ."

"Busy with my disintegrating life," I finished.

"Right. But he's an energetic and smart sweetheart. I'll bet he and Lexie would get along just fine."

I'm not usually obtuse, but I only just got where this conversation was going.

11

"You're not hinting that I should consider your dog-sitting assignment, are you, Darryl?"

"Why not?" he countered. "You'd be out of your apartment while the new tenants settle in. The place where you'd be staying is a nice one, and you're not otherwise employed right now." He glanced at me, looking a little abashed that he'd reminded me. But, hey, it was the truth.

"How much does it pay?" As if I cared.

"Fifty dollars a day." He said it as if he'd offered a million bucks. "Plus room and board. The guy's desperate."

Fifty dollars. Let's see. When I was working for my former law firm, that would have bought a client about ten minutes of my time. But that was before my license to practice law had been suspended. Before I'd resigned from the firm.

Still . . . The idea of not being at my new digs for a while, not having to deal with my dear friend and tenant Charlotte and her boytoy Yul—that interested me.

And fifty dollars plus room and board had its appeal to a lawyer who now earned nothing.

"What about Lexie?" I asked.

Was I really considering this? Darryl must have thought so, because for the first time since I'd gotten there his shoulders stopped slumping. "The guy understands that sitters sometimes bring their pets along when they stay at someone's house."

"Tell me about your client. What kind of work is he in?" If he was a lawyer, all bets were off.

It was even worse. "He's in the security business, I think. Maybe a P.I."

"Sorry, Darryl. You'd better find someone else."

"Kendra," Darryl said again, "we're friends, aren't we?"

Damn. If he started this kind of thing, I might get maudlin after all and give in. I gave a reluctant nod.

"It's a win-win-win situation. Really. You, the client, and me." He reached for the phone, then glanced back at me. "And I'm not kidding. The guy—Jeff Hubbard—is really desperate for a live-in dog-sitter. It'll be great. Trust me."

Of course I knew that when anyone, even Darryl, said "Trust me," it meant trouble.

CHAPTER 2

"Hi, I'm Kendra Ballantyne."

"Come in. I'm Jeff Hubbard." He motioned me inside his house.

He was about six feet tall, with stern eyebrows and an angular face. Nice-looking guy. He wore a rumpled white cotton shirt tucked into khakis, and he studied me as I edged past him through the door. I felt my face redden.

Not even once during the numerous occasions I'd appeared before Judge Baird Roehmann—a would-be friend who considered himself God incarnate on the bench—had I felt this nervous.

Hey, it wasn't as if I really wanted this job . . . was it?

I'd left Lexie out in my car for now. Canine introductions could come later. I heard a dog bark somewhere in the house, though. Its muffled voice was an octave or more deeper than Lexie's. The Akita was probably eager to learn who'd dared to ring the doorbell. Or maybe he was hungry. For human flesh.

What did I know about Akitas? What was I doing here?

You're exploring options, I reminded myself. *Stop sniveling.*

I hadn't gone home, such as it was, to change, so I was still wearing my T-shirt and jeans. That was fine for a potential dog-sitter's garb, even if it wasn't exactly a lawyer uniform. But Jeff Hubbard didn't have to know of my former life.

The house was nondescript inside and out. It was a pseudo-Mexican ranch-style house in the flats north of Ventura Boulevard in Sherman Oaks. The walls were textured beige, decorated only with wrought-iron sconces bearing unlit light bulbs. My walking shoes made no noise on the hardwood floors.

"Why don't you go in there?" Jeff pointed to a large room off to our right. I walked down a couple of steps into the sunken living room, whose focal point was a huge stone fireplace. Around it, on a bright, southwestern-style area rug, were a couple of chairs and a grouping of white sectional sofa pieces around a coffee table that was a polished portion of rough-hewn log.

Then there was the wide-screen TV and whole wall of sound equipment.

The place smelled as if a fire had been lit recently. I inhaled the scent of burned eucalyptus.

"Have a seat." Jeff gestured toward the sofa. He sat opposite me in a chair. "So, Darryl told you about my dilemma?"

"You need a pet-sitter."

He nodded. "Someone with experience. References. You know."

I did indeed know. I squirmed under his narrowed blue eyes. "I . . . well, I have a dog of my own, so I'm experienced in taking care of pets. I own a house"—more or less—"so I know how to take care of one—you know, keep the plants watered, the—"

"I know who you are, Kendra Ballantyne."

Shit. Why hadn't he spared us both this uncomfortable moment by just telling Darryl to take his suggestion and shove it? I started to rise. "Sorry for taking up your time." I tried so damned hard to slip a litigator's frostiness into my voice, but it didn't work. It was too quiet, and there was a woefulness to it that I hoped he didn't hear.

"Please, sit." Maybe I imagined the softening of his stern glare. Maybe I was just being naively optimistic. "Did Darryl tell you anything about me?"

I didn't sit. "He said you're in the security business. A detective."

"And what kind of a detective would I be if I didn't check the background of someone I considered hiring to watch my most valuable stuff?"

I gave a wry smile. "A pretty bad one."

"Exactly. So, although it was damn quick, I took a look. I know you're the Kendra Ballantyne who got in trouble at your law firm for leaking a confidential memo to the other side in a big case."

16

Bile rose into my throat, and I drew myself up righteously. "*Allegedly* leaking. It was a lie. I *didn't* sabotage my own case."

Jeff's careless lift of a shoulder told me he'd read otherwise. According to the allegations against me, I'd been guilty of arrogance, attitude, and a big, fat argument with John Germane, the martyred CEO of the company that was my client.

I *had* argued with the scheming and supercilious Germane. As to the rest, if I'd ever had attitude, by now it had been humbled right out of me.

"There was a break-in," I continued.

"Right." He didn't put the usual sarcastic spin to the word, but I knew he was just humoring me.

The prevalent theory, reported in the media, was that I had manufactured evidence of the burglary after the fact. The truth was that other evidence appeared to have been manufactured against *me*.

"And you had no idea," he continued, "that the leak would cause a mistrial in the case after you'd all but beaten the other side's pants off?"

I'd done that, the theory went, as revenge against Germane for telling my partners to remove me from the case at the last minute so I wouldn't get the credit and kudos for the win. If it cost his company megabucks, my inflated ego would have been assuaged.

Or maybe my motive had been less obscure, suggesting another popular hypothesis: I'd simply taken a bribe from the plaintiff to turn over the memo. Germane had heard about it, and *that* was why we'd fought and he wanted me off the case. Never mind that I didn't need the money—not then, when I'd been riding high. Or that no amount of money could have convinced me to do what I'd been accused of. Or that said plaintiff was insane.

"Look, Mr. Hubbard—"

He ignored my rising fury. "And you didn't know that something in that memo would make the plaintiff so enraged that she'd shoot Germane?"

"How the hell would I have known that?"

I was halfway out of his living room before he blocked me. "My point exactly. How the hell would you have known?"

I blinked at his too-cute smile. I wanted to smack it from his face. But I hadn't been a litigator for nine years without learning when to swallow my wrath and say a very polite "Yes, your honor," no matter how much I ached to slug the judge or kick opposing counsel in the balls.

I didn't care about working for this guy. Even so, I needed the job. So I said, "I'll take that to mean you're reserving judgment about my part in what happened."

He nodded. "Unlike the Bar Association."

Which had been all set to take me to trial before the State Bar Court to deprive me of my law license. The charges: failure to competently perform legal services. I guess you could say that, if I'd purposely thrown a client's case. The Rules of Professional Conduct provide that one violates the concept of

18

competence if one hasn't the mental and emotional ability reasonably necessary to do the job. Being justifiably miffed wouldn't be a defense, even if I'd committed the foul deed. And if I did it for money, they'd throw in moral turpitude, too.

Because things had looked bleak—they'd had evidence, for heaven's sake, though only hell knew where it came from—and to avoid a messy trial, I'd settled, admitting nothing but my own innocence. I'd agreed, kicking and screaming but with little choice, to three months' suspension of my license, plus a year's probation.

It could have been worse, if criminal prosecutors had leapt into the fray and I'd been arrested and convicted of fraud, or even conspiracy to commit murder. I could have lost my license alto-gether—and a lot more—although I was innocent of everything.

But the terms of the settlement had still been the final straw. My firm, which had stood behind me because their malpractice insurance carrier had to back me anyway, finally had justification to unpartner me. They let me resign with what dignity I could muster, and left me too broke to pay my many bills. I'd had to resort to bankruptcy to stave off the slew of creditors. I'd gotten the suspension postponed for a while, for all the good that had done me.

"Unlike the Bar Association," I agreed, finally responding to the patient Mr. Hubbard.

"Besides," he said, "even if you screwed up

before, I figure you won't dare do it again. At least not so soon. You're prettier than your pictures in the articles on-line, by the way."

How condescendingly male! I glared, and irrationally blushed. "Mug shots aren't exactly flattering," I stormed.

Why had he said that? To get me into bed? Sure, I needed some money to survive, but I wasn't desperate enough to sell my body . . . yet.

"No, they're not flattering," he agreed, looking as smug as if I'd voiced my thoughts aloud, "but I also found the photos from some of your past successful cases."

Now I *knew* he was lying. Prettier now? Heck, some of those post-trial pictures had been quite becoming, portraying me as the professional counsel I was. My hair was longer now and back to its natural shade of nondescript dark brown. No bleaching, no highlights. Who could afford a hairstylist when my gourmet fare for the fore-seeable future was likely to be peanut butter sandwiches?

And makeup? Well, I had to admit I still indulged. Not even now could I bring myself to go out with a totally naked face.

"So you could use a temporary job," Jeff said, at last returning to the crux of my reason for coming here. "And I need someone to house-sit. I'm leaving in about . . ." he looked at his watch, "twelve hours for LAX. I'll be gone two weeks this time and have several more trips scheduled nearly back-to-back. So if Odin likes you and your dog, then we can scratch each other's backs, so to speak. As for references, Darryl speaks highly of you, Kendra."

Thank God. Thank Darryl.

And that was how it began. When we finally met, Odin barked at me, but when I held out my hand, knuckles first, for a sniff, he approved my aroma enough to roll over on his back to let me rub his stomach. And when Lexie and Odin met in Jeff's vast backyard, their ears went back, their tails wagged briskly as they sniffed each other, and then they started to play.

Dog-sitter? Why not? I had nothing better to do for now.

I might even develop on expertise in pooper-scooping. And who knew what other new vistas might open to me?

CHAPTER 3

Lexie and I went home for the evening.

Though the moving van was out of the driveway, my nice, convenient parking space beside the garage—the two spaces inside were leased with the house—was occupied by a big, black Bentley.

The rest of the driveway was filled, too, with an assortment of automobiles of similar ostentation.

"Lexie," I said to my dog, who was eagerly wriggling to get out of the car, "talk me into not breaking that damn lease right now."

If she'd spoken English, I'm sure she'd have reminded me that I just had to put up with this, at least in the short term, overnight. We had someplace else to stay starting tomorrow.

"You're right," I told her. I parked on the crowded street and went through the gate—left open, in violation of the lease. Lexie and I went up to the front door of the house and rang the bell.

I braced myself for Charlotte to throw herself into my arms and beg my forgiveness. Instead, I got Yul.

He was about six feet tall, with short golden

hair, and dark, scowling eyes. He was dressed in a red muscle shirt and shorts. "Hi, Yul," I said. "Would you please have the person who parked in my space move the car? Oh, and I'll need the other cars moved, too, so I can get to the space. And the gate—it's supposed to be closed."

The expression on his face was blank. He looked down at my hands as if he expected me to be carrying something—a food delivery, maybe? But all they held was Lexie's leash, which Yul's eyes followed to the end. Recognition dawned. He might not recognize his reluctant landlady, but the pup looked familiar. "Oh, yeah. Sure. Sorry."

That had to be a record: four words strung together, more or less.

While I waited for the space to be made available for my car, Charlotte darted from the house and hugged me hard, apologizing profusely. "No problem," I lied.

"Would you like to join us?" she asked. I looked at the crowd jockeying cars behind me and jockeying drinks and hors d'oeuvres inside. Beautiful people, all of them. And years younger than me.

I'd not thought myself over the hill at thirty-five, but if I hung around here I might get an age complex on top of all the others I'd adopted lately. "No, thanks. A housewarming party already?"

"No, this is just a moving-in party," she said. "Housewarming's next weekend."

I didn't let myself ask what the occasion for the party would be the following weekend or the one after that. That night, as I lay in bed trying to sleep despite the party noise and music from next door, I thanked my lucky stars that Jeff Hubbard needed a house-sitter so quickly, and that he hadn't let a little thing like my suspension from the State Bar stand in the way of hiring me.

The next morning, I packed a few things. Mostly for me. Lexie always traveled with her fur coat, so all she needed were her bowls, food, and leash. I threw sweats, T-shirts, and more jeans into an overnight bag, along with undies, cosmetics, and a nightshirt.

In my old life, I was used to packing bags for an overnight out-of-town meeting, making sure I'd brought suitable law-garb for every occasion: casual breakfast meetings, dressy depositions, even dressier court appearances, and moderately dressy dinner meetings. Plus all the night stuff, hair stuff, stuff in general. And briefcase with laptop. Files . . .

I decided I could get used to traveling light. Except for my purse. Nothing could convince me to give up my big one.

Jeff was dashing about his house when we got there. He gave instructions about the dog and the house, showed me the security system, then tossed me the keys and left. He was going away for a couple of weeks, yet he took hardly more than I'd brought while traveling light. Odin stared glumly after him till I gave both dogs some rawhide chews Jeff had pointed out.

That night was a heck of a lot better than the previous one. Lexie and I slept in a room at Jeff's place that was half guest room, half storage room. Boxes were piled along one wall, labeled neatly with names and dates.

Though my curiosity was stoked, I didn't even consider looking into them. I, of all people, knew what trouble could result if the wrong folks saw information that was none of their business.

Still . . . Why had Irving O'Shay, a movie director with mega-credits and reputed multi-megabucks hired Jeff Hubbard as his security consultant? I could guess, but . . .

I swear I didn't peek.

Then there was Philipe Pellera, the latest Latin craze, a recording artist with bucking hips that burned CDs and DVDs all by themselves. What inflamed him to engage Jeff Hubbard's services?

Nope, I still didn't look.

Nor did I try to hack into Jeff's computer. He'd asked if I'd brought my own, which I hadn't. It didn't dawn on me as I'd left home that I might miss surfing the Net. Not to worry, Jeff had said. I could log onto his computer and use his Internet Service Provider. There were files I wasn't to see, but that was okay. He had them protected by ironclad systems.

Nothing, of course, was ironclad to the right people. Or the wrong people, depending on how one looked at it.

I'd assured him that hacking wasn't my habit or

my inclination. And judging by the way he remained unconcerned, maybe he *had* figured out something ironclad enough not to worry about a lowly former litigator finding a way in.

It would have been much simpler for me just to peek into those boxes . . .

Instead, I showered and planted my nightshirt-clad bod in the narrow but surprisingly comfortable twin bed against the opposite wall. Lexie liked the bed, too. She kept my feet warm all night.

I awakened refreshed and, for the first time in months, optimistic. I'd survived another day and had started a new chapter in my life. *May it be more forgiving than the last,* I prayed.

Lexie pranced at my feet as I threw on sweats, and we went down the hall to fetch Odin. The Akita's nighttime domain was Jeff's much larger, much neater bedroom, even when his master was out of town. I suppose I could have camped out there instead, but just then I needed space of my own, however cramped, temporary, and filled with stuff designed to tempt even me.

Both dogs and I headed for Jeff's kitchen. It was small and functional, and I suspected the microwave oven got more of a workout than the stove. I glanced at Jeff's written instructions that backed up his verbal ones. Odin's food expectations were noted in detail, which was good, since my mind had been spinning with his directions as he'd tossed them to me so hurriedly. Now, I followed the instructions explicitly, gave Lexie her breakfast, then took the dogs for a walk.

It was an experience: a large, sleek red and white dog with a curly tail asserting dominion over the neighbors' property by leaving his scent and lunging at other dogs who dared to be out on a leash that morning, and my yappy, less aggressive, little Lexie. We managed fine, even with my stooping, plastic bags in hand, to collect what the dogs tried to leave behind.

Nice neighborhood for a walk, too—flat and pleasantly residential, with gnarled oaks, towering eucalyptus, and vibrant gardens.

Ages ago, when my life was normal, the time walking Lexie was spent mulling over my next maneuvers in my most pressing cases. Lately, I'd tried hard to keep my mind blank, to prevent it from dwelling on the disasters multiplying about me exponentially with every hour.

To my delight that day, despite all the attention I'd needed to pay to the pups, I found myself considering the future—and not with dread. What was next? Could I do this pet-sitting bit for a while? Maybe, but I had to do more to get a real income, so I could take back my home . . . my life.

An ancient truck rolled by spewing fumes and coming dangerously close to dropping gardening equipment from its bed. I moved the dogs out of the way.

Would I go back to my old law firm? Not hardly. Marden, Sergement & Yurick wouldn't want me.

More important, I no longer wanted *them*. Who needed them, when most people there refused to stand behind me and loved the idea that there was a convenient scapegoat to attribute all problems to? Stick everything on Kendra: the leaked info, the ensuing murder, the resulting loss of clients and income.

So . . . a different law career?

For the first time that morning, my cheerfulness faltered, which also caused me to hesitate, which created a yanking at the dogs' necks. Both stopped and stared at me accusingly.

"Sorry." And I was. For now I was thinking yet again about the demise of my career. What law firm in its right mind would want someone whose license had once been suspended—in theory voluntarily since I settled without a trial, but in fact under duress? And what client would want to hire me even after it was reinstated, assuming I had the guts to go it alone as a sole practitioner?

Damn! What was I going to do?

It was then that Odin spotted a cat and started to give chase. That meant so did I, and a thrilled Lexie.

When the dogs finally sat at the curb, they were panting, but with their tongues hanging out they seemed to be laughing. Smiles are contagious. I found myself returning theirs with one of my own.

"Guess you showed me," I said. "To be successful

at this dog-sitting gig, I've got to pay attention, right?"

Odin woofed. I'd have sworn it was in the affirmative.

"Okay," I told the dogs. "Let's resume this discussion later, shall we?"

It was time to go back to Jeff's and make some calls.

I hadn't checked in with the people I needed to keep in contact with for maybe a week. Of course I'd had to scrap my cell phone—too expensive. And I hadn't hung out at my new digs over the garage long enough to take calls. Mostly, I didn't want to talk to anyone while my misery was such a living disease that it probably would have slithered through the phone lines and infected anyone who didn't hang up on me. I hadn't even hooked up my old answering machine.

Jeff had a phone in the living room, on the rustic coffee table in front of the huge TV. I switched on a talk show for company in the background, then listened to some other poor saps' problems for a few minutes while I drew up the courage to pick up the phone.

First thing, I called Esther Ickes. It had felt odd to me as an attorney when I'd had to hire myself a lawyer, but as the old saying went, "She who represents herself has a fool for a client."

Esther was no fool, though I wasn't sure about her client. But no matter how brilliant we both might be, how excellent a bankruptcy settlement she'd finagled, the only way she'd been able to keep the State Bar from taking me to trial was to strongly suggest settlement. And no wonder, considering the magnitude of the phony evidence proffered against me. Now she needed to know where I was just in case the truth suddenly fell from the skies. I wasn't holding my breath.

She wasn't in—probably out arguing on behalf of some other pathetic person struggling to salvage her career—so I left word that I had a new phone number where I could be reached. Temporarily. And then I called my former firm.

There weren't many people there that I wanted to talk to ever again. But if anyone needed to get in touch with me, they would undoubtedly contact my former secretary, Susan Feeney.

Susan, who'd been a legal secretary when I'd been screaming my lungs out as a high school cheerleader, wasn't exactly the maternal sort, despite her age. But in her own gruff, no-nonsense way, she'd supported me through all the chaos and calamity.

I blinked hard when, after I'd punched in my former phone number, she still answered the call, "Kendra Ballantyne's office."

"Susan, it's me."

"About time you called," she harrumphed. "What happened to your answering machine? You have a pen and paper?" When I assured her I did— after finding a pencil and two-week-old newspaper under the sofa—I took down the list of messages and numbers she rattled off.

"Thanks," I said when she was done. I wouldn't return most calls, of course. Some were from reporters who must be hurting for something exciting to write about if they still wanted to interview me. I was old news.

I recognized a few names from cases I'd had to pass along to other attorneys at the firm, and I identified those to Susan.

"Yeah, that's what I thought," she replied. "Avvie checks the list often, but I figured you'd want to know who called anyway."

"You're right," I assured her. Avvie Milton was a senior associate. She'd become my protégé of sorts, second chairing in many of my cases. She was the right one to make sure nothing was overlooked for the clients'—and therefore the firm's—sake.

"Okay, formalities are over," Susan finally said. "Where are you? What are you doing?" And then, gruffness smoothed away from the corners of her tone, "You okay?"

"I'm fine," I assured her. Amazingly, it felt true. I explained where I was, what I was doing. "It's for a couple of weeks at least and gives me room to think."

"You're dog-sitting?" She made it sound as if I'd told her I was taking it all off at a strip club.

"Yeah," I replied, not offended. I'd react the same way, if I were still in my old life looking at someone else who'd had it all and lost it. But I was alive. I still had Lexie. I had food to eat and someplace to sleep where reminders of my old life wouldn't be staring me in the face—or shouting "Party time!" in my ear. And most of all, for the first time in what felt like eons, I had hope.

"Yeah," I repeated, so cheerfully I nearly made myself gag, "I'm dog-sitting!"

CHAPTER 4

That night, after a final walk with the dogs, I fed them their dinners and stuck a packaged gourmet meal from Jeff's freezer into the microwave for myself. Then came the phone calls. The first was, not unexpectedly, from Jeff himself.

"Things okay?" He sounded rushed.

"No problems," I assured him. "And I've got your cell phone number at the top of your instructions, just in case."

"Right."

In other words, he didn't have to call to check up on me again, since I'd let him know if there were any emergencies.

No doubt I'd hear from him again. Tomorrow. Maybe first thing. And every day thereafter, at least once a day.

That was okay, I told myself. I'd actually done the same thing with the neighbor kid I'd hired to watch Lexie now and then when my work took me out of town.

Then came Avvie Milton's call. "Kendra, Susan told me where to reach you. How are you?"

With Avvie, that wasn't simply a social question. We'd grown friendly in the couple of years she'd seconded me in the most intricate cases at Marden, Sergement & Yurick. I'd been the one to back away during my recent misfortune. Though she'd been sympathetic, even outraged on my behalf, she hadn't stood up for me with the senior partners. I understood, at least on some level. Mostly, it was hard to see her segue into the lead in all my cases. And she'd seemed relieved at my retreat.

"I'm fine, Avvie," I assured her, trying my damnedest not to grit my teeth. I didn't need her cheerfulness or concern.

Or my jealousy. She was where I still wanted to be.

No I didn't, I reminded myself. Not at that firm. No way, no how. And did I really crave the pressures of litigation right now?

We chatted a while longer. I waxed eloquent over how much I enjoyed my more relaxing existence. I promised to keep in touch, but I kept my fingers crossed, in case I decided not to. That way, it wouldn't really be a lie.

"I spoke to Baird earlier," she told me as we ended the call. His Honor Baird Roehmann, the cantankerous, confrontational judge who, off the bench, was also my friend. Or wanted to be. "He wants you to call him."

So I did. I had a brief conversation with his answering machine, told him where I was, that I was fine, that we'd talk soon.

The third call I got that evening was the biggest surprise.

"Kendra?" said a familiar voice after I'd said hello. "It's Bill."

"Hi, Bill," I said warily, my mind racing at this one. Why was he calling?

Bill Sergement was a partner at my former firm. He was also a former lover.

Success in the first lawsuit I'd won nine years earlier had been seductive. I'd felt on top of the world. And when one of the firm's senior partners turned seductive, too, I'd considered it a perk of the job. He was good in bed, and he could help my career advance rapidly. And, in fact, I suspect Bill had a lot to do with my making partner as fast as I had.

Bill and I were an item for a year or two before drifting apart as bed companions. We had remained friends as well as business associates, and I'd often had long strategy sessions with him over dinner in the intervening years.

I'd suspected Bill was also bedding some of the other more junior associates as they joined the firm. Definitely Avvie, though we never talked about it.

Meantime, Bill had married—a grade school teacher, not a lawyer. They had a couple of kids now. Whether or not he continued sleeping through the associates while married . . . well, I didn't know it for a fact except for Avvie, but I sure suspected it.

Not that it mattered to me and my career.

What did matter, though, was that, despite our

long friendship, Bill hadn't stuck up for me, either, during my recent tribulations.

Bill Sergement's nickname was "Drill Sergeant," and he came by it naturally. He was the one who ran partners' meetings.

If he'd voted to keep me in, the others would have followed. If he'd voted me out . . .

"So, Kendra," he said now in a hearty voice that made me highly suspicious, "I hear your new career has gone to the dogs."

"Absolutely." I could feign heartiness, too. "One thing about dogs is that they are loyal."

A pause. Then, in a more subdued tone that I might have mistaken for sincerity if I didn't know better, Bill said, "I'm really sorry about all that happened, Kendra. I wish we knew the truth about who leaked that document."

I noticed he wasn't saying he was sure *I* hadn't. I muttered something noncommittal.

"Anyway, if there's ever anything I can do for you . . ." His voice trailed off, implying I only needed to ask.

"If you hear of anyone needing a house-sitter, let me know," I said. "Thanks for calling, Bill. Good night." I hung up softly before he could get in another word.

I went to bed that night in Jeff Hubbard's half guest room, with Lexie at my feet, my mind tumbling over thoughts of what Bill Sergement really had wanted.

★   ★   ★

Three weeks later, I was still residing in the guest room at Jeff Hubbard's place. He'd been back once for a few hours, then left again for another assignment. He might as well have been a lawyer, because all he talked about was who his clients were and what he was doing for them. I learned zilch. But it was sheer nosiness on my part when I asked.

Lexie and I popped in now and then to my house and the garage apartment. I was never able to guess when Charlotte and Mule . . . er, Yul, would be out or asleep. Didn't showbiz types stay out all night and sleep till noon? Not these two, at least not consistently. I kept running into them, sharing hugs with Charlotte and attempts at conversation with Yul.

For now, I preferred Jeff's place.

Despite Odin being triple my pup's size and an alpha male, he was an amazingly friendly fellow. I only had to feed him, walk him, brush him, play with him, as I did with Lexie, and he tried to become a lap dog just like her. Good thing none of my former opposing counsel got to see me curled up on Jeff's couch with the dogs jostling for position on my legs, or they'd have gotten the impression that I was a big softy. Which I was—but only for dogs. Not for the other side in litigation.

And that wasn't the end of it. When I'd called to thank Darryl the next day after settling in at Jeff's, he asked if I wanted another pet-watching job, one I could do while house-sitting for Jeff

37

and Odin. Another *paying* job. How could I refuse?

And then he referred another customer my way. And another.

Now, after three weeks, I found myself dashing from one client's house to the next. Some just wanted their dogs walked in the middle of the day while they worked. Others, going out of town, needed me to visit twice daily to feed their pets and walk those that needed walking.

Some I had to clean up after. Others required me to coax pills down their throats. I brought in newspapers, checked mail, whatever.

What a different world from being a litigator. Oh, it was just as fast-paced, in its way: Although so far my customers were all in the eastern San Fernando Valley, they weren't that close together, and I had to keep on the move. I mostly left Lexie in Jeff's kitchen, shut in by a removable plastic gate. Odin got the run of the fenced-in backyard.

I found myself enjoying it. The stress was there, sure, but different from what I'd left behind. I had time to think about what had happened to me, what I'd do when Jeff Hubbard returned on a long-term basis, though Darryl assured me he could refer me to any number of customers who'd want me to stay in their homes while they were gone. I'd even have references now. And there was always home-sweet-garage waiting for me.

Did I want to do this forever? I'd learned the

hard way not to worry about forever. One day at a time was just fine. And one day at a time, I was beginning to feel alive once more.

That was why I was grinning as I turned the key in the lock at Carl Cuthbertson's.

I'd felt humiliated when I first talked with Carl about pet-sitting for him. He'd been referred to me by Darryl, just like the others.

The big difference was that Carl had been a client of mine.

Rather, his company, a small boutique Hollywood production outfit that had produced a popular TV sitcom a few years back, was a law client of Marden, Sergement & Yurick. When it sued a competitor for stealing a feature film script, I handled the case.

And negotiated a nice, juicy settlement.

Carl and I had gotten along famously . . . before. I'd even referred him to Darryl's spa when he'd told me he lived nearby in the Valley and had a dog. And to my surprise, he'd handled my now-fragile pride quite gently, making it clear that he never had any doubts that I hadn't done the nasty things that the media—or the Bar Association—had said.

I was pleased to take him on as a client once more.

His house was in Toluca Lake, an upscale area between Burbank and North Hollywood, though Carl's house wasn't on the lake, where the real elite live. Nor did it appear particularly upscale, though the homes in the area weren't cheap.

Certainly they were above my current means, even if I wanted to consider selling my leased-out house. But then, these days, everything was above my means.

Carl was on a one-week vacation, due back tomorrow. He had a graying black mutt whose name was Cheesie, for reasons he hadn't explained. Cheesie didn't like cheese, but took her allergy pills in chunks of hotdog. When we went for a walk, she barked at the sheltie next door but ignored the yapping miniature poodle on the next block. She always greeted me at the door with a gruff bark, followed by an ecstatic episode of lying on her back while I rubbed her tummy.

But not today.

"Cheesie?" I called, standing in the tiny, tiled entry. "Cheesie, where are you?"

I heard a whine from somewhere. Uh-oh. Was I about to face my first crisis in my new career? Was Cheesie sick? I had insisted on veterinary information from all my customers and I kept a copy in my car and in the kitchen of each house. But I figured I'd better check out the situation, see if there was anything I should panic about.

"Cheesie," I called.

Another whine.

"Keep it up," I urged, hurrying down the hall toward the source of the sound. Maybe she had simply gotten locked in somewhere. But all sorts of horribles flashed through my mind. Was she injured? Had she eaten something she shouldn't? Had she had a heart attack?

I thought I'd prepared myself for any eventuality, but I was wrong.

I found Cheesie in a bedroom. She stood, whining, over Carl Cuthbertson. He lay on the floor. Completely still.

There was blood all over his chest.

And it clearly wasn't Cheesie who'd creamed him.

CHAPTER 5

I called 911.
 I was a civil litigator, not a criminal attorney. And I had no time and even less inclination to watch cop shows on TV, although I had as a kid. But I knew enough not to disturb the crime scene.

Except, of course, to kneel at Carl's side on the disarrayed area rug and check for signs of life.

The side of his neck was cold and pulseless. His wrist, too. I was sure it would take more than trying to breathe life into those blue lips and pounding on his bloody chest to bring him back.

A miracle, maybe. And I'd been short on those for months.

"Oh, Carl," I whispered sadly, hearing a whine in response. Not from Carl, but Cheesie, who leaned her warm, furry body against me. I turned from Carl and wrapped my arms around the shaking dog as we tried to glean comfort from one another.

I didn't inhale too deeply. The room was filled with the metallic scent of blood and the distasteful aroma of all that happens when a body relaxes in death. I kept my eyes firmly turned from Carl's bloody chest and the equally bloody long-bladed knife on the floor beside him.

The doorbell rang. With Cheesie preceding me and barking, I went to answer it.

Two cops stood there, uniformed alike, but not a matched set—a tall, black woman and a stocky white man. "Did you call in an emergency, ma'am?" he asked.

"Yes," I acknowledged hoarsely, leading them down the hall.

A guy in a gray suit nodded a greeting at the lady cop who'd kept me company and then turned his attention to me. "I'm Detective Ned Noralles." I'd have guessed that he was African-American, by his coffee-toned skin. But his name sounded Hispanic, and that aspect of his background seemed affirmed by his high, flat cheekbones and straight hair. In any event, he was good-looking enough that I noticed even under these God-awful circumstances. He flashed his credentials. The shield was LAPD. "I understand you discovered the victim."

I nodded.

"And you are. . . ?"

"Kendra Ballantyne." For the next few minutes, he led me through the basics—who I was, what I was doing there. He took notes on a small pad of paper with a pen that said Hilton Hotels. Did cops cop pens from hotel rooms like ordinary citizens?

I made a mental note of one good thing: He

43

hadn't read me my Miranda rights. What I said couldn't be used against me, and I wasn't in custody.

Yet.

Despite eschewing cop shows since my youth, I'd developed images of criminal interrogations—all unpleasant. But Detective Noralles seemed sympathetic. Like I was a victim, too.

Or was that kind demeanor just meant to throw me off guard?

Though Carl's trashed bedroom made it seem obvious that he had come home early to find a burglary in progress and was killed by the intruder, his murder was yet another act for which I was blameless, but could nevertheless be blamed.

"I've come here around the same time every day," I responded to one of Noralles's questions. "I have the pets I care for on a schedule." I didn't know if the animals cared, but that way I got to everyone as often as promised.

"Do you keep a written log?" Noralles asked.

I nodded.

"Can I see it?"

"Sure." There was no pet-sitter-client privilege, after all. Gee, if I did this long enough, maybe I could come up with a whole set of ethical rules for my new profession.

Sure. A whole new set of rules I could be accused of breaking.

"It's in my car," I told him.

"I'll get it from you later."

As I spoke with Noralles, I heard activity in Carl's hall and saw flashes of light from cameras. It looked as if they took photos of everything, not just the spot where the murder occurred. Most people I saw through the door wore suits as Noralles did, even the women. Other detectives investigating the crime scene?

One guy with a badge on his belt stopped for my fingerprints and a hair sample. "If we find your prints or anything else around here, we can seperate them from those that could belong to a suspect," Noralles assured me.

Maybe. But it didn't help my state of mind when a different detective reported to Noralles that the victim had, indeed, been pronounced dead at the scene. Apparently stabbed to death with the knife on the floor beside him, though tests would be run to confirm it.

No sign of forced entry. It could have been done by someone with a key—like me.

Rather than waiting for Noralles's accusation, I said, "I've been in and out of Carl's twice a day for nearly a week. I have a key and wouldn't need to break in, but if I'd intended to loot the place, I'd have had plenty of chances before it was nearly time for Carl to get back from his vacation."

"Okay." I got the impression he didn't accept what I said as true, only acknowledged that I'd said it.

"And Cheesie's not afraid of me," I pointed out. Despite all the activity, Carl's canine companion stayed by me most of the time, and if she wandered off, she always returned, demanding comfort. "If I'd killed her beloved master, wouldn't she be miffed instead of offering me her doggie allegiance?"

"Okay," Noralles said again. His expression was as bland as the single word he spoke. He looked down and riffled through his notes. "Nothing else right now, Ms. Ballantyne, but if I need to get hold of you—let's see, your home is at . . ." He rattled off my home address. "Nice area," he finished, head tilted as he seemed to wonder how a pet-sitter could afford such posh surroundings.

"I live in an apartment over the garage." Why did I feel compelled to say that? At least I didn't regale him with an explanation of how I'd come to reside there. I knew Detective Noralles would eventually find out who I was and how my reputation had been flushed down the toilet, thanks to my alleged breach of ethics.

"Okay," he said.

"And right now I'm living at one of my clients' homes." I gave him Jeff Hubbard's address.

"You're staying at Hubbard's?"

"You know him?"

"Everyone does," he said cryptically. Did that raise or crater my stature in his estimation? "So I don't have to hunt it down, give me the phone number."

I did. My cell phone, too, since I'd restored service on a budget plan for pet-sitting customers to contact me.

Surely someone guilty of stabbing a nice fellow like Carl Cuthbertson wouldn't be so cooperative with the cops, right?

When Detective Noralles mentioned that I should avoid discussing this case with the media, I chomped on my tongue to avoid laughing. As if I would tell the damned microphone-wielding carrion-crunchers anything after their earlier eagerness to damn me with innuendoes.

And then the detective was through with me . . . for the moment. He walked me to my car, and I showed him my log of visits to clients' homes.

"I'll take that." He held out hands with long, thin fingers. I noticed in the sunlight that a few silver hairs shone in his short, black cop-cut. He looked young for the authority he exuded—maybe mid to late thirties. I guessed that the stresses of his job sent worry-signals to his hair follicles, ordering them to turn him an early gray.

"No, I need it to stay on schedule," I told him.

I didn't win. Not exactly. He agreed to take me somewhere close to copy it.

But first, one of us had a call to make. Fortunately, it wasn't me.

Among the emergency phone numbers Carl had left for me was his daughter Laurie's. She lived in Thousand Oaks. I'd met her during the lawsuit I'd won for Carl.

Now, she needed to know about her dad.

While Noralles spoke with her, I took Cheesie for a short walk. I needed to clear my head, and

Cheesie needed to clear her bladder. When I got back, my head was as muddled as before, but the dog was more comfortable.

Detective Noralles, though, was pissed. "You shouldn't have left without telling me, Ms. Ballantyne." His tone suggested that I should have asked permission, not just notified him.

"Then consider yourself told that I have to get on my way. I've lots of animals to care for, and I'm running really late." I winced at my own words. *Sorry, Carl.* It wasn't as if finding him that way was a mere inconvenience to my busy day.

"All right. I'll go with you in a minute to get that daybook copied."

His "minute" was half an hour. He disappeared down the hall toward the bedroom, and I waited in the living room with Cheesie. And waited.

Finally, he reappeared and drove us down Riverside Drive, Toluca Lake's main commercial drag, to the nearest copy shop. When we got back to Carl's, his daughter Laurie had already arrived. Chubby and clad in a flowered sundress, she stood outside, talking to a guy in a suit. Another detective, I assumed. They turned toward us as we approached.

"Detective Noralles, this is Mr. Cuthbertson's daughter, Laurie Shinnick," said the short guy, whose dark eyebrows were bushier than his receding hairline. Polite introductions followed, as if we'd convened for a party instead of a murder investigation. Sure enough, the other suit was a detective, Howard Wherlon.

As we established each other's credentials, I felt Laurie's sharp glare peel off the outer layer of my skin despite the tears in her close-set brown eyes. I gathered she'd jumped to conclusions about my real purpose for hanging around and hoped to slash a confession out of me.

More of my skin was accessible now than when Laurie and I last met. Then, I was suited up for a court appearance, a jacket over a dressy blouse and stockings on my legs. My hair and makeup had, as always, been jury-impressing perfect. Now, I wore my usual dog-walking garb of T-shirt and jeans. And the last time I'd combed my hair was in the ladies' room at the fast food place where I'd grabbed a salad for lunch.

"Hello, Kendra," she said. "Detective Wherlon said you found my father." She stopped and swallowed and looked away.

"Yes," I said gently, gulping again at the lump in my own throat. "I'm very sorry. Your dad was a very nice man. I—"

"*Too* nice," she spat, rounding on me. "I told him over and over to be careful and not assume what-ever people told him was true. You'd have thought someone who did so well in show business would know better. He didn't learn his lesson when that script got stolen from him, back when you were his lawyer. He told me you were pet-sitting now, and I warned him about what I read in the papers, about how you did terrible things to your own client. I said he shouldn't trust you, even though you got him lots of money in that lawsuit. And now—were you trying to get that money back? Did you come here to hurt him?" She burst into tears. It wasn't a pretty sight. I saw red blotches on her round face before her pudgy fingers covered it.

But I wasn't exactly model material either when I cried. And right then, I felt like doing just that.

Especially when I saw the two detectives exchange glances. Now they had a hint of my less than stellar reputation. I was sure they'd dig into it further before many hours had passed.

Gathering all the litigator's aplomb I had left, I said calmly, "You're right that someone's to blame for what happened to your father, but it's not me. I liked him. He was a really kind man, willing to take my word for what happened and trust me with his home and dog. I won't try to defend myself to you about the spurious accusations against me. But there's no way in Hades I would have harmed Carl Cuthbertson. *No way.*" I emphasized the last two words, looking from one detective to the other. As if they'd believe me any more than Laurie did.

Then again, they still hadn't arrested me.

I didn't want to press my luck, and I had to get on my way. A lot of furry clients were probably standing around with their legs crossed.

First, though, I said, "Laurie, are you going to take care of Cheesie?" I knew she worked outside her home and had a kid or two, so Carl had never wanted to bother her with taking care of his best friend while he traveled. But now that he was gone, would she adopt this sweet, living remnant of her dad's life?

"Yes." Her tone was still abrasive and insulting, her watery glare accusatory, but I ignored it.

"Fine." I wasn't sure what I'd do if she'd said no, but I wouldn't have left the poor, masterless pup alone. I reminded her of Cheesie's routine and turned to Ned Noralles. "You know how to get in touch with me, Detective, if you have more questions. And now I need to get back to work."

No one slapped handcuffs on to restrain me. No one even contradicted me. I felt their stares, though, as I briskly strode to my Beamer.

I drove to the end of the street and around the corner before I began shaking so hard that I had to pull over.

"Damn!" I shouted in the solitude of my car, grateful no one else could hear. The only thing good about the horror that had happened was that surely nothing worse could go wrong.

CHAPTER 6

I didn't have time to worry. Too many fuzzy friends were waiting. I looked at my list of client names and addresses. I'm an admitted listaphile. Or perhaps a listaholic. Everything I do, everything I know, goes on a list.

This time, I hoped to instantly envision a more efficient way to visit everyone. But I'd already plotted the fastest course. I steered the Beamer toward where I'd originally intended to go after Carl's.

Carl. That sweet old man . . .

I grabbed my cell phone, opened the flap, and spoke a name to activate its automatic dialing feature: "Esther."

I'd called my attorney so often over the last few months, it was a wonder my recently reactivated phone didn't dial her by default the moment I lifted its flap.

"Ms. Ickes' office," answered a familiar voice.

"Janet? It's Kendra. Is she there?"

"No, sorry, she's in court. Anything I can help with?"

I doubted Esther's secretary could convince Detective Ned Noralles and company that I was incapable of murder—though I feared such skill might be beyond even the redoubtable Esther. And though Esther had preserved my license to practice law, preventing my disbarment, not even she'd held out hope that it wouldn't be suspended.

I left an urgent message for Esther to call when she could. I needed to prepare her to bail me out if I was taken in for more than questioning.

If? Hell, the way things had been going, *when* was the question.

After hanging up, I spoke another name into my phone: "Darryl."

A female voice answered, "Doggy Indulgence Day Resort. How can we indulge your best friend today?"

"Hi"—I took a guess—"Kiki?" Darryl had just hired the would-be starlet with that unlikely name; a blond, blue-eyed babe who gushed all over his clients. She might not make it in movies, but Darryl's dogs would undoubtedly vote for her in a puppy popularity contest.

"Yes?" She obviously didn't recognize my voice.

"This is Kendra Ballantyne. Is Darryl available?"

"Oh, hi, Kendra." Since I was neither client nor client's owner, the enthusiasm in her tone ebbed. "I'll check."

In less than a minute, Darryl answered. "Kendra? Where are you?" He sounded a touch irritated. Had one of the dogs called him to complain that I was late?

"On my way to Alexander's." Alexander was a

pit bull who adored people—and ate smaller dogs for lunch. Or at least he wanted to. That was one reason I'd taken to leaving Lexie at Jeff Hubbard's house while I worked. Alexander's owner would be home in a couple of days, and Lexie would be able to join me once more.

"Jeff Hubbard called. He's home and wanted to know when you'd get there." Speak of the devil.

Swell. I hadn't expected Jeff till after the upcoming weekend. Since he was in town, I had no doubt that he wanted to chew me out for leaving Odin and Lexie alone for so long. They were becoming such buddies that I'd decided to try leaving Odin in the kitchen with my Cavalier. One or both might not have been able to hold their stuff for so many hours, despite how well-trained they were.

On top of that, now that Jeff was back, Lexie and I would have nowhere to stay the night but our garage-top apartment. Sure, it was Thursday, not Saturday, but I had a feeling Charlotte and her strong-and-silent twerp would have invented an occasion for a party. It had been that kind of day.

"But think of how much worse it was for Carl," I whispered.

"What, Kendra?" Though I still clutched the phone in my free hand not steering the Beamer along Burbank Boulevard, I'd nearly forgotten Darryl.

He would hear about it in the news anyway. And

54

right about now I needed a stiff shot of Darryl's sympathy. "Darryl, Carl Cuthbertson is dead. He was murdered."

"What?! What happened?"

I gave a quick rundown of what I knew, which amounted to only an iota more than diddly-squat. I couldn't help finishing with, "Of course the police didn't believe my story. And Carl's daughter gave them enough hints that it won't take Sherlock Holmes to realize that I'm that infamous unethical attorney in the news a few months back."

"Damn! But you're okay?

"More or less."

"I'm sorry, Kendra. He was a nice old guy. And for you to have found him like that—"

"Yeah. Thanks, Darryl. I'll call Jeff now." Maybe sympathy wasn't what I needed. I felt sobs starting deep down inside, and I had no time for a crying jag while turning onto a busy stretch of Sepulveda.

No crying I'd ever indulged in before had helped me get around or over the accusations of unethical conduct against me.

Then again, neither had stoicism.

I hadn't programmed Jeff's phone numbers, either house or cell, into my phone. Why bother? I didn't need to call his house while I stayed there. And he phoned me nearly every night, so his cell number hadn't been necessary, either.

But I'd entered his stats on my essential list. I pulled into a strip mall parking lot, dug it out with shaky fingers, and pressed in his number. "Hi,

Jeff? Kendra. Darryl said you were back and wanted to talk to me."

"Hi, Kendra. Yeah, I'm home and I've walked both dogs. They seemed happy to see me, but other than that it looks like you've done fine by Odin and the house. I appreciate it."

But . . . ? I waited for the other gumshoe to drop. Surely the private investigator in whose house I'd been staying hadn't told Darryl he needed to talk to me immediately so he could express appreciation.

"The thing is," he continued. Ah, here it came. "I'm only here overnight, then off on something else. Can you stay? It'll be another week, maybe two. Odin seems happy, so I don't want to change things, okay?"

I'd been right. There *was* something else on his mind. The remarkable thing was that it was something I wanted, too.

And then I had an off-the-wall idea. Could I trust the guy?

Hell, he trusted me with his house and his dog. "Well . . ." I added hesitancy to my voice as I watched a kid exit a shop with a huge pizza box in his hands. My stomach rumbled, and I realized I'd skipped lunch. And I never ate much for breakfast. But it would be a while before I'd have time to eat again. "I'll try to accommodate you, Jeff. But there's one big *if* I can't control."

"Anything I can help with?"

Ah-hah. I had him.

Maybe.

"Maybe," I echoed my thoughts. "The thing is, something horrible happened today. I had nothing to do with it, but I'm afraid I'll be arrested for murder."

Silence. What had I expected? That he'd just take it in stride and swear he'd find the real killer so I wouldn't have to be scared anymore?

Well . . . yes. That had been my fantasy.

"We'd better talk," he said. "I'll be here for the evening. We'll get some take-out, okay?"

"Sure," I said calmly. "By the way, the detective in charge of the case knows you. Noralles. Maybe you could call him and get a rundown on what the police think."

His barked laugh fell short of reassuring me. "Not likely. Did you mention my name to Ned?"

"No, he recognized the address where I was staying."

"Don't count on associating with me to clear you."

"Why?" Just what I needed. Two males obviously full of antipathy toward one another.

"I'll explain later. But, hell, why not? I'll call, see what I can find out. What time should I expect you?"

Since I was parked, I was able to check my indefatigable list. Six places left to go. Fifteen minutes per stop—sorry, animals. I'd spend more time with them in the next few days to atone for today. Ten minutes to travel from one place to the next. "Give me a couple of hours," I said.

"Fine."

"Oh, and Jeff, since I'll be late, could you feed Odin and Lexie?"

Not only was I asking him to do his job on my behalf, I was asking him to do *mine*. The one he was paying me for.

But he wanted a favor from me, too.

"Sure." He paused. "Kendra?"

"Yes?" He said my name casually enough to cause concern.

"Why don't you pick up our dinner?"

CHAPTER 7

Since Jeff wasn't specific in his supper request, I made the big decision: We'd have Thai. I needed to indulge in those great, fat mee krob noodles in a mildly spicy sauce. Comfort food.

Judging by the smile that softened the planes of his face when he peeked into the large bag, he was pleased.

So were Lexie and Odin, the big beggars. Though the kitchen's sliding glass door was open to the backyard, both canines crowded around, nuzzling my legs and wagging their tails. "I thought you both ate already," I grumbled cheerfully. Their expressions stayed innocent and pleading. "Well, there might be extra rice . . . We'll see."

In five minutes, we were sitting at Jeff's round kitchen table. It was sprinkled liberally with small, white cardboard boxes and chopsticks. The aroma was sheer heaven: oriental, spicy-sweet, and tummy-rumbling tempting.

Before dinner, I checked my makeup, added extra concealer to diminish the sad shadows spreading beneath my blue-green eyes, and combed my hair, wishing it were blond again. So I looked fairly decent, despite not being lawyerly ladylike. "So tell me about where you just were," I said to make conversation as I ladled Thai treats over white rice. I avoided serving a description of Carl with our supper, even though the suspicions against me were the impetus for our eating together. "What's in Akron, Ohio?"

"Business." Jeff mounded vast helpings onto his plate. If he ate like that all the time, he had to work out a lot to keep so trim. Or maybe his six-foot frame simply supported a heck of a lot of food. He was dressed casually in a short-sleeved denim work-shirt and frayed jeans a lighter shade than mine.

"I figured. Oops." I'd missed my plate, and both dogs scrambled for the grains of rice that rained to the floor. Lexie got there first. Odin sat politely and regarded me with soulful eyes, as if I'd fed my pup on purpose. What could I do? I dribbled more rice, and he pounced. This time Lexie glared.

"Forget it," I said to her. Then, to Jeff, "Tell me about your business."

"How about some wine first? Merlot?"

"Amen."

In a minute, I was sipping a flavorful vintage from his multi-faceted wine goblets.

"Cheers." He lifted his in a toast.

"To Carl Cuthbertson," I said.

Jeff clinked his glass on mine. "May his afterlife be awesome."

I laughed. I'd figured Jeff to be near forty, judging by the experience I saw in his guarded blue eyes. His hair was a little long to be fashionable, a shade too dark for blond, and too light to be brown. Though I didn't know—or care—if he believed in an afterlife, I appreciated the sentiment.

Of course there wasn't much I did know about Jeff, except his address and his Akita. And his attractiveness. "Why Ohio?" I asked. "Are you licensed there?" I knew of California's licensing requirements for P.I.s, as I had hired them now and then to track down dirt on the opposition in the cases I had litigated.

"I'm only licensed here, but I design and install security systems, too. I was actually putting together security for a movie shoot, a big-budget feature." He named a couple of production companies that even I had heard of.

"Whoa. The big guys. Why Akron?"

He guessed the town was eager enough for business to be more accommodating than Hollywood these days. "Or maybe the script dictated it. I never learned what the story was about."

It dawned on me then that it had been ages since I'd had dinner with a good-looking guy for reasons other than a case. And as we talked, Jeff looked into my eyes. I looked back.

There were vibes between us. At least I thought so, assuming I could even recognize vibes anymore.

Though I'd had relationships now and then, my sex life was nearly as terminal as Carl. No time.

No interest. Most of all, no trust in my own common sense, thanks to that pathetic fling with Drill Sergeant. I'd become more like my divorced attorney mother than I'd ever imagined, living for the law and loving it. But that was all before.

"My next job is in Seattle," Jeff said while scraping the last of the pad Thai from a small box. "It should be particularly fun. The client's hired me to break into his offices."

"Huh?" I blinked. "Why?"

His grin was smug. "To see if the security system he got from someone else is as foolproof as promised. I've promised it isn't."

I asked the ins and outs of breaking and entering at the owner's behest, and he described some colorful experiences. Enjoying a slight buzz from the wine and Jeff's company, I relaxed enough to laugh as he spoke.

Until he stopped talking about himself and turned the discussion to me.

"Okay, tell me how you found Carl Cuthbertson."

I sighed and glanced at Lexie. My sleeping pup was of no assistance. "Not much to tell." I described my current routine, where Carl fit in. How I'd left Lexie here to avoid the pit bull on my route. How Carl's dog Cheesie hadn't greeted me in the usual way.

How I'd found Carl.

"I called 911 and checked to see if he was alive, though I was pretty sure he was gone." I swigged the last sip of wine in my glass. "He was."

"What else did you see in the room?"

"Like the murder weapon?"

He nodded.

I described the bloody knife on the floor. "It looked like a standard kitchen knife, the kind usually found in butcher block holders."

"Was it Carl's?"

"I think so, though I didn't go into the kitchen to check."

Jeff leaned forward in his chair, hiked up his sleeves, and rested his partly bared forearms on the table. "Okay, and this is important. How were you getting along with Carl?"

"Fine, though I hadn't heard from him while he was gone. He was visiting friends in San Diego and wasn't due back till tomorrow. He was a law client of mine before . . ." Heck, Jeff knew my background. There was no reason to dissemble. "Before my license was suspended. He and I kept in touch because I knew he had a dog and I'd recommended him to Darryl's place."

"Darryl and you are good friends, aren't you?"

I nodded, wondering where that nonsequitur had come from. "Carl had asked Darryl about a dog-sitter, like you did, and Darryl told him that that's what I was doing these days. Carl didn't hold the nasties I was accused of against me, so he hired me." I figured my expression, as I glanced at Jeff, must look rueful. "Sorry. That's probably more than you wanted to hear."

"You're doing fine. By the way, Ned Noralles

called me before I got around to calling him. Asked questions about you."

Oh, shit. My dinner froze into an ice ball that pressed on my inner organs.

During my previous problems, nearly everyone I knew was interrogated about my ethics, after I'd been accused of breaching them. Were friends and acquaintances now going to be asked if I were capable of killing?

If so, that surely meant I was a serious suspect.

A Matterhorn-sized weight settled in my gut. "And you said . . . ?"

"I stated facts. You came recommended, my dog likes you, and I have no complaints or fears for my life when you're around. You'd never mentioned Cuthbertson to me before, and I have no reason to think you offed him. Period."

Not a glowing endorsement, but not an accusation, either. And the guy had been a cop. He probably knew how to handle a grilling without getting steamed. "Thank you."

"Then I did some digging. You're not his only suspect, but Noralles was happy to describe what he had against you—mostly means and opportunity. But the motive didn't cut it."

Grateful, I forbore from gagging, and asked, "What did he think my motive was?" *My* motive!

"Burglary, since the bedroom was trashed."

Indignation made me half stand. The movement woke the dogs. Lexie put her paws on my knees, and I pulled her into my lap for comfort.

64

"That's just stupid. I hardly fit the bill for murderer-slash-burglar."

"I agree, but the guy's a—never mind."

"What's between you two?"

"Nothing good." Jeff stood, obviously intending not to discuss it further.

"I gathered you weren't close, but will he lean on me harder simply because I work for you?"

"Not if I can help it." Standing at one of his tile counters, Jeff filled both goblets again.

"But he might?"

"He might." Jeff turned his back to put the wine away. When he faced me, his expression was grim. "Picture him and me in LAPD uniforms, with different partners, but called to the scene of the same drive-by shooting. We had both paid our dues as patrol officers, done great on written and oral tests for promotion to detective. Our background checks were fine, and we were ranked near the top in the same band. That's a group waiting for promotion. In this shooting, I found evidence pointing to the suspect before the detectives arrived to investigate. Noralles sabotaged it so I wouldn't get credit. When I found out, I didn't go through channels to report him. I handled it myself." He flexed a fist. "Damn, but it felt good, even though I got disciplined. He made detective. I quit the force."

"Sounds like you're the one with the beef, not him."

Jeff's grin was so full of smugness I could have

carved some off with one of his dull butter knives. "The guy prided himself on being a martial arts pro. Studied it for years. Black belt in everything. Figured it'd help him be a better cop, I guess. And I've seen him in action, and I have to admit he's got style. But I decked him. He's never forgiven me."

I laughed, then sobered. "He doesn't really think I killed Carl, does he?"

Jeff's glee turned to sympathy. "Ned Noralles likes to take the easy way in a case, which is probably why he didn't find that evidence I mentioned in the first place. You're an easy target."

I took a deep breath, despite feeling as if I'd forgotten how to inhale. "So what do I do to erase the bull's eye on me?"

"I've promised to take that Seattle assignment, so I've got to leave tomorrow. Otherwise, I'd look into your case just for the fun of thwarting Noralles again."

I tried to conjure a tactful way to say, *Thanks, but I've got enough troubles, so don't toss me into the middle of a testosterone war with the main cop on my case.*

But Jeff hadn't stopped talking:

"I'd love to see Noralles's face if you get the evidence on who really did it—especially with my help." His grin was as contagious as a cold between kissing cousins.

Not only that, it was really sexy. My return smile must have shown my interest. Either that, or Jeff shared those uninvited vibes.

66

He stood and leaned across the table toward me. I did the same. I closed my eyes as we kissed—just as Lexie, still in my lap, decided to bark excitedly, as if she was jealous.

Maybe she was. Whatever her reason, I was both thankful and regretful.

"Bad idea," I told Jeff.

"Good idea, bad timing," he countered.

"Maybe."

"Let's keep it in mind," he said. As if I could help it. "For now, hold on."

To what? My hormones? My sanity?

He went to a drawer in a kitchen cabinet, pulled out a pad of paper and a pen, and placed them in front of me.

"What's that for?" I asked.

"We're about to strategize, Ms. Ballantyne, about how you'll investigate Mr. Cuthbertson's demise. Take notes."

Ignoring his arrogance—and the fact I was supposed to forget that all too brief lip-lock—I prepared to do as the expert investigator said. Make notes, create a new list.

If what he said made sense, it couldn't hurt.

CHAPTER 8

Eventually, fingers tingling from writing so fast, head swimming, eyelids drooping, I'd had enough. We went to bed. Lexie and I. In the guestroom.

I slept amazingly well, considering that I was a murder suspect, and the guy who'd tweaked my sex drive more than any I'd met in ages lay in bed right down the hall. But his officious attitude had deflected any interest I had in yanking open his bedroom door and throwing myself on top of him. Thank you, Mr. Arrogance-Personified Hubbard.

He was up and about by the time Lexie and I appeared the next morning.

"I'm making myself an egg-white omelet," he said. His hair was long enough to look sufficiently sleep-rumpled, inviting my well-rested fingers to comb through it. He wore khaki shorts, and his short-sleeved brown shirt was unbuttoned, giving me a glimpse of what lay beneath—a chest with contours to cry for.

Good thing I was fully dressed—beige denim slacks and a blue shirt with all buttons fastened except for the top one.

That didn't keep him from eyeing me lustfully. I felt my face flush.

"Care for one?" One what? Lay? Oh, omelet. Sexy, and he cooked, too. Or was he planning on lecturing me about his expertise in choosing omelet ingredients, as he had with everything else?

Fortunately, I had a good excuse to beg off. Pets pined for my attention even more than I pined for Jeff's.

And I intended to start my own investigation into Carl's murder that day. Top suspect? Ha! I'd find a way to send Noralles sniffing after someone else.

I brought Lexie along, simply wanting her company.

Having a Cavalier King Charles spaniel around had long been my sole concession to the possibility that I might be lonely. Not that I ever dwelled on such a thing. And not that my life wasn't fulfilling when I'd bought her two years earlier. But my friends were mostly business associates. And my lovers—what lovers?

But having someone at home to talk to . . . nothing beat that.

I first learned about Cavaliers by seeing them in artwork from the seventeenth century, when King Charles II of England had popularized the small spaniels he adored.

Then there were more recent photos, in which people in yesterday's headlines were equally fond of the breed, like former President Ronald Reagan and Frank Sinatra. So were current stars like Courtney Cox and her husband David Arquette.

Most significant had been meeting one on Ventura Boulevard. Not alone, of course, but walking her owner, a Cavalier aficionado who waxed eloquent about their loving nature.

So, as was my wont, I did detailed research, bought my pup from a reputable breeder, and brought her home.

Now, if only she spoke English, I was sure she'd give great advice about avoiding Jeff and learning the truth about poor Carl. I still wouldn't bring her near my petulant pit bull client, but it was easy enough to keep her cool in the car during my morning rounds. The early June-gloom overcast air hadn't had had a chance to heat up after the comfortable L.A. night.

As we drove, I listened to my favorite middle-of-the-road music station. My fingers kept twitching toward the controls. There were two local all-news stations. Others ran updates on the hour. Had the media started spouting their usual sensational semi-truths about what had happened to Carl? Probably. I'd know by now, if I'd thought about turning on the TV news last night. But, hey, I'd seen what had happened firsthand. I didn't need someone else's lurid interpretation. And fortunately, none of them had found me to hound yet.

In a short while, I parked my Beamer beneath a

blooming jacaranda tree. The car would be coated with purple petals when I returned to it, but so be it. The spot was shady.

I poured water from a bottle into a small plastic bowl for Lexie and made sure windows were open enough to let air in without letting her out. "I won't be long," I promised.

I heard Alexander bark as I strode up the path to his Sherman Oaks cottage. The pit bull had heard me arrive. No security system to disarm here; Alexander *was* the security system. He waited beyond the front door, slobber sluicing from his wide muzzle. He rolled over so I could rub his tummy. "Hiya, Alex. Been a good boy?"

When I'd leashed him for his walk, my cell phone sang "Ode to Joy." Figuring I could both talk and walk, I let Alexander lead me out and onto the sidewalk as I grabbed the phone from my pocket.

"Kendra, what happened?"

"Avvie?"

"You're all over the TV today. The *Times,* too. Again. What happened to Carl Cuthbertson? I know you didn't do it, but all the media say you're a suspect."

Despite my former assistant's recent friendly words of support, I wondered if she were simply assuaging her curiosity. Did she genuinely care that I was being falsely accused again?

"Of course I didn't hurt Carl. I found his body, though." I shuddered, just as Alexander saw a cat and tried to take off down the street after it. Attempting to control the dog with one hand and the phone with the other, I said, "Can't talk now. I'm walking a dog." Rather, Alexander was walking me. "I'll call you."

"Can you join me for lunch today?"

Once upon a time we'd lunched together almost every day. Was Avvie now attempting to atone for her obvious absence from my new life? Curious—and needing a little company that wasn't canine—I kept on trotting while I totaled up pets still to see, and my progress so far. "A short one," I finally said.

"Great! Will you come to the office?"

"Yeah." No doubt she figured her time was worth more than mine. Right now, in dollars and nonsense, it was. But I gave in, otherwise I might have looked like I gave a damn about being falsely accused again. Besides, I had an idea.

"Noon?" Avvie asked.

"That'll work. See you then."

I glanced at my watch, did a quick calculation. I'd have to shave time from my rounds, but not much. "Hungry, Alexander? I'll give you a treat if you let me take you home now."

The big dog bounded down the street as I trailed behind.

I was heading for the next pet-stop when my cell phone rang again. "Who is it this time?" I asked Lexie. On the passenger seat, she cocked her head as if trying to grasp the question. Pulling to the curb, I checked the number. It was Darryl.

"Hi," I said. "And before you ask, no matter what the papers say, I won't change my story. I didn't kill poor Carl."

"Hi to you, too." He sounded amused. "And though a hundred people have told me what they saw on the news this morning, I've made it clear you can't believe all you hear and read."

"Good boy," I said.

"You make me sound like one of your charges. You've been dog-sitting too long."

"You talked me into it," I reminded him.

"Yeah, and I'm about to talk you into something else."

"What?" I asked suspiciously.

"Have you ever met a ball python?"

Good thing the car wasn't moving or I'd have slammed on the brakes. "I'm dog person. I'm already tending cats and looking in on an iguana and some birds. But I draw the line at snakes."

"Even for a hell of a lot of money?"

I hesitated. "Define 'a hell of a lot.'"

The figure he mentioned fit in that category. I whistled. "Why—?"

He interrupted. "A new customer just came in. Can you come by this afternoon? I'll have the guy tell you about Pythagoras."

I snorted. "Pythagoras the python? Why not Monty?"

"It's been done."

"I'll stop by because I've other stuff to discuss with you. We'll talk about the great mathematician python then."

"What do you want to discuss?"

"You'll find out." I hung up and drove faster than I should have toward my next client.

CHAPTER 9

By the time I was headed for my former office later that morning, I had more time on my hands.

Not only had Carl's murder, and my purported part in it, made local news, but word was out elsewhere, too. When I reached one client's house that morning, the schnauzer's owner was already home—she and two of her brawniest friends, in case I really was into stabbing my customers, though she never said that. She'd been in Palm Springs, heard the news last night, and was home by ten A.M.

On top of everything else, would Carl's death be the end of my new enterprise?

I believed so even more strongly when someone I was supposed to start sitting for next week called to cancel. Maybe the rest of my customers were too far away to fire me this quickly, but their repeat business could be crumbling.

Damn. "And I really liked this gig," I told Lexie as we exited the Harbor Freeway. I'd even resumed a smidgen of my former self-assuredness, since pet-sitting was something I was good at. So what if it didn't have the cachet of being a high-powered civil litigator? It also didn't have the pressures. Or it shouldn't have . . .

I hadn't killed Carl, of course, yet a boxcar-sized burden had sat on my shoulders since his death. Guilt? *Yeah, kinda, Kendra.* What if I'd gotten there sooner? Could I have saved him? Was it my fault that—*Can it, counselor.*

Reaching downtown, I nearly pulled into the familiar parking lot beneath the Marden firm's building till I glanced at the rates. I no longer had a monthly pass and couldn't count on the firm validating my ticket. I crossed over the freeway and parked in a bargain lot that required sole-power to reach a downtown destination. Lexie didn't seem to mind.

I wondered how my former colleagues would react to my bringing my family along to work.

Family? Hell, I actually had a family, though not in L.A. And definitely not as close as Lexie. What would *they* think of my being accused of murder? My remarried dad in Chicago hadn't exactly been full of hugs and support during my prior troubles. I'd figured his wife wouldn't let him. Showing me affection would have been too hard on all my little half-siblings.

And my happily unmarried mom, a lawyer herself in D.C., would have been mortified to own up to knowing someone whose law license was suspended.

At least I'd gotten calls from my brother Sean

in Dallas. Offers of help, too, though I couldn't figure out what a motel mogul could help with, besides money. And that wasn't the kind of help he'd offered. Not that I'd have accepted.

Traffic noise and car exhaust from the freeway below assaulted my senses as Lexie and I walked over the bridge. Downtown L.A. is a mélange of modern skyscrapers, interspersed with low-rise buildings waiting to be gutted and replaced by new behemoths or turned into residential lofts. Some oozed character, like one with two reclining male nudes on the façade.

The Marden firm was in a prime location in one of the newest buildings. In the opulent lobby, I picked up Lexie and strode briskly by the security desk. Fortunately, no one paid attention. Were they as cavalier about would-be terrorists as they seemed to be about Cavaliers-in-arms?

We took an otherwise empty elevator to the twentieth floor. In the interests of looking semi-professional, I'd stuck on a tweed suit jacket I kept in my car over my shirt and slacks. I used to shove pens, paper, and paperclips into the deep front pockets. Now they usually held leashes and house keys and the plastic poop bags that were de rigueur for dog walking.

I still carried the same large purse I'd used to tote all I needed as a lawyer. Hadn't even cleaned it out. You never knew when you might need an electronic planner or voice-activated dictation recorder.

When the elevator door opened, familiar brass letters on the teak wall proclaimed that we'd indeed reached the law firm of Marden, Sergement & Yurick. The deep breath I took was loud enough that Lexie looked up. If she spoke English, I was sure she'd say, "You've nothing to be ashamed of. Go get 'em, girl."

"Great advice," I whispered, standing straighter.

As I walked through the open glass door, Cathy, the MSY receptionist, looked startled to see me. Or maybe she was startled to see a black, white, and red bundle of fur wriggling in my arms. A relatively recent secretarial school grad, Cathy began working at the firm only a short while before my troubles began. As a result, she'd only known me as a beleaguered attorney and not the firm's premier litigator. She sat behind a tall wooden desk. The waiting area's leather chairs and sofa awaited the next influx of clients.

"Hi, Cathy," I said. "I'm here to grab Avvie for lunch. Could you let her know I'm here?"

I put Lexie down, holding her leash as she sniffed the plush beige carpet. I hid my grin at Cathy's dubious expression. She looked worried that my dog would have an accident. Lexie was well-trained. If she did some business on that beautiful, costly carpeting, it would be no accident.

The door to the inner sanctum opened. Avvie poured through it along with Bill Sergement and my former secretary, Susan Feeney. Bill was first

78

to reach me. Ignoring Lexie, who sniffed his wingtips, he folded me into his arms before I could back away. "Kendra, hi. I just heard about your latest trouble. Anything we can do?"

Sure. Take up criminal defense fast and get the police off my case.

I gave him a polite return hug, then pulled back. "Thanks, Bill," I said, suspicious of his sincerity.

No matter how relaxed Bill was, he always looked harried. Maybe that was because the hair behind his far-receded hairline never lay quite flat. Or the fact that his white shirts were always rumpled and unbuttoned at the neck, usually with the loose knot of his necktie dangling beneath.

Avvie came closer. So did Susan, who eyed Lexie cantankerously.

"Kendra. So glad you could make it." Smiling beatifically, Avvie took my hands and squeezed them, leash and all.

Avalyne Milton looked the way a lady litigator for a mega-power firm should look, thanks to me, though I was sure she'd conveniently forgotten that. When she started at MSY, she'd had long, flowing hair and wore the latest of youthful styles, which included very short skirts. I'd convinced her to get her hair styled and to wear lawyerly suits. Her overeager demeanor had transfigured with her new look into cool, calm confidence.

"I'm glad we could get together, too," I told Avvie. Over her shoulder, I noticed Susan hovering.

Maybe Susan Feeney had been a legal secretary

a lot longer than I'd been a lawyer, but I was with the Marden firm first. An alum of one of L.A.'s largest law offices, she'd been hired a couple of years after me. She wore her iron-gray hair in a sleek cap that slid into curves at the sides of her face. Her wide mouth was parenthesized by deep grooves, and her light-brown eyes were prone to stab at attorneys and clients alike. Even when I'd had to tell her what to do, she always gave the impression of having whipped me, and others she worked for, into shape.

"Hi, Susan," I said with a grin.

Her return smile was brief. "Here are your messages," she said. "A lot of reporters called this morning wanting to talk to you. I didn't tell them how to reach you."

"Thanks." I hadn't realized how much I'd appreciated Susan's brusque efficiency till I no longer had her to look after me. Not only that, despite the fact that she wasn't a kid, she had a knack for knowing how to use all the latest gadgets in modern technology. She'd taught me plenty, from upgrades to word processing programs to tricks to speed up Internet use.

Impetuously, I went over and gave her a hug. She wore one of her usual collared blouses, but had relaxed enough to exchange her former long, dark skirts for slacks. I was gratified when she deigned to squeeze back a little. And then she stepped briskly away, proffering messages on old-fashioned pink message slips despite her proclivity for technology.

"That's all so far today," she said. "But keep in touch."

For Susan, that seemed almost gushy. "Sure, and you know how to reach me if anyone important calls." I said that to her rigid back as she walked through the door toward the offices.

Bill waved as he headed back toward his office. "Don't be a stranger," he called to me. "You're always welcome here."

Right. Like monkey-pox-carrying prairie dogs would be . . .

"The whole gang's here," Avvie said. "They'd love to see you." She knelt on the floor to pet an ecstatic Lexie.

Yeah, sure. The "gang" consisted of other attorneys, paralegals, and secretaries who'd mostly avoided looking me in the eye after I was accused of unethical behavior. It would include senior name partner Royal Marden, but most likely not the "junior," Borden Yurick, on medical leave for a supposed mental illness. Rehab? Maybe, although I couldn't picture old Borden on booze.

I'd loved to have thumbed my nose at everyone, but I passed on the unpleasantries in favor of something more useful. I said, "I'm hungry. Let's go eat."

"Okay, I'll get my purse."

In a low voice, I asked, "Do me a favor?"

Her glance was justifiably suspicious. "What?"

The phone rang, and Cathy answered. Good. She'd be preoccupied.

"I know the firm still represents Cuthbertson Productions," I said to Avvie. "I'm not interested in any current matter, but I'd appreciate it if you'd bring the files about the case I worked on. I need a refresher on who's who at the company."

"You think one of them killed him?" Avvie's eyes were wide.

I shrugged. "Will you bring the files?"

"Why not?" She headed back into the office.

Good thing her question was probably rhetorical. I could think of a lot of reasons.

And a big, fat, glaring one was that it might be unethical.

We ate at the outdoor area of a café on Seventh Street, where diners with dogs weren't anathema. Lexie lay obediently under my seat, not too proud to accept scraps from my Cobb salad.

Avvie and I chatted about law and life like we used to, though the conversation too often seemed strained. In silences, I studied files, jotted notes.

Avvie grabbed the check before I did. It wasn't charity, I told myself. She was paying old debts. She could believe she owed me something for showing her the complicated ropes of litigation. So what if that had been part of my position as a member of the firm? I'd done a damn good job.

Plus, we'd actually discussed a legal dilemma she had.

"Let's split it," I told her.

"Next time," she lied, slipping her credit card

into the folder containing the check. "Besides, I can stick it on my expense account. You advised me on getting Judge Roehmann to recuse himself in the Pherson case."

As if Baird Roehmann would take a hint like that. "Like I said, good luck."

"You and the judge have a history, don't you?"

"You could say that." Some of my hardest fought cases had been before the tough judge whose prematurely silver-haired good looks were an unprofessional subject of discussion at local lady litigators' Bar Association meetings. Something I'd never mentioned was that the moment those trials were over, I received calls from the gorgeous judge inviting me out for drinks.

The first time, I was curious enough to accept. But not curious enough to jump into bed with him, as he'd apparently intended. I'd done that with another law professional who had control over my career. Never again.

How many others at the ladies' bar group had been similarly approached by Baird? My subtle attempts to find out suggested that I was a select group of one. If so, why?

More likely, the other ladies lied.

I'd never revealed the entirety of the encounters to Avvie. And while I was enmeshed in my ethics dilemma, that mogul of the local bench had again propositioned, then turned his back on, me.

Right now, I simply finished, "He's a good judge, seems ethical on the bench." Off the bench, though . . . "It shouldn't be hard to convince him not to hear a matter where one of his neighbors is a defendant, since he's likely biased in her favor." But would he be? He might consider a recusal motion a slap at his ability to keep personal biases from beneath his judicial robes.

Baird Roehmann apparently believed he had a lot of interesting stuff under those robes . . .

A few minutes later, Avvie signed the credit slip, stuck her folders back into her briefcase, and stood up, slinging her purse over her shoulder. Lexie sprang from beneath my chair.

"Keep in touch, Kendra, okay?" Avvie put her hand on my arm, solemnity and sympathy in her hazel eyes. "And if there's anything else I can do to help you, let me know."

"Thanks," I said. "For lunch and for the help and—" I sounded pathetic, even to myself.

"Oh, I nearly forgot to tell you," she said, interrupting. "Some detective called the office. Nogales? Something like that. He said not to mention it, but he's made appointments with a few of us this afternoon. He's got questions about you and your role at the firm and your representation of Carl Cuthbertson. Don't worry, though. Everyone's on your side."

I managed another thanks and a smile as Lexie and I walked away. If I fell apart, it wouldn't be in front of Avvie.

CHAPTER 10

I still had an hour before afternoon rounds, so Lexie and I drove by my house and made sure it was still standing.

It sure was—with a couple of clearly marked media vans lining the street. Lying in wait for Charlotte or me? I didn't want to walk up and find out, so I decided to head for Darryl's.

But before I could swing my car onto Ventura Boulevard, my cell phone rang. I glanced at the number on the screen. It was the number I most *didn't* want to appear. "Hello?" I said brusquely.

"Ms. Ballantyne, this is Detective Noralles." No kidding. "I've got a few more questions and wonder if you could come to the North Hollywood station tomorrow at ten A.M? I realize it's Saturday, but maybe that'll be even more convenient for you."

Weekends made no difference to a working pet-sitter. And I had a choice?

He'd have had his MSY meetings by then. Maybe I'd be able to extract any info he'd learned.

Damn! Those meetings had sat on my mind like a lead-bottomed baboon since the moment Avvie had defied the detective's demands and mentioned them to me.

"Sure, *I* could come tomorrow," I responded, "but I don't know if my attorney's available."

A brief silence. "Of course you can bring your attorney, though what I want to ask shouldn't make you feel compelled—"

"Detective Noralles, as you undoubtedly recall, *I'm* a lawyer. My area isn't criminal law, and even if it were, I'm sure you're familiar with the tired old adage about lawyers who represent themselves."

"Yes, and I know you're not a fool, Ms. Ballantyne."

"Amazing that we agree on something, Detective. I'll call later and let you know when we can be there."

Shit. I'd begun shaking, which didn't bode well for driving. Lexie sensed my anxiety, and she whined. "No more calls till we're stopped," I assured her. Only after I pulled up in front of Jeff's place did I say Esther's name into my phone.

Gee, big surprise. My high-powered attorney was in court again. I told her secretary Janet what I needed and was promised a return call that afternoon.

Damn. I really felt unnerved about a command performance before Noralles. Good thing I was already on my way to territory that was friendly—at least till I denied Darryl his request. As a lawyer, I'd met lots of snakes in the grass. That didn't mean I had to get to know a real one now, up close and personal.

Before getting out of the car, I called to get another appointment for the next day—at Carl Cuthbertson's production company. I hinted about being an agent representing a former reality-TV star with an idea, called myself "Kenni Ballan." Could I come talk to them?

I heard her hesitation. "Charlotte LaVerne referred me," I blurted, hoping the woman I was talking to knew something about my tenant and the show she'd been on.

"Okay, come on in," she finally said, surprising me a bit despite my determination. It was Saturday, after all. Good thing showbiz types never rested.

And with Noralles on my case, I needed to dive into my own inquiries as to who'd had it in for Carl.

A short while later, I braced myself as Lexie and I prepared to walk in Darryl's door. Sure, I needed a little moral support. But I didn't need to look like it. I stuck on my former litigator's jury-face. Very friendly. Very sincere. Very guarded about what hid behind it.

Darryl greeted me at the door, wearing his usual green knit logo shirt, jeans, and a big, welcoming smile beneath his wire-rimmed glasses. "Hi, Kendra. You okay?"

"Of course," I lied. "You?"

Lexie tugged on her leash. With a fond shrug, I let her go. She headed to where a large mutt and tiny Yorkie disputed companionably over a fraying rag bone. Lexie proudly swooped it up in her short muzzle and trotted into a corner as the other dogs leapt after her. Soon, they were engaged in a tug of war that seemed both friendly and aggressive.

Darryl motioned to an attendant to keep an eye on the game. Then he spoke softly. "Anything new about the Carl Cuthbertson situation?"

"Not much. The cops have stormed the Marden firm and want to talk to me again."

Darryl's eyes scrunched in concern. He motioned for me to follow him.

"The detective in charge has a lot of questions," I said when he'd closed his office door. "And today they seem to concern the firm, and I'll be on the hot seat tomorrow."

"Are you sure—"

"That I want to go? As much as I'd like to gargle lye. I'll drag Esther along to keep the interrogation friendly."

As he sat behind his messy desk, I planted my jeopardized butt in the soft chair across from him, wondering if it would be the last comfortable seat I'd have access to for a while.

Darryl stayed quiet, unusual for this effervescent business owner who loved to play with his guests even more than he enjoyed their owners' money. Or so he claimed, though he never hesitated to hold out his hand for the aforementioned fees.

"So what about—" I began.

He started speaking at the same time. "Are you okay for money to pay your lawyer, Kendra?"

He'd offered help before, but I'd refused. His suggestion to earn money by pet-sitting, though, had been a horse of a different color . . . green. "I'm doing fine that way now, thanks to you," I said.

"Taking care of animals isn't as lucrative as being a lawyer." He rested his thin arms on the paper piles on his desk as he leaned toward me. "And I know a couple of your new clients—"

"Fired me." I sighed. "Did they call for new referrals?"

"Yeah." His mouth tightened. "I didn't want to lose their business, or I'd have given them referrals, all right." His sudden smile floored me with its evil sparkle. "In this business you hear about owners' nightmares. Sitters who take advantage of having house keys, stealing, that kind of thing."

"I figured." Surely he didn't really want to repay my defecting clients that way.

"Back to the question, though," he said.

"The answer is 'Kona coffee.' "

"What?"

"My favorite kind of coffee. The one you brew here for staff and visiting pet owners. Could I have a cup?"

"You're changing the subject."

"You got it." As I rose, I smiled. "Like I said, I'm fine, Darryl. Thanks for asking."

He stood, too. "You'll never ask for help, will you?"

89

"If I do, we'll both be sorry."

He walked through the pup-filled main room toward the kitchen.

"Kendra?" called a loud female voice. "I thought I might find you here. I heard about Carl and you on the news."

Cringing as all human eyes in the place focused on me, I turned to see Shirley Dorian walk through the spa's outer door, her silver miniature poodle Rosie in her arms. I wondered if I should just gather up Lexie and leave.

Shirley had called during my ethics investigation and gave me her vote of confidence. But she'd first been a good friend of Carl's. He'd referred her to me as a lawyer a year ago, when her show biz public relations company was sued for defamation. I'd become as friendly with her as with Carl, and I had recommended Darryl's place for Rosie when I learned she lived in the San Fernando Valley.

But now Carl was dead, and if she listened to the media, she probably thought it was by my hand. I guess I'd know soon enough.

"I'm glad I caught up with you," she said as she reached my side.

Shirley exemplified the adage that people adopted dogs that looked like them. Shirley was short. Her hair was poodle-curly and formed a wiry gray helmet about her round face. Her nose was smaller than her dog's, but her mouth was as wide, and almost always open. She wasn't known for quiet ways or tact. That was why she was a pillar of the

PR industry, I supposed. Before, I'd admired her for her outspokenness. Was she about to lay into *me* now?

"I called your old office," she continued, "but they wouldn't give out your cell phone number." Rosie wriggled, so Shirley let her down. The small silver dynamo dashed to the sofa, leapt up with the bigger guys, and lay down. "I tried your home and didn't even get an answering machine. Tell me what happened."

Darryl sidled to me as if in support. But though Shirley was frowning, I didn't feel any ire.

Quietly, carefully keeping emotions at bay, I related how I'd found Carl. She studied my face with small, glistening eyes behind black-rimmed glasses, as if assessing my truthfulness. I felt Darryl's attention, too. These two people were— or had been—my friends. Would they believe me? *Please let them believe me . . .*

"I believe you, you poor dear," Shirley said as I finished with a mention of my upcoming police tête-à-tête.

I blinked in surprise. She smiled, baring large, even teeth. "You did a damn fine job defending my ass in the lawsuit brought by that piece of feces former client of mine. Carl spoke highly of you, too. Why the hell would you have killed him? Plus, I was always impressed by your intelligence. If you murdered anyone, you'd keep your own nose looking clean and frame someone else. Right?" She looked at Darryl.

"Damn straight." He grinned back.

"So look, Kendra. I didn't realize you were pet-sitting while your other troubles get straightened out till I heard it in the news. I'm going to San Francisco next week, and the neighbor I usually trade pet-watching with is recuperating from surgery. Will you take care of Rosie for me?"

"Sure." I was certain to have time, with other customers leaping off like frightened fleas.

Unless I was in jail awaiting trial for murder . . .

"Great. Give me your phone number and we'll work out the details."

Grinning so hard my face nearly cracked, I complied. She gave Darryl instructions on what to do with Rosie for the rest of the afternoon while she dashed to a meeting. Then she was gone.

And I had another client. A new one. An old friend. I walked to Rosie and petted her wiry curls. She woke up enough to roll her eyes at me. Mine were a little misty, but I ignored them. Time for Lexie and me to get back on the road.

When I went to say goodbye to Darryl, he was near the door. With him stood a guy whose width rivaled his not-so-imposing height. He had a brown mustache and glasses, and wispy hair stuck out from his head. I jumped to the conclusion he was a techy geek, partly because of his Coke-bottle lenses and the pasty shade of his skin above his white shirt and charcoal slacks. The only thing interesting about him was his narrow necktie, patterned with pale magenta swirls on a stunning, glossy blue background.

And then the necktie raised its head, looked at me and stuck out a forked tongue. I gasped. And then I knew. "Is—is that Pythagoras?" I croaked.

"Yes." The man beneath the python rushed toward me and shook my hand. "Are you Kendra? Darryl's told me about your pet-sitting service. If I weren't desperate, I wouldn't leave Py at home, but I'm going to my mother's wedding, and she doesn't tolerate reptiles well."

"I see," I managed. Had Darryl suggested that snakes were my best friends?

Smoothly, Darryl said, "Kendra, this is Milt Abadim. He set up my books and does my taxes. Keep him in mind for your accounting."

No wonder he named his snake after an ancient philosopher who'd developed geometric and mathematic theorems, if my memory of undergrad history wasn't mush.

"When Milt comes here to work, Py's always with him. The dogs don't bother him, though they get a little edgy when they see Py."

Like me. Still, I'd never imagined a snake to be such gorgeous colors. "Does he bite?" I asked.

"Only when he's scared." I wasn't reassured. "But then he mostly curls up into . . . well, a pretzel. Or a ball. He is a ball python, you know. They twist themselves when they get nervous. That's how they got their name. They're also sometimes known as royal pythons, did you know that?"

I gathered that Milt, instead of twisting himself into a ball when nervous, let his tongue run loose.

"He's not very old. That's why he's only about three feet long and sort of thin. Females are bigger. They come in lots of colorations, not just how Py looks—mostly browns and rusts and even albino—but I like his more exotic colors. Or did you know all that?"

"No, I didn't. Milt, I'm afraid I—"

"Here." By the panic in his eyes, I'd say he guessed I was about to refuse the job. By the panic in my eyes as he lifted the snake from his neck and put him around mine, he could guess why.

Only I didn't feel so panicky with Py around my shoulders. He wasn't very heavy. And when I lifted my hand to touch his bright blue skin, he wasn't slimy.

"He likes you," Milt said, sounding relieved.

The strange thing was, I liked him. Kind of. Or at least I wasn't as freaked as I expected to be with a reptile wrapped around my neck.

Not until he started slithering down one side, over my right boob and downward. "Hey!" I stared down, horrified, and watched as he slid head first into one of the pockets in my jacket.

He disappeared there. How could something that large disappear into my pocket? Yes, it was a deep pocket, but . . .

"Maybe he is feeling a little stressed," Milt admitted. "I'm sure he wanted to make a good impression. Is he twisted into a ball in your pocket?" He held out his hands as if intending to reach in and check, but his gaze fixed first on my bosom, and he backed off, face flaming red.

Drolly, I met Darryl's eyes. He winked, the louse. He'd put me into this position, and he was enjoying every moment of it.

Still, I owed him. A lot. So I reached down and pulled the top of my pocket out as far as it would go. I looked inside.

Sure enough, Py had rolled himself into a coil, his screwdriver-shaped head pointed up as if he were watching to see what I was going to do.

What could I do? I was unexpectedly charmed by this snake. "Let's make a date for you to teach me how to take care of a ball python, Milt."

I only winced once when he started describing what Py ate.

CHAPTER 11

L exie and I got back in the Beamer. Then came the beginning of the barrage of phone calls.

The first was from Detective Noralles, reminding me to pick a time for tomorrow's session. His windows of opportunity were narrowing, though it was the weekend. Didn't the guy have a hobby?

I eliminated a couple of his possibilities, then said I still needed to get back to him with my lawyer's availability.

I'd no sooner hung up than I heard from that lawyer. We settled on one of Noralles's times. I was glad when Esther said she would call Noralles back.

Lexie and I headed toward the next pet-sitting house. Before we got there, I heard from another client with an excuse to fire me tactfully: His boss cancelled his vacation next week. I expressed condolences, almost sounding like I believed him.

Damn. I'd begun to keep a mental list. Shirley had joined me, but so many other clients were tap-dancing away. What would I do if even my new career collapsed?

As we pulled up to the Valley Village home we'd aimed for, another client I'd sat for last week called. I cringed. But he couldn't fire me. I didn't have a current assignment for him.

To my surprise, he asked about Carl's death, and he apparently empathized with my situation. "I know you'll be busy straightening out that mess," he said, "but if you could look after Lester for me, I'd appreciate it." Lester was a basset hound whose morose visage disguised a sweet, happy-go-lucky personality. Trying not to sound too effusive, I promised Lexie and I would take wonderful care of Lester again.

The score was evening out.

Though I liked "Ode to Joy," I was getting tired of so much bliss. I shut off my cell phone so the voicemail would kick in. Next, I needed to concentrate on taking care of Cicely, the Shih-Tzu, at the house we'd just reached. I brought Lexie in. She and Cicely got along famously—a little mop of white fur playing with my tricolored pup on the blue tiled kitchen floor. Cicely's potty training left a lot to be desired, and the kitchen smelled like it, but hey, I'd cleaned up worse in my day. Though not as often as lately. The three of us took a short walk. When we got back, I mopped to mask the odor while Lexie and Cicely romped.

Back in my car, I cringingly checked my cell for messages. Esther had called to confirm the time for the police interview tomorrow. "Hell, what a euphemism for interrogation," I told

Lexie, who cocked her head attentively and wagged her tail.

Another client had called to hire, not fire me. I was smiling at how things were sort of looking up when I pulled up in front of another client's house in Van Nuys—a cat-house, dominated by four felines. After returning to my car, I turned my phone back on.

The next time "Ode to Joy" serenaded me, it did not portend anything close to joy. It was Carl's daughter Laurie. "What does this dog eat?" she exploded. "I even brought the dog food from Dad's kitchen, but she hasn't touched a bite."

Cheesie hadn't eaten in two days? And what about her medication? "She's grieving, Laurie," I said. "Tempt her with treats. Even table scraps. And make sure you use a piece of hot dog to get her to take her allergy pill. If she doesn't get anything down tonight, I'd take her to a vet tomorrow."

"Vets are expensive," she grumbled. "And dogs don't have emotions like people do. I'm the one who's grieving over Dad. Do you know, they haven't even released his body for burial yet. Something about needing to complete the autopsy because his death was a homicide. It's not right."

"It's probably the law, Laurie. And you're wrong about dogs. I once had one who—"

"Well, if this one doesn't snap out of it, she'll wind up in a shelter. With my kids and work and dealing with Dad's funeral, I can't handle another problem." Her voice had risen, and she almost shrieked the last few words.

Poor Cheesie.

"Tell you what," I said calmly, though if she'd been closer I'd have considered kicking her. "If you get to the point that you can't keep Cheesie, let me know. A good friend of mine owns a doggy daycare facility, and he'll find her a good home. Okay?"

"Who the hell pays good money to keep their dogs in daycare?" Laurie grumbled. "I've got my youngest in kids' daycare, and it costs a fortune."

"To some people, their pets are like their families."

"Pathetic," Laurie spat. "Anyhow, I'll keep in mind what you said about a new home." A pause. "You're not planning to take her, are you? I mean, the police think you were involved in my dad's death. It'd look bad if I turned his dog over to you."

Lord, I was starting to loathe this woman. I wanted to feel sorry for her, losing her father that way. But I could see now why Cheesie was more family to Carl than his daughter had been.

"I don't have room for Cheesie in my life right now," I said coolly, "but I'll help find her a new home, if that's what you want. And for the record, I didn't hurt your dad, Laurie. I really liked him." *Maybe more than you did.*

Fortunately, she hung up. I was broiling, sitting in the car. And the heat was less from the beating sun than it was from talking to that miserable excuse for a daughter.

Sometime later, "Ode to Joy" pealed again. I was finally on my way home, navigating surface streets toward Jeff's.

"Kendra, this is Baird."

The Honorable Baird Roehmann, judge of the Superior Court of the State of California.

"Hi," I said unenthusiastically. Was he going to suggest he'd somehow get the heat off me if I slept with him? He'd hinted as much when I was under siege by the State Bar. When I'd half-jokingly said I'd take him up on it, he'd backpedaled—fast. I'd imagined him on a unicycle in his trailing black judicial robes and had laughed in his face despite the worries on my shoulders. Other than that fiasco of a phone call, he'd offered me no support, immoral or otherwise. And now, all that seemed trivial to a potential murder suspect.

"Kendra, I heard the news about your finding one of your former clients dead."

"He was a current client, too, Baird."

Silence. "But your law license is suspended." As an officer of the court, he'd be obliged to report any infractions to the State Bar.

Only I hadn't breached the terms of my suspension. "Carl Cuthbertson was also a pet-sitting client. That's my job now."

"Oh." I could imagine what he was thinking. Baird lived for the law. The world consisted of two groups: those involved in the judicial process and those who weren't. The elite were judges, followed by lawyers, then support staff who took care of those who really mattered. Everyone else had a hierarchy, too, but their functions were primarily as suspects or victims in criminal cases, and plaintiffs or defendants in civil courts. No one else was worth worrying about.

I'd become a pet-sitter. Maybe I no longer existed to him.

Maybe that was a good thing.

The silence stretched. I heard fidgeting on the seat beside me and glanced over. Lexie watched me carefully, as if sensing the shift in my mood.

Well, hell, I really didn't give a damn what His Honor thought of me. "Did you want something, Baird? I'm on my way to see a dog about a walk." Odin was waiting for Lexie and me, and he'd want exercise and attention.

"It's a great idea for you to keep busy," he finally said. "I was calling mostly to say that I'm on your side. No matter what else you did, I don't see you as capable of murder."

What a glowing endorsement.

"Thanks, but you realize that means you'd have to recuse yourself if you're the judge selected to hear my murder trial."

Another silence. Surely he wasn't really mulling that over.

"And speaking of recusing yourself," I continued, "I had lunch with Avvie Milton. She said one of your neighbors was involved in a case before you."

"Avvie has her own agenda," he huffed. "And I'll do what's right." His voice lowered. "Kendra, anytime you'd like to get together, let me know. I can't fix things for you, but maybe I can provide . . . well, a shoulder to lean on. A distraction, at least."

An eager body for sex, was what he meant.

"Thanks, Baird. I'm okay for now. But if I ever need someone to talk to—or whatever—I'll let you know." With a shake of my head, I flipped my phone closed.

Only one more call of note that day. It didn't come till I was back at Jeff's, trying to relax and not think about my pending "interview" the next day. The caller? Jeff himself.

I sat in his living room. When his home phone rang, I pushed the mute button on his wide-screen TV. The news commentators began to benignly mouth their usual stories of the day's horribles. Maybe I'd always keep the news on mute after this. I answered the phone.

"Kendra? It's Jeff. How's Odin?"

That very dog was curled up beside Lexie and me on the sofa, though I didn't mention it to Jeff. He was one of those finicky owners who seemed to consider his pet less than human, and therefore not entitled to be on the furniture.

Of course Jeff's sectional sofa was white. But hey, the dogs were clean—sort of.

"He's fine," I responded, smiling at the Akita. Odin caught my eye without raising his head. His curled tail made a half-hearted attempt to wag before he went back to sleep.

"And you? Anything new today?"

"Well, I agreed to take on a snake as a pet-sitting client."

"I mean with your case."

"I didn't stab anyone today, so it was relatively quiet."

"Kendra . . ." He drew out my name ominously, and I grinned. The guy even sounded sexy when he was exasperated.

But he wasn't here, and it was a good thing. I didn't need a complication like sex right now, no matter how much fun it might have been.

"Tomorrow's a big day," I told him, then I mentioned my upcoming interview by the police and their additional MSY meetings. "I also made an appointment at Carl Cuthbertson's company. I'm getting in on false pretenses—is that a crime, or just a private investigator's ploy? I figured they wouldn't see me if they knew I was the miserable jerk accused of murdering their boss, so I said I had a showbiz idea to run by them. A can't-miss TV show."

"Good move. Now, here are the things you'll need to ask."

I sighed but nevertheless grabbed a pad of paper from my purse and took notes. Most of what he said was common sense, but a few things I wouldn't have thought of. Chalk it up to his years of experience as a P.I.

"I'll call tomorrow around the same time," he told me. "I'll want a full report."

"Sure," I said, ignoring his boss-to-assistant bark.

"Oh, and Kendra?" His tone had segued from brusqueness to something less professional. It sent a chill down my back—a very warm one.

"Yes?"

"Think of me when you're lying in bed tonight."

"Sure," I said, wondering where the heck that had come from. Wherever it was, I liked it. At a distance. "Instead of sheep, I'll count egotistical investigators climbing in windows. That'll help me get to sleep."

He laughed. So did I.

But damned if I didn't think of him after I'd showered, pulled on the long T-shirt I wore at night, and climbed into bed, Lexie at my feet.

I pictured only one egotistical investigator with really nice buns. Climbing in *my* window.

CHAPTER 12

The North Hollywood Division of the LAPD was housed in a relatively new building, and its neighborhood was as much residential as commercial.

I parked in the small lot to one side of the entry drive. Straight ahead was the large yard where police cars park. But though I was here on official business, I wasn't one of them. I wasn't even a practicing lawyer at the moment. I was a suspect.

Shit.

I'd left Lexie with Odin at Jeff's. Before heading for pet-care rounds, I'd dressed in nice slacks and a beige shirt. Now, as when visiting my old firm, I took my tweed suit-jacket from the trunk and put it on. With it, I donned my litigator personality. Crisp. Businesslike. The consummate shark on behalf of my clients. Only this time, *I* was the client. And I was relieved when, before I went inside, my own attorney arrived.

Esther Ickes' red Mercedes convertible put the other autos in the little lot to shame, even my Beamer. Hearing it purr into place, its sporty presence shouting "Watch me!" one would assume that its driver, too, craved attention.

But Esther thrived on sleight-of-hand and misdirection. For out of from behind the wheel emerged a little old lady with unabashedly gray hair, wrinkles worthy of a crumpled linen suit, and a thin, fragile physique. The briefcase she drew from behind the driver's seat looked bigger than she did.

But woe to the opposing attorney who took her at face value.

Her face lit up as she saw me. "Kendra! How are you, dear?"

"Great, all things considered."

"Well, we'll get this little inconvenience straightened out so you can put it behind you." Esther was a master of understatement, and she made good on her promises. Of course, she'd never promised to get me out of the breach of ethics claims. Getting creditors off my back by a discharged bankruptcy had been another matter.

Together, we walked beneath the square arch toward the police station's doors. Black, bigger-than-life glossy fingerprints decorated the slate sidewalk. Twenty-first century police station chic. Cute.

Briskly, Esther identified us to the uniformed officer behind the tall desk inside. "Detective Noralles is expecting us," she said.

Noralles appeared from an open doorway near the desk a minute later. "This way, please," he said. He led us down a hall, through a door labeled "Detectives," and into a large room lined with offices and decorated with a rabbit warren of teal blue cubicles. Only a few were occupied on this Saturday. Signs swung overhead, identifying each area—Theft, Auto Theft, Homicide, Major Assault Crimes, etc. Noralles opened the door to a small torture chamber labeled "Interview Room F." The sole instrument of torture, however, was him.

Actually, the interview didn't go badly. Noralles mostly went over the same ground as he had two days earlier at the murder scene. Was he trying to trip me up, see if my story stayed the same? Well, it did.

Esther mostly listened, nodding occasionally, lifting a gnarled index finger if Noralles asked a leading and unfair question like, "What reason did you have to harm the victim?" A few chastising *tsks* from Esther, and Noralles rephrased. "Did you have any reason to harm the victim?"

"No," I replied resoundingly. And though I well knew that I should only answer questions, not offer testimony, I did anyway. "Carl used to be my law client, and he was a good guy. You need to look for someone with a motive, Detective, and that's not me." The outburst earned me scowls from both sides, but I didn't care.

The detective inquired about my earlier legal representation of Carl and asked if I'd kept my nose in his business afterward. Which I hadn't. Some of his questions implied that I'd coveted

Carl's possessions. I set Noralles straight, especially since he had suggested to Jeff that getting caught stealing was my motive for murder.

I didn't think he really believed his own allegations. He was trawling for a real rationale. There was none. Or did he have something in mind he wasn't disclosing?

The session didn't actually take very long, but it felt like forever. "You're free to go, Ms. Ballantyne," the detective finally said, after less than an hour.

"Thanks," I said as I stood. "By the way, did my dear former co-workers at MSY describe what a paragon of ethics I was as a litigator? Or did they impugn my character with allegations that I actually could kill?"

"Kendra . . ." Esther's tone was admonishing.

"Okay, forget that, but do you have any *real* suspects? With honest-to-goodness motives and all?"

"We're looking into all possibilities." Noralles's voice was as bland as instant potatoes.

"What about fingerprints on the knife. Whose—?"

"Only the victim's," he admitted.

"Any others in his bedroom, which was trashed?" Chronically respectful of customers' privacy, I hadn't gone into Carl's bedroom except when I'd found him.

"Do you happen to own any latex gloves, Ms. Ballantyne?"

No fingerprints pointed to anyone, then.

"No," I responded. "So let's get back to real suspects, those who, unlike me, might have motive. How about—"

"How about feeling glad you're free to go," he said. *"For now."* The emphasis was his, not mine, and his smile seemed crocodile smug.

"Are you suggesting you don't have other suspects?"

"I'm only suggesting that I'm looking forward to seeing you again. Soon."

"The nice detective said we can go, Kendra." Esther's yank on my elbow was as authoritative as her tone.

My retort retreated and my heart sank as Noralles's malicious grin grew wider. "Say hello to Jeff Hubbard for me."

So Noralles was gunning for me because I knew Jeff Hubbard. Maybe. But I couldn't simply assume he was harassing me out of some kind of perverse payback for his past embarrassments. Hell, he hadn't even asked if Jeff and I had anything going but a business relationship. Which we hadn't. So why strike at me to get to Jeff?

For now, at least, I still enjoyed my Constitutional right of freedom to go wherever the hell I wanted. And so, after enduring Esther's anticipated admonishments, plus sending a few calculated "no comments" to a flock of media vultures who'd suddenly appeared outside the station, I made some pet visits. Then, at three o'clock, I went to keep my appointment at Cuthbertson Productions.

It was housed in a small building on Ventura Boulevard in Encino. I parked a couple of blocks away. It gave me time to hone my strategy as I strode through the busy retail area.

Strategy? Hell! My skills as an investigator were tenuous at best. I'd been a damned good litigator not long ago, but my confidence in keeping myself out of prison was slim. Still, I had to try. After all, what would happen to all my new pet clients if they couldn't count on my coming around?

What would happen to *me?*

Back to the present, Ballantyne. Strategize!

I didn't know many of the players at Cuthbertson. When it was my client, I'd dealt directly with Carl. And in that industry, underlings changed as often as TV shows were cancelled.

Carl had said he started out with ambitions of doing feature films, but he'd made money mostly shooting TV commercials. His biggest claim to fame was a sitcom in the early nineties starring an aging film luminary who'd turned to television to plump up her pocketbook in her later years. Cuthbertson Productions had been a moneymaker, but it had lacked the panache that bred Hollywood popularity. No focus. No flair.

And then Carl got hold of the feature film script that he was sure would turn everything around— a comedy with pathos, adventure, and a big, fat, meaty starring role to entice one of the industry's biggest money-magnets.

Until Conrad Taylor stole it.

Taylor's company had lured the star and filmed the flick. Marketed it. And made a lot of money from it, after convincing their staff writer that changing a minor role, characters' names, and a few other small things in a script that had allegedly come to them on spec wasn't plagiarism.

Carl disagreed and sued, and I negotiated a hell of a hefty settlement for him. If it had gone to trial, the added publicity could have ruined the rest of Taylor's shredded reputation.

Had Carl's murder been a year ago, I'd have been sure Taylor was the killer. He was still on my puny list as a "person of interest," as the police euphemistically called people they'd not yet found enough evidence against to arrest.

People like me.

But unless Taylor was driven slowly insane by what had happened in the past, he wasn't likely to have murdered Carl two days ago.

I pushed open the door to the Cuthbertson building. The place hadn't changed much in the last couple of years. The entry didn't even aspire to hold cubicles. Junior industry wannabes sat at rows of desks near phones and tried to look as if they knew something. Better yet, somebody. Even on a Saturday.

A young woman near the door asked politely, "Can I help you?" She had short, brassy hair, gold studs in each ear, and a wide band about her neck that resembled a dog collar.

"I have an appointment with Eve Adolph. My name is . . . Kenni Ballan."

"Oh, yes, the reality show idea. Please come in." She all but purred. The news had traveled fast.

And I would have to think fast, if I truly were to come up with an idea for one of those gross reality productions.

Hell, that had only been to get my toes in the door. Now that I was all the way inside, I'd drop the pretense.

"Ms. Ballan?" A modulated alto female voice got my attention. From an open door at the end of the busy reception room, a slender blond wearing a sundress and glasses glided toward me. With that slinky, steady gait, she'd either trained as a model or a ghost. "I'm Eve." I'd barely touched her cool outstretched hand in greeting before she withdrew it and turned. "This way, please."

As I followed her, I felt the eyes of the myriad of wannabes following me. Were they always that interested in a visitor?

Eve showed me into a small room containing a low table surrounded by comfortable-looking chairs. She motioned me to a seat and lowered herself elegantly into her own chair. "So," she said, "you've an idea for the ultimate reality show."

Why waste time? "Not exactly. I wanted to talk to someone at Cuthbertson Productions about—"

"About Carl's death," she finished. "You're brave

112

coming here, Kendra Ballantyne. Or stupid." Oops. She knew who I was. I suddenly had the impression I'd been lured into a lion's den instead of being a shady sleuth who'd bluffed her way into an interview. Her smile revealed perfect teeth framed by full lips painted bright pink. Her brown eyes beamed from beneath tortoise-shell frames. "We miss him, you know. He was a sweet man and a great boss. You and I haven't met before, since I started at Cuthbertson after you represented the company in that Taylor litigation, but your name's still revered here. At least it was."

"I should have used a better alias," I said.

"Do you have something to hide?" She sounded excited, though her well-trained voice remained low. "I can't imagine that you'd come here to confess to killing Carl—you're a lawyer, right? You know that you can't sell your story to get rich for doing something illegal like murder, don't you?"

I nodded, though I was beginning to feel befuddled. "I came here because I didn't kill Carl. I'm trying to figure out who did, partly to save my own hide."

"Oh." I sensed her disappointment. "I thought you'd come to sell your story for a feature film. Still, we might be able to make a deal about what happened to you before. I mean, how much did Lorraine Giles pay you to hand over that memo? Did you know it would make her so mad she'd kill your client? Or was that the whole idea? The news said you'd had a falling out and the guy—what was his name? Germany?"

"Germane," I corrected, "but—"

"Germane was going to hand the case over to another lawyer, maybe even one outside your firm."

I rose. "How do you remember all this? It was months ago."

"Carl trained us to keep tuned to the news, in case something struck us as a perfect biopic for a made-for-TV movie. Your story had it all: murder. Insanity. A lawyer who claimed to be ethical despite all evidence to the contrary—a photogenic lawyer at that." She eyed me up and down. "You've lost weight. That's good. Thin looks better on camera. We wouldn't have to get someone who really looked like you to play the part, but now that you're involved in the murder of our own boss, well, we'll have to see how this plays out. The media are hinting you're the top suspect, you know."

"Yeah, I know." I was standing now, glaring down at her. She looked right back at me, impassively. Time for me to make a move of my own. In fact, it was way past time. "So tell me, Eve, did you kill Carl?"

She rose, too. Elegantly, of course. "A police detective already asked, and I'll respond to you the same as I did to him: Why would I?"

"You tell me." Was she speaking of Noralles? Had he learned anything useful here? If so, he'd hardly remain fixated on me . . . would he?

"I wouldn't have hurt Carl," Eve responded. "And before you ask the next, obvious question about who here would, the answer is no one. Carl was about to sell the company. We all knew it, and we also knew we'd be taken care of—we'd still have our jobs, even a bonus. We'll be merged into . . . Never mind. That's not really public yet. But the fact we were looking to be bought out made a splash in the trades a few months ago."

"It did?" I didn't read the entertainment industry trade journals, but that was the kind of thing I'd have heard about. Cuthbertson was a client of MSY, and until a few weeks ago, I'd been a partner there.

"Yes. In fact, it's been almost a year, around when all that stuff about Lorraine Giles and Mr. Germane was going on."

That explained it. My mind had been otherwise engaged.

"It actually made headlines, you know—the fact that Carl was working with Conrad Taylor to find a partner."

"What! He's the louse who stole that big script. The one we sued and negotiated a big settlement from. The one—"

"The one whose film was based on that stolen script Carl really admired. Carl always said—secretly, of course—that he wasn't sure he'd have done it as well."

He'd told me that, but it wasn't the point. "Why Taylor?"

"They'd admired each other's moxie in the lawsuit. Became friends." She sat again, obviously feeling in control once more. She crossed one long leg over the other.

"He didn't tell me, even when he hired me to pet-sit." I remained standing. Petty, perhaps, but I felt I had the upper hand while I could look down on her.

"You know what a sweet guy Carl was. He wouldn't have wanted to upset you."

That sounded like Carl. Still . . . "With this big merger pending, don't you need a lawyer?"

"You're not offering, are you?" She bent her head back as if to study my face. "I thought your license was suspended."

"No. I mean, yes, I can't practice law right now. No, I'm not offering to represent you. I wouldn't anyway. I'm a litigator, not a transactional type. But—"

"I see." Once again, she stood. This time she looked at her watch. Obviously, her fun was over. Time to dismiss the object of this little game. She walked to the door and opened it. "Talk to Mr. Marden of your former firm. He was doing the paperwork."

CHAPTER 13

As if meeting with Noralles and that last statement from Eve hadn't already ruined my day, when I left the building a microphone materialized in front of my mouth. The media vultures must have flown after me. "Ms. Ballantyne, please tell us—"

"No comment," I snapped at the rapacious lady reporter, whom I recognized from Channel 9. I locked the car doors behind me and sighed. Talk about a bad day . . .

Time to get back to work, though. The animals depending on me would have called and said so, if they could.

I wished what I needed to do for them occupied more than a fraction of my brain. My overly agitated gray matter had to be glowing orange as I moved my mind along Noralles's awful attitude, the offensive journalists, and the secrets my friend and two-time client Carl had kept from me.

Pulling my car too fast from its parking space, I heard tires squeal. I waved an apology toward a scarlet-faced man who was mouthing invectives that I was better off not hearing.

Carl was involved in a transaction brokered by a guy I'd considered his worst enemy. He was using the top-name partner of my former firm to paper the deal. What *was* the deal?

I pulled again to the curb. "Avvie home," I ordered my cell phone. It was Saturday, after all.

"Hello?"

"Hi, Avvie. It's Kendra."

"How are you? Any news? Don't tell me you found out who killed Carl."

"Okay, I won't tell you."

It was a feeble attempt at a joke. I considered asking about her interview with Noralles but my curiosity about that had slipped to second place. What I wanted to demand was, *Why didn't you tell me all you knew about Carl?*

"So why didn't you tell me all you knew about Carl?" Hell, there really hadn't been any reason not to blurt it.

Pregnant silence. Then, she said brightly, "So you know about the Millipede FilmAmericam buy-out."

"Yes." Actually, I hadn't. But now I figured that Millipede, a boutique production company in the news enough for me to have heard of it, was purchasing the Cuthbertson assets.

"What we're doing is attorney-client privileged, you know."

Damn. Was she lecturing me about ethics?

"Of course it's not a well-kept secret," she continued. "Everyone knew that Cuthbertson was looking to be bought, and that Conrad Taylor was acting as broker." Everyone except me. "It made the trades months ago." Yeah, I knew that now. "One of the papers glommed on to the Millipede offer as being the one Cuthbertson would accept, but we were still in negotiations, so we could neither confirm nor deny it."

"We? I thought you were still a litigator. The transactional sorts are putting this together, right?"

"I meant the collective 'we,' the whole Marden firm. Royal's handling it, along with a couple of his associates."

Again what Eve had said.

And of course that big, fat, collective "we" of the Marden firm no longer included *me*. That scraped at the backbone of what little was left of my professional pride. "So Bill and you, and Marden and Yurick, and even Carl, figured I didn't need to know."

Another pause. "Not Yurick. Borden's still on medical leave. And you *didn't* need to know."

"Maybe, but I'm still mad."

Then it hit me. I'd just unearthed the non-existent motive Noralles had been angling for! He'd spoken to MSY people before our go-around today. Had it been why he'd seemed so smug? I assumed his scenario went something like this: I'd been kept out of the loop in this mega-sale of my former client, Cuthbertson Productions. When I heard about it, I was so peeved I stabbed Carl Cuthbertson.

A puny motive, to be sure, though it ranked slightly better than burglary. And it was just as false, except for the peeved part. But if Noralles could prove that it led to my losing it—and he clearly thought he could—my freedom would be toast.

No matter that only a crazy person would let something so trivial turn to homicidal rage. Of course I knew a homicidal maniac who'd done just that. Lorraine Giles.

"Kendra, are you still there?"

"Sorry, Avvie. It's a surprise, but I appreciate your reasoning. Carl's, too. He might have felt embarrassed about taking up with the guy we'd considered Satan incarnate last year. I'm sorry he didn't feel he could confide in me, but I understand why." If that didn't sound calm and reasonable, what would?

Maybe Avvie would testify on my behalf: *Yes, Your Honor, she sounded surprised by some of the information, but after her initial stunned reaction she took it like a trooper.*

Not a homicidal maniac.

After hanging up with Avvie, I let my mind wander as I headed for Alexander's house. Let it? Hell, it insisted on leaping from one frantic prediction for my jeopardized future to another.

Alexander the pit bull was delighted to see me. I walked him, played with him, fed him. His enthusiasm at my undivided attention convinced me to ensure that my attention *was* undivided. I owed that to my four-footed charges.

I even owed it to the slithering ones like Pythagoras the python, assuming his owner Milt hired me to keep him happy.

With colossal concentration, I almost succeeded in keeping my mind on the afternoon's tasks. For maybe half an hour. Then, while driving to my next pet household, I accidentally let it rove again. I had to reassess where I was. Where could I go with what I'd learned? How could I protect myself?

The only solution? Find Carl's killer.

So far, my pet-sitting hadn't evaporated. Even if it did, I'd have better things to do with my time than spend it in prison. Wouldn't I?

Nix the negativity, Ballantyne. I had to focus my once razor-sharp litigator's mind on finding solutions.

Could Carl have tried to back out of the Millipede deal? Cut Taylor out of his finder's fee or whatever his consideration was to be? Time passage or no, because of his earlier enmity with Carl, Taylor soared to the top of my list of those to contact.

While waiting for a light to change, I called Esther and got her machine. I told her it was important that she call back soon, since I had new information vital to my case. I also needed to attempt to talk with Conrad Taylor myself. But I only had his business info. I'd have to wait until Monday.

I reached the home of my next charges: a cagy

cat named Purrpuss and her laid-back iguana companion, Iggy. Iggy was where he belonged, in a well-equipped iguana playground on a table in the owners' study. He didn't take much tending, which was why I'd agreed to take him on with the cat of the house. But Purrpuss was another story. There were no new messes in her litter box, a good thing. But there was also no sign of her scurrying either to or from me when I opened the door.

Was she okay? Was she even there?

Oh, hell—had I blown the profession of pet-sitting already?

It took me half an hour of calling, cajoling, and nearly crying before Purrpuss deigned to appear. I wasn't sure where she'd been, but she approached while I was in the kitchen noisily rattling cat goodies in her bowl. She permitted me to feed her while I pretended that I was delighted to see her. It wasn't total pretense. I was relieved. And I had to keep my anger at her for scaring me way down deep in my pet-sitting gut.

If I'd been inclined to feline-icide, though . . .

Fortunately, the two cats at the next house were where they belonged. So was the dog after that.

I could almost relax.

When my visits were complete, I headed back to Jeff's. There, I gushed over Lexie and Odin as they gushed back over me. I took them for their walk. Fed them dinner.

And then I sat down on Jeff's white sectional

sofa in his sunken living room, planted my arms along its back, rested my head back, and waited, desperately, for inspiration.

My goose would be more than cooked if I didn't find some answers fast. And though I'd heard that geese made nasty pets, I had a vested interest in this one.

What the hell could I realistically do to save it?

CHAPTER 14

I made another list.

I'd gotten good at that while a litigator. It helped keep my mind on details, and details won cases.

So, sitting in Jeff's living room, I drew columns and started filling them in.

The first was for immediate steps. What could I do tonight?

I jotted down names of two people to call.

Tomorrow? It was Sunday. I'd cruise Carl's neighborhood and see what I could see. Talk to whoever would talk, then follow up in any way I could.

Monday? Time to seek a way to quiz Conrad Taylor.

Odin and Lexie lay on the sofa beside me. I wasn't exactly teaching Jeff's dog bad habits; I was simply refusing to insist on good ones.

Lexie snuggled beside me, sweet, warm, and wriggly. Most often, her head lay on my lap, and now and then she would open her eyes and roll them up toward me as if making sure I was okay.

She's a Cavalier. That's her job.

"So what do you think of this game plan?" I asked. Lexie cocked her head as if taking in every word, then she licked my elbow.

Odin watched the exchange with ears raised. He edged over and flopped down half on Lexie, looking up at me with his own attentive brown eyes.

I read my list aloud with both dogs listening. "Would your master approve?" I asked Odin. He didn't say no. "Tell you what," I said. "Let's go into the kitchen for a treat, then I'll make my phone calls." And that's what we did: nice, ripe cherries for me and hard, crunchy biscuits for them.

Returning to the living room, I picked up Jeff's portable phone from its cradle on the rustic coffee table. The dogs resumed their places with me on the couch as I pressed in the number for Laurie Shinnick, Carl's daughter.

"Hi, Laurie," I said when she answered. "This is Kendra Ballantyne." I waited for a scathing retort.

"Hi, Kendra." Her voice was tired yet cordial.

"How's Cheesie?" My excuse for calling. "Is she eating?"

"A little. I . . . I think she's sad. Do dogs really mourn? I know you said they do. She keeps walking around my house as if looking for something. Someone. My dad, maybe."

Tears rushed to my eyes. And not just for Cheesie. I had a feeling that the poor, ownerless dog wasn't the only one mourning, now that

Laurie'd had a chance to think about the loss of her dad. Maybe they hadn't been close, but that might make it even harder. No time to cure past estrangements.

"Yes," I said softly. "Dogs can mourn." Lexie and Odin both eyed me curiously, as if wondering why I sounded choked up. Holding the phone in one hand, I gave them each a pat. "It's surprising," I continued, "but dogs actually *have* a lot of the emotions people sometimes ascribe to them."

Silence on the other end—except for a small noise that told me Laurie was crying.

I took a deep breath. "Laurie, I know you're suspicious of me, but I'm trying to learn what happened to your father, for his sake and my own. I'd like to ask you some questions."

"Like what?" The old distrust returned to her voice.

"Do you know if you're his only heir?"

"If I say yes, will you accuse me of his murder?"

The thought crossed my mind, but I said, "I'm just looking for information. Do you have brothers or sisters, for example?"

"A brother. He lives in San Francisco."

"Were he and your dad close?"

"Closer than I was to him. Charles—my brother— is an advertising account executive. They spoke the same language, at least about commercials. Me, I always change channels or put them on mute— unless I knew they were produced by my dad. And then . . ." Her voice trailed off.

"And then?" I prompted.

When she spoke again, her voice was hoarse. "I was such a good daughter that I'd critique them. I'd tell him why I wouldn't buy the products he promoted, based on the ads he shot."

I tried to be tactful. "I'm sure he appreciated your input." Time to get into the meat of what I wanted to ask her. And it wasn't about small potatoes. "Were you aware that your father was considering the sale of Cuthbertson Productions?"

The sound I heard was more a snort than a sniffle. "Yes, he told me. Do you know, he intended to sell out to one of his biggest competitors, Millipede FilmAmericam? They do some of the splashiest commercials. Literally. They're famous for using babes in bikinis on the beach to sell nearly anything."

Did I detect disdain? But so what? It was unlikely to have led Laurie to kill her father. But her brother . . . ? "What did Charles think of Millipede's stuff?"

"So now *he's* your suspect. Well, you should know he loved Millipede, thought they did the best, most successful promotions ever."

"Was he going to get anything out of the sale?"

"If he wanted to. Charles had a standing offer to come to work for Dad. Dad would have made sure he was treated like an executive in the Millipede sale. Dad told me that every employee would get a promise of employment for at least a year, or the deal wouldn't go through."

So none, presumably, would have a motive for murder. But would that give someone at Millipede a reason to get Carl out o the way?

"The other thing you might be interested in," she said, "is that Dad admitted that the person who introduced him to the honchos at Millipede was the jerk who stole his script, the one you sued on Dad's behalf. I warned him, but—well, he never listened."

And I didn't even need to bring it up! "The fellow—Conrad Taylor—were he and your father getting along?"

She snorted again. "Like best friends."

That got me nowhere. "So with your dad gone, what happens now? Will Cuthbertson Productions still be sold to Millipede?"

"Too soon to say. Dad didn't even tell Charles what was in his will. I certainly don't know." A good reason for her *not* to kill him. She didn't know if she'd benefit from his death.

On the other hand . . . "Do you think Cuthbertson Productions would have been more successful without the sale to Millipede?"

"Probably." Aha! "But Dad was tired. He claimed he'd made enough money, wanted to retire, travel more, get to know my kids and Charles's better. Even if he'd kept the company, if he wasn't actively involved, who knows what would have happened to it?"

If she killed him now, the company hadn't time to go downhill. But that only made sense if she knew she was an heir. Propping the phone receiver between my ear and shoulder, I jotted on my list, *Find out if Laurie could have known the contents of Carl's will.*

"All this is really helpful," I said to Laurie.

"It is?"

"It gives me other avenues to explore. How about disgruntled former employees of Cuthbertson Productions? Do you know of any?"

"I never kept track of anything about Dad's company."

"And you don't know of anyone else with a motive to kill him?"

"No," she said. "Including you. At least not on the face of things. You're not in his will, are you?"

Oh, lord, I hoped not! "We weren't that close, Laurie, just business associates."

"Okay. Well, I guess you should know that my dad's body was finally released. His funeral will be the day after tomorrow."

"Where will it be, and what time?" My clambering clients would just have to be patient. I had every intention of paying my last respects to Carl.

"It'll be announced in the papers tomorrow, but I really don't want you to come. It'd look bad. So, you're not invited, Kendra."

CHAPTER 15

I tried not to let my feelings feel decimated. I tried to put myself in Laurie's flab-footed shoes. With no success. I hurt like hell, damn it.

Would I honor her wishes? Yeah, for Carl's sake. I didn't want to create a scene as his life was celebrated for the final time.

It was getting late, near the time Jeff usually called. I wouldn't dump my depression on him, but I needed to run my latest findings by him. Sure, I was in his employ, but I wanted him to exercise his investigative skills a little further on my behalf.

No sense standing on formalities, and I just couldn't wait, so I called him.

A breathless woman answered his cell phone. "Jeff Hubbard's line." She ended with a giggle.

And I wanted to throw up.

Jeff saw other women when he traveled? Hell, why not? Nothing else was going right. Or maybe this *was* right. I should feel relieved. He was hardly seeing me here, and then only as the person he'd hired to be at his dog's beck and call.

Plus, he'd given me free P.I. advice while paying

me. He also handed me a place to stay where I wouldn't have to watch my tenant throw parties for practically any occasion.

And the fact I found Jeff sexy? Or that he'd kissed me, and told me to think of him in bed? It was normal, hormone-induced banter between two healthy adults. In no way did it constitute an intimate relationship.

It wasn't a relationship at all, except of the business kind. As it was supposed to be. And I'd no intention of giving in to any of my baser impulses where Jeff Hubbard was concerned.

Except the impulse, right now, to hang up.

But that wouldn't get me what I needed. Other than a modicum of satisfaction.

All this flashed through my miserable mind in about half a second. "Hello," I said in a haughty litigator's intonation. "This is Kendra Ballantyne. To whom am I speaking?" Okay, so I hadn't totally convinced myself I didn't give a damn that some marshmallow-voiced babe was answering Jeff's phone. But did I really want to know the name of his latest bedmate?

A noise at the other end sounded like the growl of a sick lion. Then, "Hello? This is Jeff Hubbard. Who's calling?"

"Jeff?" I made myself speak brusquely. "Kendra. Did I call at a bad time?" Like, did I catch you with your pants down, or only unzipped?

"No, now is fine. I was doing last minute checks on a security system I'm installing in an all-girl fitness spa. I put my phone on a table, and one of the women who heard it ringing thought she'd be helpful, and—"

"I see." Despite everything, I grinned. He was obviously embarrassed about whatever I'd caught him at. "An all-girl fitness spa? That locker room has to be a bear for installing . . . *security* stuff. Or is it a 'bare'?" I heard background noise that sounded like running water splashed with female catcalls.

"'Fraid you've guessed the naked truth." He caught the differences between the homonyms without my spelling them out. I heard the laugh in his voice. So much for his fleeting embarrassment. "I'm not charging these clients a lot because of the other job benefits."

"I'll bet. Want to call back when you can keep your mind on the conversation instead of your . . . installation?"

He choked, then shot back, "Why? Is something wrong?"

"No," I lied. "I just wanted to report findings to my P.I. advisor."

"I'm walking out the door as we speak." The background noise abated.

"Were you really in the women's locker room?"

"Yes. But before you get the wrong idea, the fitness club is brand new, opening tomorrow. It was built by female labor. And today they're checking all the equipment."

"Yours?"

"So to speak. I designed the security system, including coded membership cards, fire alarms, entry metal detectors, the works. I'm showing the owners how to use it—fully clothed, damn it. All of us."

"Better luck next time."

"Yeah. So what's the scoop?"

Yawning, Lexie changed positions, snuggling more with Odin than me. Fickle friend.

I took a deep breath to still my beleaguered brain, then I gave Jeff a rundown on my daunting discussion with Noralles, my stonewalling the persistent media, my investigative efforts, and my conversations with Avvie and Laurie. I kept my exposition light and entertaining. No sense giving substance to my gloom. "Tomorrow's Sunday. I'll have to wait till the workweek to follow up with Royal Marden on his representation of Cuthbertson Productions, and with Conrad Taylor, Carl's newest best friend. Can you check out what Taylor and this Millipede outfit are up to? And Laurie Shinnick and her brother Charles Cuthbertson? We might find some interesting stuff."

"Sure. I'll get my research geeks on it. Too bad it's too soon for Carl's will to be in probate. I want to know who his heirs are."

"Ditto. Can you check how he took title to any real property, like his house? If it's in a trust he established for estate purposes, we might be able to learn its beneficiaries."

"Right. I've already got people tracking what's out there on Cuthbertson Productions. So far, they've got info about the company's films, the lawsuit you worked on, and the stuff on the sale that made the news. I'll tell them to concentrate on rumors and innuendoes and less-reliable sources. That way, we'll learn industry scuttlebutt on the company's proposal to sell out."

"Good. Can they do much on Sunday?"

"On-line, they can do it on Christmas Eve while watching Santa scoot down the chimney."

I was silent for a moment, then said, "Keep a running tab. We'll compare what you owe me for pet-sitting with what I owe you for investigating, and I'll pay the difference as soon as I can."

"I'll take it out in trade."

An interesting proposal. Especially considering the kind of trade that phrase usually referred to. . . . But I'd already gotten way past that in this conversation.

And his continued comment provided any clarification I needed. "With all my travel lately, your pet-sitting's really been a great help."

I looked at Jeff's white and red Akita flopped at the far edge of the couch, my tri-color Cavalier curled at his side. "Yeah, Odin, Lexie, and I are getting along fine."

"I'll call tomorrow night around this same time," Jeff said, "to let you know what I've found out."

So what if I barely slept that night, spinning

scenarios both positive and pessimistic? The fact that it was Sunday didn't change a pet-sitter's program, either. Animals still had to pee, poop, eat, and exercise. No weekends or holidays off.

Because I'd been forced to stint lately, I spent extra time in the morning with each pet I tended, particularly the dogs. Nothing like good-humored canines to help combat grim reality.

It was nearly eleven o'clock when I was done with the first rounds of the day. I had the choice of going back to Jeff's, reading the Sunday *L.A. Times*, and moping, or getting in a little amateur investigating.

Guess which I chose. After a quick drive past my former not-so-humble abode for my rent check from Charlotte, I headed to another familiar neighborhood: Carl's.

The place appeared mostly as it had a few days earlier—pleasant and upscale.

No media vans, thank heavens, but yellow police tape still cordoned off Carl's property, and I'd ceded the key to the cops. Going inside would have done me no good anyway. Crime scene investigators were unlikely to have left any clue that would clear me.

No, my intent was to scour the neighborhood. Rather, the neighbors. As if the cops hadn't already canvassed them. But I'd spent time here. Something helpful might occur to me.

The homes around Carl's were mostly two-story, probably built in the mid-twentieth century, for they didn't have the cookie-cutter pseudo south-of-the-border look of newer developments. A couple were charming, with peaked roofs and tall chimneys. No unmanicured lawns anywhere.

I exited my car and walked slowly down the sidewalk. An older lady with a black Labrador retriever came toward me. I thought I recognized the Lab, if not her.

"Hi." I held out my hand for the dog to sniff. "What a pretty dog. What's his name?"

"You're the girl who walked Cheesie, aren't you?" The woman studied me with narrowed eyes. She wore thick glasses and an attitude. "The one who killed poor Carl."

"You're half right." I tried to keep my smile friendly. "I was pet-sitting while Carl was out of town. I found him." My shudder wasn't solely for effect.

"The cops think you murdered him." She studied me as if memorizing my features in case she had to describe them on a witness stand.

"They're wrong. I'm here to find out if anyone saw anything that could help prove my innocence."

"Nope, no one around here did." She sounded definite.

"That remains to be seen. I'll be knocking on doors, so tell me where you live so I won't bother you again."

"So you can break in and kill me, too? Forget it. In fact, if you don't leave right now, I'll call the cops."

136

"Fine. Ask for Detective Noralles. He knows who I am." *And he'd love to have something new and fun to charge me with, like harassment, so he can haul my ass off to jail even faster.*

Over her shoulder, I saw two other women walking briskly toward us. The chunkier woman had a scarf over her head and wore a Dodgers T-shirt. The other was small, thin, and wrinkled and bounced with a brisk energy. They started to go around us, but the smaller one stopped. "Something wrong, Clara?"

"That's it. Give my name out to a murderer." The woman I'd been talking to snarled so irritably that her Lab sat and whined.

"What?" The smaller power-walker looked aghast, her watery blue eyes huge. "Is this—?"

I held out my hand. "Kendra Ballantyne, pet-sitter. Do you have any animals at home who need care when you travel?" I might as well toss in a plug. Maybe that would put the women at ease.

"Poor Carl was found by his pet-sitter," said the chunky woman. Her face screwed up, as if she was about to cry.

"That would be me. But contrary to what Clara and the news say, I didn't harm him. Ask Cheesie."

"Carl was very dear to me," she continued, as if I hadn't spoken. "I cooked dinner for him often. He particularly liked my cherry cobbler. If he'd lived, we might have gotten to know

137

each other better, but we were taking things slowly . . ."

"He was just being polite, Isabelle," said her wizened companion, obviously intending her rapier words to burst her friend's balloon. "And you know it."

Before this community gathering turned into a catfight, I wanted my questions answered. "Wouldn't you like to help me find who killed poor Carl and put the scum away for good?"

"Yes," said Isabelle.

"Let's keep out of it," said her companion.

"We've been questioned by the police already, Vivian," Clara said, stressing the name of the woman who'd just spoken, in obvious payback. "We promised to tell them if we remember anything significant."

"Of course you should tell the police." I directed my comment to Isabelle, the only one who seemed somewhat rational. "But it won't hurt to tell me, too." I pulled a case from my pocket and handed her one of my new pet-sitter business cards with my cell phone number and e-mail address on it. Then I jotted down her info, too.

"I don't know that I'll be able to help you, Kendra," she said. "But I'll let you know if I think of anything."

She glared defiantly at her two neighbors. Clara with the Lab looked at me. "If we find Isabelle stabbed to death in her house, we'll know who did

138

it. So don't try anything around here again, you hear?"

I heard. And I left praying that no one I ever encountered met the horrible fate Carl had.

CHAPTER 16

Jeff called that night as promised. As usual, I'd looked forward to hearing from him. Since more shit had happened since we'd last spoken, I didn't look forward to describing my progress. Or lack thereof.

"I walked the streets near Carl's house today," I said after Jeff asked about the day's dirt. Wearing a short terrycloth robe, I had my legs tucked under me on the white living room sofa, with both dogs beside me. Of course.

"Learn anything interesting?"

"Only that I'm persona non grata." In more places than one, I thought, considering Carl's impending memorial. "The neighbors adored Carl and are ready to throw my bones to the wolves—or dogs—if it turns out I'm the one who offed him."

"And no one saw anything?"

"Not that they're telling me."

I glanced at the TV, which I'd put on mute when the phone rang. Law enforcement types slid with backs against building walls, guns drawn. With only a touch of imagination, I could picture Noralles outside of Jeff's house, ready to serve a warrant to arrest me.

I flicked the remote to change channels. Ugh. Another reality show. One woman was surrounded by a pack of fawning men.

"Sorry you didn't learn anything useful," Jeff said. "Neither did I. Everything my research geeks have found indicates that Laurie Shinnick, her brother Charles, and Carl's buddy Conrad Taylor aren't candidates for halos, but neither are their tails forked."

"Not even Taylor's?" Dismay pealed in my voice, but, hell, I'd litigated against the guy. And I was sure I'd glimpsed some nasty-looking horns on his high forehead, whether or not his tail was spiky.

"Don't give up, darlin'," Jeff said. "As someone a lot more literate than me once said, 'Tomorrow is another day.'"

"Right," I agreed. *Darlin'?*

"Hey, Kendra? What are you wearing?"

"Less than I intend to tell you about, *darlin'*." I stretched out the final word, then softly hung up. And smiled. The guy had definitely moved my mind from devils to a different kind of deviltry.

But it wasn't thoughts of Jeff, alone, that kept my eyes gaping at the textured ceiling deep into the night.

I kept counting cops ready to storm in and serve Noralles's arrest warrant.

Monday. Morning rounds. First, I opened the door

of my Beamer, parked in its now-usual spot on Jeff's street, to let both Lexie and Odin leap in. I felt I had souls on my side when I could look toward my car and see both pups posed there, noses poked through the windows I'd cracked open for ventilation.

I tended all the critters on my current list, made sure they had no legitimate gripes, then we headed back to Jeff's.

I'd stewed all morning about two calls I needed to make.

But before I got to them, I received one from Noralles. The display of his phone number got my nerves jumping. His voice shot them to Santa Barbara.

I was in Jeff's kitchen, after letting the dogs out into the big backyard. I watched them cavort, wishing I were with them as Noralles spoke. "One of Carl Cuthbertson's neighbors called in a complaint, Ms. Ballantyne. Is there some reason you returned to his neighborhood?" *Like, did you forget something when you murdered him? Or was it simply that perpetrators always return to the scene of the crime?* My own battered brain stuck those unspoken barbs into his mouth.

Hell, why not tell him the truth? "I was hoping to find out something new to lead to Carl's killer, detective, since I gathered when we spoke on Saturday that you're stalled on assuming I'm the best suspect."

"I wouldn't say I'm *stalled* on it, Ms. Ballantyne."

142

Oh, but he sounded so smug. "It's just that my job is to go where the evidence leads me. We'll talk again soon. Meantime, leave the detecting to me." *Like hell.* "And by the way—"

"I'll give your regards to Jeff Hubbard." I hung up.

Damn! My knees went aspic, and I propped my weight against the wall.

Take control, Ballantyne. Of something, at least. Maybe I should both fire Jeff and quit as his pet-sitter. But that wouldn't necessarily neutralize Noralles.

I wobbled to the living room to make my long-anticipated calls.

The first fueled my frenzied frustration. I phoned Conrad Taylor's office. Ethically, I might have asked if he had an attorney. The rules dictated that if a lawyer knew someone was represented, she couldn't talk directly to that person without his attorney's permission. In theory, no civilian was astute enough to speak to a big, bad lawyer without the shelter of his own sage attorney's protection. But I rationalized that such caution here was unnecessary. Right now, I didn't represent a client with opposing interests.

Hell, right now I couldn't represent a client with *any* interests.

I decided to chance it, got myself psyched on how to request a meeting. Something about the deal he'd worked on with Carl, without being specific. Maybe he wouldn't know I had nothing to do with it.

As it turned out, my self-psyching was all for naught. He was out of town. Not due back until the end of the week.

I didn't leave a message.

Then I called my former firm. I didn't ask for Avvie, since she'd have wondered why I asked the question I needed to have answered. Or maybe she'd know and admonish me to stay clear. Instead, I asked my former secretary if Mr. Marden was in. He was. I thanked Susan, settled the canines safely at Jeff's, and headed downtown.

Cathy, the receptionist, didn't seem surprised to see me this time. She only raised her brows when I asked to see Royal Marden instead of my usual stable of non-supporters.

She'd been there long enough to recognize that Royal had been a royal pain in the ass during my Bar Association ordeal. Good thing he wasn't a litigator, for he seemed of the mind that where there was smoke, there was fire. Worse, a claim meant liability. An accusation equaled guilt.

Perhaps his law school—though Ivy League and one of this country's most reputable—had failed to teach him basic criminal law. The U.S. legal system does advance the presumption that people are deemed innocent until proven guilty.

Hear that, Noralles?

I'd readied all sorts of enticing reasons for Marden to see me, assuming he'd balk. To my surprise, after only a five-minute delay, Cathy told me to go on in.

Since he was the first of the named partners, his office was the most ostentatious, at the end of the hall. It comprised a corner, of course, and its windows provided a glorious vista of downtown L.A.

I'd never been an aficionado of antiques, but I was sure his elegant rosewood desk was hand-hewn by some well-known designer of centuries past. The chairs facing it were less opulent but of the same rich red wood, upholstered in gilt-trimmed stripes. On his desk, stacks of manila folders were topped by stylish paperweights.

"Hello, Kendra," resounded his modulated voice as I walked in. "To what do I owe this visit?"

He even sounded elegant. Looks—that was another matter.

I'd never had the guts to ask Royal why his parents had been audacious enough to call him "Royal." Or maybe he'd been a better-looking baby than adult.

He was tall, and he chose his wardrobe as carefully as he did furnishings. But even hand-tailored suits couldn't hide his potbelly and they did nothing to combat his homeliness: pudgy cheeks where his beard erupted each afternoon, a hook nose, small, myopic eyes that squinted even behind his fashionable wire-framed glasses. Lovely teeth, though, and I'd heard him tell someone they were all his own.

Since much of litigation was stage presence, I wasn't surprised he'd chosen transactional law. When it came to contracts, he knew his stuff.

145

"Hi, Royal. I've been mulling over what to do once my suspension is up and wanted your advice."

Actually, though I hadn't considered asking him, I did respect his shrewdness and ingenuity in his areas of practice and his many, many contacts. Maybe he really could give me ideas for my future.

His frown nearly made his eyes disappear into his flesh. "The partnership voted to accept your resignation before you left, Kendra, so if you're asking whether we could extend employment to you again—"

"Oh, no," I said hastily. "I just know how active you are with the L.A. County Bar Association and State Bar committees. I hoped you'd suggest people to talk to when the time comes." Of course, all those contacts of his were probably why he hadn't stood behind me. It was too embarrassing to have a junior partner at one's own firm the subject of an ethics investigation.

"And your suspension is up when?"

I was sure he knew. But I wanted something from him, so I didn't let my irritability show. "The agreement was for three months. Nearly one has passed, so there are two more to go."

"But if you're indicted for murder . . ."

This was the opening I'd hoped for, just not the approach I'd have chosen.

"That's possible," I admitted, staring straight into his little, self-righteous eyes. "Not because I harmed Carl Cuthbertson, but because I was at the right place at the wrong time. I was pet-sitting for him, you know."

"So I heard." He leaned forward, clasping plump fingers together on his desk to display the squatly masculine diamond rings on both hands. "In fact, Carl told me about it."

Good. So he was admitting that he'd represented Carl. Or at least that they'd been in contact.

"I've been checking into what Carl was up to when he died. Of course the police are investigating, and since they haven't arrested me, they must have doubts about my guilt." Sure they did.

"Or they haven't found enough evidence yet to make their case." He was smiling, damn him. Did he really think I did it?

"They won't." I refused to let my anger show. "But while I've checked around, I've learned some interesting stuff, like that Carl made peace with his old nemesis Conrad Taylor."

I paused to see Royal's reaction. There was none. Might he have made a good litigator after all?

"In fact," I continued, "I heard you're papering a deal that Taylor brokered, where Carl was selling his interest in Cuthbertson Productions. How was the deal going? Were he and Taylor really getting along? And what about the people Carl was selling to—might one of them—"

Royal stood. Still smiling, he leaned forward. The only sign he wasn't just having a great old time was that his hands fisted on his desk. "You know I can't tell you anything about a client's business, Kendra, even though that client's deceased."

I spoke through teeth I carefully kept from gritting behind my own false smile. "I'm not asking for the terms of the transaction, just everyone's attitudes. Or give me names and I'll check them out. I'll talk to Taylor, of course, when he's back in town, but the others—"

"You don't really think I'd sic you on the guys across the table, do you, Kendra?"

"It's just a business deal, Royal." My voice was raised despite my efforts to modulate it. "I'm talking about my life."

"And about my client's murder," he said coldly.

"Carl was my client first. And I know how I was getting along with him—very well. What about you, Royal? Was he happy with the way you were handling his deal? Or was he threatening to fire you and blemish your oh-so-important reputation? Maybe you had reason to kill him."

"Don't be ridiculous," he hissed. "Next you'll accuse me of giving that strategy memo of yours to Lorraine Giles."

I sat for a moment, pondering this as I had pondered it before. It was the first step in the chain of events that had led to the murder of another firm client, or at least its CEO.

Someone gave that strategy memo to the loony plaintiff. There'd been other false evidence planted against me. Who'd done it? Someone from this firm? That would explain how the evidence was obtained. Could it have been Royal Marden? If so, why?

Why not?

"How well did you know Lorraine Giles?" I asked him.

"You'd better leave." His posture was never more imperious.

I shot him a real, if icy, smile. "I'd come here to ask you a few, simple questions that might help me investigate Carl's murder. But your concealment of the things you *can* reveal has made me wonder. The mystery of the leaked memo may never be resolved, but this one's right in front of me. *Did you kill Carl, Royal?*"

"Get out!" he shouted.

I was already on my way toward the door.

The odd thing was, before then, I hadn't focused on Royal as a viable suspect—even though I'd stuck him on my list simply because he was there. I'd considered him too remote from all the pertinent players. But in the purpling of his face and shifting of his eyes, I'd seen fear behind his arrogance.

Had I scored a hit before I even knew I was aiming?

CHAPTER 17

I couldn't leave without stopping to see Susan, in case she'd taken more messages for me. She was on the phone when I popped my head into her cubicle.

"I'll let her know you called," she said, then hung up. "Hello, Kendra. Cathy sent me an e-mail that you were here with Mr. Marden." Jungle drums, high-tech style. Probably everyone else knew I was around, too. "I have a few messages for you." She pulled pink slips from a small rack at the edge of her organized desk.

"Thanks." I glanced through them. Nothing out of the ordinary. A legal recruiter. A couple of reporters. I stuffed them into my purse. "Everything okay around here?"

"As okay as always." Not exactly a glowing report. "And you? I keep hearing you'll be arrested any moment for Carl's murder, but I can't believe it. Neither can anyone else." From Susan, that was a glowing endorsement, and I appreciated it even though it was a gross exaggeration. Some people believed everything they read about me. Royal Marden, for instance.

"Thanks," I told her again.

"I'm just sorry you had to take on something like . . . pet-sitting." She spoke the phrase as if it was covered in smelly dog poop and she'd no idea how she had gotten something so vile in her mouth.

"That's the least of my problems," I said lightly. "I'm actually enjoying it. May even stick with it after my law license is reinstated."

Her light brown eyes gaped in utter amazement, but before she could comment further, Avvie appeared, followed by Bill Sergement. The three of us chatted in the corridor between lawyers' offices and support staff cubicles, with Susan pretending to ignore us. I asked casually about cases I'd had to hand over, told amusing anecdotes about my latest clients and their owners. A couple of other lawyers, a paralegal or two, edged by, tossing me surface-friendly greetings.

It wasn't like working here—brainstorming a case, sharing enthusiastic camaraderie that only litigators who loved their work could understand. Still, it prodded some pleasant memories, leaving me wistful. I'd shot far beyond being one of MSY's top guns, whether I liked it or not.

But that wistfulness went away fast when the bunch of them broke away. Time to get ready for Carl's funeral.

"With all the media attention, I think it's best for the family if I don't go," I responded to the questions of whether I'd be there. "Carl would understand."

Especially because it was his family who'd invited me to stay away.

On the way to my car, I got a call from Darryl. He asked if I could stop over after the funeral that afternoon. I gave him a time, did more pet visits, and picked up Lexie and Odin before heading there.

"You're a mess," Darryl told me when he'd extracted himself from the dogfight he'd broken up. It wasn't an observation about my appearance, I knew, though he'd skimmed me first, squinting his blue eyes beneath his wire-rims. "Come into my office."

I let Lexie and Odin disappear into the canine crowd, to be supervised by Darryl's able staff.

"What's up?" he said when he'd shut the door behind us.

I took a seat. "Well . . . I had a great time this morning jabbing at the head partner at my old firm. Plus, I've been making calls and visits and trying to figure out who the hell killed Carl. I'd love to be able to serve up the perfect suspect when the cops come to arrest me—like in ten minutes." I glanced at my watch. "And in case you're wondering why you didn't see me at Carl's memorial, his daughter invited me to stay home."

"Hell, Kendra, I'm sorry." Darryl looked at me with a quirky expression I couldn't interpret.

"What?" I asked.

152

"Yeah," he said finally. "Why not? I want to introduce you to someone. Wait here."

When he came back into his office, he was accompanied by a woman with short, curly hair and a long face. She looked older than me, but she was dressed in one of the faddy cropped tops that teens wore these days. It seemed to suit her.

"Kendra, this is Fran Korwald. She owns Piglet, a really cute pug."

Instead of beaming about her pride and joy, Fran began to cry quietly and with dignity. Tears rolled down her cheeks before she could extract a tissue from her tote bag and hide behind it. The small square of paper was soaked fast.

I met Darryl's gaze over Fran's bent head. He wanted something. I owed him. One of us would be sorry. . . . Me. But, then, what else was new? I sighed, then asked as obediently as any well-trained pup, "What's wrong, Fran?"

Darryl beamed. He showed Fran to the chair beside mine and resumed his own seat.

"I'm sorry," Fran said in a moment. Her eyes were red-rimmed, and the smudges around them revealed she'd been wearing mascara. "I doubt there's anything you can do, but Darryl said you're a lawyer." I opened my mouth to interject my current reality, but she continued. "I know you're not practicing law now, and I already have my own lawyer anyway."

My curiosity was piqued. If she was represented, why was my former career a consideration?

"I'm in the middle of a divorce. It's been relatively amicable till now. Rubin and I were married for six years. I want kids. He doesn't. We knew that before but thought we'd find a way to compromise. We haven't. There's more to it, of course, but we both decided that our differences now outweigh our feelings for one another. So, it's over."

"Mmm-hmm," I encouraged.

"Have you ever been married, Kendra?"

That came out of left field and conked me over the head. "No." I chose not to explain that, though the idea of having a family someday held some appeal, the concept of trying to share space permanently with a man—any man—would take a lot of getting used to. Not that I was anything like my mother, but I knew she was a lot happier without the shackles of wedded non-bliss. And why she'd chosen my father to bind herself to, even temporarily, remained beyond me.

Still, my brother Sean had been married for four years and actually seemed happy about it, at least so far. Maybe the sex was good. My sister-in-law, a CPA, appeared to get her way a lot without antagonizing him.

I realized Fran was talking and tuned out of my own thoughts. "Even if California wasn't a community property state, we're both reasonable people. We've worked hard to make sure everything's divided exactly in half, even selling our house to split the equity. But . . ." Her voice trailed off, and she swallowed a woeful sob. "There's no way of dividing Piglet. We could treat her like a child and share custody, but Rubin is planning to move to Alaska, of all places."

She sounded the way most of my friends and acquaintances who've become single once more sound about their exes—amazed at and irritated by their idiosyncrasies.

"I don't want to keep putting her on planes," she continued. "It's not like she really is a child we could explain this to. She'd be traumatized being stuck in a crate in some dark compartment with strangers around. And that's the one thing Rubin refuses to give in on. He wants Piglet. But I can't give her up. She's like my baby. I don't know what to do. He's holding up the divorce till we get this resolved, and I can't go on like this."

Spite, malice, and a pug named Piglet. "How could I help?"

"I don't know." Her voice was a wail till she got it back under control. "But Darryl said you're a dog lover and a good lawyer who fell on hard times. If there's anything you can think of, please, please let me know."

I sighed. "I'll give it some thought."

"Here." She handed me a business card: Frances Korwald. Personal Trainer and Massage Therapist. No wonder she looked good in a teenage outfit, despite the deep lines etched on her face.

"No guarantees I'll be able to help," I said. "And even if I think of something, I'm not practicing law at the moment, so—"

"What I really need is someone with common sense. Someone who cares." She smiled at me rather tremulously. "Darryl thinks the world of you."

And with that, she left his office. I wanted to kick him in the shins, or someplace worse. After an endorsement like that, I'd feel like the lowest form of animal life if I didn't come up with a way to help Fran.

I didn't intend to stay around and damn Darryl after Fran left. What was the use? But I doubted I'd do her much good.

"Any ideas?" he asked me when, a short while later, I started to round up Odin and Lexie.

"One, though it's not well-formed yet."

"And that is?"

"Sweet revenge on a certain doggy day spa owner."

He laughed. So did I. Kind of. But I still felt bad for poor Fran. And if she really dared to rely on me, I definitely felt sorry for her.

As the dogs and I prepared to go, Shirley Dorian came in. "Oh good, you're here," she said. "Can you come to my house tomorrow? I'm leaving the day after for a short trip and want you to watch Rosie for me."

"Sure." We made appropriate arrangements.

And she wasn't the only one. I swallowed hard when Milt Abadim also stopped me at the door, his brilliant blue decorative snake about his neck. The time had also come for me to start looking in on Pythagoras the python.

Look at it this way, I told myself. I might not have to worry about my imminent arrest for Carl's murder. Maybe this time tomorrow, I'd be constricted to death, thanks to good old Py.

CHAPTER 18

After leaving Darryl's with the dogs in tow, I did the usual drive-by of my house, slowly, watching for media vans. Fortunately, there were none. Maybe they were all camped at Carl's memorial.

I missed my spacious castle in the hills. But these days, I was content to wave as I went by.

Only today, Yul stood outside the front gate, looking affronted. Had Charlotte kicked her boy toy out? If so, was that a good thing? For all I knew, Yul was the tidy one who made sure the place stayed in one piece.

Assuming it *was* still in one piece . . .

I pulled my car to the gate. "Hi," I called cheerily, the dogs wriggling beside me as their tails wagged contrapuntally.

Yul bent to peer into my car. He looked puzzled.

"Kendra Ballantyne," I reminded him. "Your landlord."

"Oh. Yeah. Hi." The passage of a few weeks hadn't increased his fluency. Probably not his intellect, either.

"Is everything okay?" If Charlotte had intentionally locked him out, I didn't want to let him in.

"Yes. No. I mean, Charlotte's at the airport. Headed for Europe. Forgot her passport. Sent me in a cab to get it. Only I don't have the opener."

Or the cab. I wondered how he planned to catch up with her. He was obviously emotional, for he'd surpassed his former speaking record.

Of course he could be lying. "Does she have a cell phone?"

He nodded grumpily. "But she can't get here in time to open the gate."

"What's her number?"

He told me, and I used my own cell to call her.

"Hello?" Her voice suggested she hoped I was male and available.

I told her who and where I was.

"Oh, thank heavens you're there." Recognition and relief tinged her tone. "I realized later that Yul could have trouble getting in."

She hadn't thought about calling him on his own cell? Or maybe she hadn't sprung for one for her pet stud.

"No problem." I pressed a button in my Beamer and the gate swung open.

Yul rushed in, waving in a manner that could have been either a thanks or a half-hearted "up yours." I noticed a large SUV sitting there. Aha! That was why he'd let the taxi go.

I left the dogs in the car and followed Yul into the

house. No landlady's notice of entry, so my pursuit was probably a no-no except in an emergency. But this *was* an emergency. I had an urgent urge to make sure the place was being well-treated.

Inside the front door, I called, "Yul? Everything okay?"

His far-off, shrill reply was unintelligible. In moments he reappeared, a small leather case in his hand. "Got it. Sorry. Got to run." He stood in front of me, herding me outside.

I'd barely had time to glance around. Didn't even leave the entry. My prized crystal light fixture was still there. The rustic tile remained intact, covered by an ugly throw rug.

A million invented reasons to stay sluiced through my mind. But seeing nothing wrong, I decided against them. If I'd seen anything amiss, it would have been another story.

"Right." I pivoted and preceded Yul outside. "Wish Charlotte bon voyage for me. One of these days, when she's back in town, we'll have to get together for coffee."

"Sure." I barely heard the word as he slammed the front door shut on my last longing gaze inside.

For future reference, I showed Yul the trick of getting onto the grounds by a code for a side gate that I'd sometimes supplied to trusted gardeners. With a mumbled "thanks," he shot toward the waiting SUV and roared away.

The next day was a useless Tuesday. I managed

to stay out of jail and keep my pet charges happy. Or at least I didn't get complaints.

I even prepared to watch Py the python by receiving instructions from his owner.

I watched Milt Abadim defrost a dead mouse in his microwave and test to make sure it was neither too hot nor still frozen in the center—either of which could lead to a big python tummy ache. Assuming a python had a tummy.

Milt showed me Pythagoras's tank, a large affair in the living room, the pièce de résistance of his modest one-story North Hollywood abode. He didn't lay the mouse carcass inside. He wanted to demonstrate all I'd need to know before Py's attention was distracted.

"Is that Astroturf?" I asked. The tank was lined in a brilliant green substance that resembled grass.

"That's right. Py loves it. It's his favorite substrate—that's the stuff at the bottom of his tank."

There was a large container of water at one side of the glass enclosure. The rest was a maze of ceramic caves and other habitat areas that I supposed were a python's most prized surroundings. It was kept warm and snug, and Milt instructed me how to make sure the temperature remained a cozy range that differed on the two sides of the tank, thus giving cold-blooded Py a choice of how warm he wanted to be.

"He'll sleep when he's cold," Milt told me. "But watch out about getting him too warm. Put him near a cozy fire, for example, and he's up right away and ready to party."

A python party. What an image.

I should have been glad the mice he was fed were already dead. That way, I didn't have to stick something cuter than the snake in with it for its supper. From what Milt said, live mice might have the effrontery to fight for their lives, thus injuring the predatory python.

"We'll get along fine," I told Milt, who placed Py around my neck to get him used to me. I didn't even flinch as the brilliant blue and magenta snake twisted around my torso. My warmth wasn't enough to get him in a party mood, for he settled down—a good thing. But I was relieved when Milt put him back in the tank with the mouse cadaver.

"Bye, Py," I said as I hurried to leave. "Enjoy your gourmet meal."

Wednesday promised to be a more exciting day. No new nasties from Noralles, and a phone call confirmed that Conrad Taylor was back in town.

Of course his receptionist prattled about how busy he'd be, so if I wanted an appointment to pitch my brilliant client's film script, I'd have to wait a few days.

Hollywood agent? I didn't exactly lie. I simply dropped a few notable names of people I didn't actually know and let her draw her own conclusion.

"So," I told Lexie and Odin after I changed clothes, "Mr. Taylor will have to find time to see me. Otherwise, I'll take the decade's best script someplace else." Lexie cocked her head, and one of her black, floppy ears hung down even lower. If she'd spoken English, I was sure she'd congratulate me on my ingenuity. Odin opened his mouth as if to assert his opinion. He stuck his tongue out at me, and I scowled.

"I could up the ante and suggest I now have control over Carl's company . . ." My voice trailed off as I considered how to do this without hard-to-sustain prevarication. The dogs didn't give the idea a glowing reception.

But my determination to deflect Noralles from me and find a more suspicious suspect had become a driving force. My arsenal of litigator's moxie engaged, I arrived at 11:45 at the Conrad Taylor Enterprises office in a primo Century City high-rise along the Avenue of the Stars. Taylor had certainly come up in the world, and not just because his suite was on the tenth floor. When I'd sued him for Carl, he'd worked out of his Burbank apartment and had no "enterprises." Script-stealing was apparently good business. Brokering mergers of entertainment industry companies, too. What else did Taylor dabble his dirty little fingers in? I had to find out.

I couldn't tell from the tiny reception area how large the office was, but even the rental of such lavish oak furniture wasn't cheap. The receptionist exuded a wannabe starlet vibe from every pore. Not to mention her long, blond hair and cleavage-squeezing red dress.

"Hi," she enthused, displaying teeth so white they glittered in the recessed lighting. "Can I help you?"

"I'm Kendra Ballantyne. I reached Mr. Taylor earlier on his cell phone. He said he could squeeze me in before lunch."

A puzzled expression darkened her features, which were so artificially enhanced that she could have strode onto a movie set without a stop at the makeup artist. "He didn't tell me he expected you."

"No? Well, I won't take up much of his time." I headed confidently for the door separating reception from office.

Conrad Taylor sat behind a vast desk that might have hailed from the same oak grove as his reception area furniture. Piles of scripts covered it. How many had been stolen from producers? It was possible, though, that Taylor had gone legit.

I remembered him as vaguely nerdy, but he'd either gotten contacts or laser surgery, because he no longer wore glasses. He was on the phone gesticulating wildly with the arm not holding the receiver. He wore a light blue shirt with enough buttons open to reveal a hint of highly buff pecs, no chest hair. His hair had silvered at the temples. Geez, the years had turned him into one good-looking guy.

Except for his mouth. Maybe it was because he was angry with whomever he spoke to, but the petulance I saw switched off any smidgen of attraction I felt.

His eyes latched onto mine and switched into me-hunk-you-woman mode. I guessed he didn't recognize me, which might be a good thing. But I'd already decided my approach would feature candor. Or a semblance of it. I reached down deep into my purse. It didn't hurt to be prepared.

Taylor hung up and smiled at me. "What can I do for you?" His sham-silk tone suggested that the best favor he could bestow would be to tear off my clothes and regale me with the greatest sex ever, right there on his office floor.

I approached with hand outstretched. "Hi, Conrad. Good to see you again. Kendra Ballantyne."

His come-hither leer melted like torched ice. "The lawyer."

"That's right. Carl Cuthbertson's lawyer." I didn't put it in past tense. Maybe he wouldn't know I no longer worked at MSY.

"But Royal said you're not practicing law anymore. Right?"

Okay, so he did know.

"Not at the moment, which makes this convenient. I can talk directly to you, not just with your lawyer." Maybe. "But if you have any concerns, let's get your lawyer on the phone right now and get his okay."

"No need. What do you want?"

"I've come about Carl. You know he's dead?"

"I went to his funeral. I also heard you killed him."

165

I inverted my wince into a droll smile. "Not hardly. Carl and I were buddies back when we sued the pants off you—so to speak." I forbore from leering at his open shirt. Or his pants. "We were still friends when he died. But I found him, so the police stuck me on their suspect list. I didn't come to tell you that. I need to know what's going on with the deal you brokered for selling Cuthbertson Productions, now that Carl is gone."

Taylor snorted. "Same as when he was alive."

"Yeah? Who are you dealing with?"

He leaned toward me, dark brows lowered Neanderthal-like. "Didn't your former boss Royal tell you what was going on?"

"Some." Which was vague enough not to constitute a lie. "And I've been talking to Carl's daughter, Laurie Shinnick." Also not really a lie.

"The deal ran into hitches. Millipede wanted more concessions, and Carl said he'd already gotten his ass reamed enough."

So Carl had felt he'd negotiated sufficiently. Had the game been over when he died? And how much commission might Taylor have gotten for brokering if this deal went through?

Enough to murder for, if it was in jeopardy?

I wanted to stand and do a dance step. I'd kept my fingers crossed that Conrad Taylor would be a viable suspect in Carl's murder. Now I knew it. He had a motive.

I thought I'd maintained my litigator's face, but my expression must have given me away.

"Don't get any ideas that I had it in for Carl, though," Taylor said. "We became buddies after our big misunderstanding that you were involved in. I understood his position and tried to move Millipede off theirs. It was all on hold while Carl took his vacation. While he was gone, I visited my kids in Big Bear."

There went Taylor's opportunity. Maybe. Big Bear wasn't far away. He could have come back, killed his buddy Carl, and returned to his kids.

Before I could lob more questions at Taylor, the receptionist came in to announce that his lunch date had arrived. For real or for relief? Who knew?

I said goodbye, thanking Taylor for his time and the information.

I didn't quite dash to my car, but came close. For once, I was eager to call Detective Noralles.

I reached deep into my purse and turned off the voice-activated recorder I'd snapped on before. Nothing there amounted to a confession of murder. But maybe, just maybe, what I now knew about Conrad Taylor and the demise of this deal could blow some of the heat off me.

CHAPTER 19

I should have known better.

First, Noralles wasn't in when I called as I headed for afternoon rounds. Then, he returned my call at the most awkward moment imaginable.

Lester, the basset hound, had decided to take a dump on the curb by a neighbor's property. I had of course come prepared to scoop it up. But that proved difficult when the neighbor's Great Dane took umbrage at the affront. Scaling the white picket fence around his grassy yard in a mighty leap, he lunged after Lester. As easygoing as Lester is, he refused to roll over in apology.

So there I was, standing by the street, separating snarling dogs, praying the Great Dane wanted neither basset hound nor human hand for supper, and trying to do my neighborly duty. And my cell phone rang right then.

Making sure my body shielded one dog from the other, I held the filled plastic bag with the same hand that dragged Lester by his leash and managed to answer, "Kendra Ballantyne. Please hold."

Fortunately, the Great Dane only guarded his own yard. He didn't follow. But it was more than a minute before I could talk.

Noralles was peeved. "I'm returning your call, Ms. Ballantyne," he said frostily when I finally said hello.

"Thanks for waiting." I oozed false gratitude. "I have some information for you."

"And that is . . . ?"

"Just a second." Passing an open garbage can, I dropped the filled plastic bag into it. As Lester and I moved forward, I described my conversation with Conrad Taylor. "He didn't say how much he stood to lose thanks to Carl's not signing the deal as Millipede offered. But Taylor wasn't happy that Carl took a vacation in the middle of negotiations. Or that Carl may have decided that the negotiation *wasn't* in the middle, but the end."

"And . . . ?"

"He had a motive to kill Carl, Detective. Money. Actually, the likelihood that there would be no money."

"Mmm-hmmm." Noralles's tone was condescending.

"You need motive, means, and opportunity to hone in on a real suspect." I prayed I sounded more patient than I felt. "Taylor has a motive. As to opportunity, he'd become a friend of Carl's, so he could have had a way to get into the house. Maybe Carl even gave him a spare key when he traveled. As for means, anyone could have grabbed

169

that knife from Carl's kitchen and brought gloves." I paused to let Noralles comment. He didn't. "So what do you think?" I prompted.

"We're aware Mr. Cuthbertson was in discussions about selling his company," he finally said. "In fact, I was surprised you didn't seem to know about it when we talked."

I'd wondered whether that was what he'd angled for when he interrogated me. The unsupportable, unmentioned motive he ascribed to me: anger that I wasn't Carl's lawyer on the deal?

"We're looking into that situation," he continued. "But so far, we've found nothing in the negotiation to connect it with what happened to the victim."

I just handed you the damned connection! I wanted to shriek. Instead, I applied an important part of my litigator's litany: Even a stupid judge can throw you in jail for contempt of court if you argue with him. Ergo, no matter how much you hold that judge in contempt, swallow insults, smile, and say, "Yes, your honor."

Not that Noralles was a judge. But he *was* judging me, and he had power over at least my short-term fate. And so I said sweetly, "Sorry if I wasn't clear, but you might want to dig a little deeper, in case there was a connection between Conrad Taylor, his irritation that the deal wasn't going as he'd planned, and what happened to Carl Cuthbertson."

"Thanks for the insight," Noralles said. "I'll take into consideration."

Like hell he would.

Damn! Wasn't there *anything* I could do to get this guy off my butt and onto a trail toward Carl's killer?

My cell phone sang as I headed toward Jeff's. "Hello?" I slowed for a light changing in front of me.

"Hello." Then nothing. It was a female voice, but I couldn't identify it.

"Who's calling?" I asked.

"Isabelle."

Was this a game of Twenty Questions? More likely, it was a knock-knock joke. I played along. "Isabelle who?"

I expected something like, "Is a bell playing in the old church yard?" or an equally lame response. Instead, I got, "Isabelle Lane."

Was that a street name? "Where is it located?" I asked.

Silence. Then, "This is Isabelle Lane. I live near Carl Cuthbertson."

Oh. It was one of the ditsy women I'd met in Carl's neighborhood: I'd thought Isabelle the least batty of the bunch. Guess that was a clue about how clueless I really was.

"Hello, Isabelle. How are you?" And why are you calling? Have you remembered seeing who killed Carl?

"Very well, thank you. You asked me to call if I recalled noticing anyone around Carl's near the time he died."

"That's right." Anticipation lunged inside me, though I grabbed it and held it still. It was almost a week since Carl's murder. If she knew anything significant, why did it take her this long to remember?

The light turned green, and I slowly stepped on the gas.

"Well, it may be nothing, but I was watching Oprah and it jogged my memory."

Great. She'd seen Oprah in the neighborhood? I couldn't wait to give that news to Noralles.

"There was a man on who wore a suit," she continued.

"Mmm-hmmm," I encouraged without enthusiasm.

"Carl always had a lot of people come by. He was in show business, you know. Did a lot of deals, he told me when we had dinner together. You know, he was very interested in me. But I didn't think of him that way. I mean, he was nice looking but—"

"I understand," I interrupted. Wherever this tangent might lead, it wouldn't be somewhere I wanted to go. "Tell me about this man in a suit." I propped the phone under my chin as I made a left turn.

"Well, he came the week Carl was out of town. He promised to call when he got back, you know, to take me to dinner." Carl, I assumed, and not the suited stranger. "That's why I knew he was gone. That and because I saw you walking Cheesie."

172

"Right. So did the man knock on the door?"

"Yes, and when he didn't get an answer, he went around the side of the house. I had a phone call then and went inside."

So she didn't see him leave? "Was this the day Carl died?"

"Could be, or a few days before. I don't recall."

Just in case . . . "Would you recognize the man again?"

"Goodness, no. My eyes aren't very good, you know."

Of course.

"I hope this is helpful," she said.

"Absolutely," I lied, then thanked her.

If she'd said it was definitely the day Carl had died or described Conrad Taylor, I would have called Noralles. As it was, the only person I could think of who I'd wanted to consider a suspect and who habitually got dressed up was Royal Marden. But no sense siccing Noralles on him just because I'd started to dislike him.

Not without a better reason than that he happened to wear a suit.

At least someone was excited about my conversation with Conrad Taylor, though, like me, he didn't figure Isabelle's big revelation was worth beans.

"Good job, Kendra," Jeff said when he called that night. "I'll have my chief geek focus on checking out Millipede and the aborted deal."

I couldn't remember when strokes like that— over the phone and not in person—had turned me on so much. Or maybe it was Jeff Hubbard's deep, distant voice.

Or maybe it was just that I was too damn horny.

I fidgeted on the sofa, disturbing the two dogs snuggled together at the other end. Lexie and Odin were becoming such close friends that I wasn't sure how they'd react when it was time to split them up and move back to my garage.

Though one of these days Lexie might go into season, and I'd have to separate them. I'd never heard of a Cavakita or an Akalier, and I wasn't about to encourage the birth of the first.

"Thanks," I said into the phone to Jeff. "But your friend Detective Noralles was less than enthused." I related that conversation to him.

"Yeah, Ned considers keeping an open mind tantamount to taking a slug in the skull."

"Nice image."

"Anyhow, I have some information for you." His favorite computer geek had delved into on-line services that dish out personal poop on everyone. He had a complete history on Carl Cuthbertson, from all his addresses for the past twenty years to credit and business credentials. "I'll send the printouts to the fax in my home office. Maybe something will jog your mind about who else might have had it in for Carl."

My bet stayed on Conrad Taylor, but if I couldn't convince Noralles, I could at least keep trying to muck up his interest in me by stirring in a cloud of other candidates. "Great," I said. "Anything on Carl's daughter Laurie or his son Charles?"

"I'm sending info on them, too. Plus that executive at Cuthbertson Productions you mentioned, Eve Adolph. And a printout of who lives at which homes in his neighborhood."

"Your pet geek's been a busy boy."

"That's pretty sexist, coming from a lady lawyer. My best geek is a girl. Woman, actually. Althea. She's in her fifties."

"I'm impressed." And I was. I'd found the sticky threads of the World Wide Web fun to crawl through, but usually crept off on a tangent before finding what I really needed.

"I took a quick look through the info," Jeff continued, "and nothing jumped out at me, but I don't know the players. Maybe you'll see something that'll make one of these people a clear candidate to be our murderer."

"Right. I'll let you know."

Not long after we'd hung up, the fax's phone rang. Soon, pages poured out. When the last came through, I took the stack into the living room and leafed through it. No blinding flash of intuition.

"Maybe I'm just too tired," I told the dogs, who wagged their respective tails. I took them for their last walk of the night, then I got ready for bed. I flipped once more through the printouts, stacked them on the nightstand in frustration, then turned out the light.

"Come on, Carl," I whispered into the room's silence, waking the dogs but not, as far as I could tell, the dead. "Something's got to be here. Give me a hint. Tell me who killed you."

I sat up straight in my nightshirt when I heard a ghostly whoosh. Carl?

Nope. Only Kendra being clumsy. I'd dropped a couple of pages and they'd fluttered to the floor.

With a sigh, I picked them up. Who could sleep with all this fun facing me? I'd study them right now.

Something had to be there . . .

CHAPTER 20

I spent hours studying every punctuation mark on the printouts and the details between. Lots of commas, dashes, colons. Words, too. Mostly names. And an innumerable amount of numbers. All I got was a nearly sleepless night.

In the morning, I sat at the table in Jeff's compact kitchen, making notes on the few interesting things I'd found, jotting a list of what to follow up on.

"You've had your walk and breakfast," I told the pacing dogs. I glanced at their water bowls. Filled. They simply wanted attention. "One more short walk later, before I start my rounds," I promised. As if they understood, they lay down. Lexie rested her head on top of my bare foot.

I put the prime pieces of paper on top of the pile.

Laurie Shinnick had a spendthrift husband with a penchant for sports events. Maybe I could see why he had to attend all Dodgers games, home or away, but there was an amateur Australian soccer team from Sydney that counted him as one of its greatest fans.

Might Waylon Shinnick have offed his father-in-law in the hope that his wife's inheritance would satisfy his craving for Australian airline tickets?

People had murdered for more stupid reasons. Like looney Lorraine Giles.

Laurie worked part-time at a local fast food joint and full time as a secretary in a dental office. With a husband like Waylon, no surprise she'd had concerns about how much Cheesie ate. Maybe I'd send her an anonymous bag of Iams.

Then there was Eve Adolph, VP of Cuthbertson Productions. No wonder she'd reminded me of a gliding ghost. The woman was into the occult. Records unearthed on her included invoices from hokey on-line sites that professed to put one in touch with people who've passed on. Might Eve have decided she'd communicate better with her boss if he was dead?

There was nothing else interesting about anyone at Cuthbertson. A lot about another candidate, though—Surprise!—Carl's former foe and current best bud, Conrad Taylor. According to the Internet info, he'd been a busy boy over the past year, establishing himself as a player in the entertainment industry. He owed a lot to Carl's stolen script. Had Conrad paid Carl back by pretending to put deals together for his new pal, then deleting him from the competition? That remained my pet theory.

All I had to do was prove it.

★　　★　　★

178

A few days passed, including the weekend. Not that premier pet-sitter Kendra Ballantyne had time off, but I finagled a few minutes to plow through printouts and check off items on my list of questions on those who might have had it in for Carl.

But nothing useful rose to the surface and blew bubbles in my face. Not a damned thing more to turn over to Noralles in the hopes that he'd lay off me. Not even the paltriest smoking pistol to point to Taylor.

But something else gnawed at me. That was why I'd come to Doggy Indulgence to talk to Darryl. This afternoon, I brought not only Lexie, but Odin, too. I'd heard from Jeff over the weekend. Could I stay on for yet another few days?

"I said yes, of course," I told Darryl as we sat in his office. "As long as he wanted. Longer."

"You've talked to Charlotte?" he asked dryly. He sat behind his desk, hands folded as if he'd nothing better to do than talk to me. But I heard the ruckus in the next room, and I knew his staff was engaged in entertaining the dog pack to keep them from killing each other—all in the spirit of enjoying their daycare experience.

"My tenant's back in town already and all atwitter preparing for her next big bash."

"How many is that since she moved in?" Darryl's thin face looked amused over a situation that was driving me bonkers.

"Too many. And this one's guest list includes all the people in her reality show. It'll be televised."

"Great! Go home and hold up a placard with your phone number. 'For the Valley's best pet-sitter, call Kendra at . . .'"

My expression said it all, for he hushed, spare eyebrows raised above his wire rims. "I'll change the subject," he said sagely. "Any ideas yet on how to help Fran Korwald?"

"In her custody case over pug Piglet? That's why I wanted to talk to you. I've done some Internet research." And yes, I'd trotted off on tangents, but I managed to return to where I needed to be. "Fascinating stuff. Do you know that pet custody, and not only in divorce cases, is a growing area of the law?"

"Do tell." His words were sarcastic, but he leaned forward, his attention engaged. And why not? He might learn stuff to benefit his business, advising clients what to do if someone tried to take their most prized possession.

"There've been custody battles all over the country. The ones that get to court are mostly in divorces, though even splitting lovers and former roommates fight over who gets Fido. One big divorce case was in Southern California—San Diego, not L.A. Pets are personal property—possessions under the law—but courts are recognizing that people love them like they love their kids."

"More."

"At your rates, I'd guess so."

"So how did the cases turn out?"

"They vary," I replied, "but judges are beginning to apply similar standards as in child custody battles. What's in the best interest of Puppy or Kitty?" I described the cases I'd read about. Some resulted in shared custody—one owner winding up with primary custody and the other entitled to visitation, like with kids. "That was what it was coming down to for Fran, only it won't work well with her husband moving to Alaska."

"Those cases sound like the people were wealthy enough to make their lawyers rich while they battled out who got the pooches. That's not Fran's situation. She does all right as a personal trainer and massage therapist, but she's not exactly Ivana Trump. And her soon-to-be-ex Rubin isn't The Donald. He's in the travel industry, moving to Alaska to manage the Anchorage office of some sightseeing company that's starting a specialization in wilderness tours."

"No kidding? People pay to get lost on glaciers or mauled by bears?"

"Apparently."

"Ugh. In any event, I don't have an inexpensive answer for Fran yet. But if you see her, tell her I'm working on it."

"She'll be thrilled. Thanks, Kendra."

"No problem." If I'd seen Fran, I'd have thanked *her*. I've always enjoyed the part of being a lawyer that involves researching precedents, then developing a way to use them to a client's advantage. Legal arguments were my joy. They let me take what I'd learned in law school—where students are taught to "think like lawyers"—and expand on it with my own imagination and ingenuity. Immodestly, I'd felt I had a lot of those commodities. Before.

But like with pre-pet-watching physical fitness, I'd been afraid I was getting out of shape. I'd missed exercising the litigator's part of my brain and feared it had atrophied from disuse.

Now I had a real problem to research, though I couldn't present it to Fran as I would if she were my client. At hundreds of dollars an hour . . .

"Anyway," I told Darryl, "no answer for her yet. But—"

"But you'll have one," he said with the slow, bright smile that had soothed me during the worst of my prior nightmares.

And I realized, as we stood so I could retrieve my dogs, that the conversation had taken my mind off being a murder suspect for ten whole minutes.

I wished later that afternoon that I'd had something to take my mind off my pending duty.

Hard to believe that nearly a week had passed since Milt Abadim had shown me the particulars about tending to Pythagoras, then left me in charge of his pet.

Okay, so why was taking a dead mouse from Milt's freezer and sticking it in his refrigerator to thaw overnight worse than being pooper-scooper to a pack of dogs?

It just was.

The worst wouldn't be till the next day, when I had to stick the thawed rodent into the tank. Thank heavens snakes only ate once a week.

I looked in on the brilliant blue and magenta serpent. He seemed to know that I was there, for he raised his head and stuck out his forked tongue. But he didn't budge from his ball position.

I checked his tank's temperature and the amount of water in his bowl for soaking his long bod. Everything looked fine.

"See you tomorrow," I told him.

He looked absolutely thrilled.

I headed for a new address later that afternoon, a place I hadn't pet-sat before.

I heard my newest charge before I saw her. Rosie the miniature poodle had been placid at Darryl's spa, but now she was defending her home. Noisily.

"Hi, Shirley," I said when my former law client opened the door to her sprawling hilltop hideaway. Like me, she had a Hollywood zip code, but her home was located on the Valley side of Mulholland, only blocks from the boundary of Studio City.

Rosie was a yapping silver armful. She wriggled, and Shirley, a red apron over her shirt and slacks, put her down. Rosie lunged. I held out my hand for her to sniff. Apparently she remembered me, for she sat and looked up as if puzzled about why I was there.

Shirley laughed. "Come in," she said. I did, Rosie at my heels.

Their home was as gorgeous inside as out. It boasted vaulted ceilings with crystal chandeliers, hardwood floors with brilliant-colored oriental rugs beneath exquisitely simple furniture. . . . My mind went on immediate overload.

Especially when I inhaled the bittersweet scent of chocolate that permeated the place.

Shirley caught my look of ecstasy. "Come into the kitchen," she said. "I'm baking brownies to bring along."

Her kitchen was a showpiece. It was tiled and cluttered with every gleaming metallic appliance imaginable. The huge cooking island in the middle would have made me drool even without the chocolate aroma. It, too, reminded me of my own abode—the house, not the garage—but far exceeded its space and amenities.

Despite her short physical stature, I knew Shirley had a huge professional one. Her PR firm was sought by major Hollywood studios. She'd hired the Marden firm without blinking to defend a suit by a disgruntled director, a former client of hers who'd claimed a press release circulated by Shirley's firm had libeled him. The jury had, with a quick, decisive verdict, suggested that the guy should have been thrilled to be mentioned at all by Shirley's agency.

Carl Cuthbertson had referred me to Shirley. I'd referred them both to Darryl's for their dogs.

Poor Carl . . .

"Everything okay, Kendra?" Shirley asked.

My mind whizzed back to the present, not difficult when she offered me a warm brownie. I bit into it and purred like one of my kitty clients. "This is great."

"Thanks. I've always figured it's a good idea to charm the cast and crew on a film shoot for later publicity. Pretend to be a pussycat bearing treats, then come down like a tiger to make sure they all promise to grant the media interviews we schedule."

Speaking of felines . . . I laughed. "So that's why you're off to Las Vegas?"

She nodded. "I'm flying this time, or I'd bring Rosie along. It'll be a quick trip, just a couple of days, but there'll be a lot more visits during the shoot. I'll need your services a lot."

"Just say when."

She gave me the particulars of caring for Rosie. I got the requisite list with the usual necessities— vet's phone and Shirley's cell numbers, security code and all. She showed me how to work her security system and handed me house keys.

"I'll need you to come starting tomorrow," she said.

"Great." I went over a couple more points and gave Rosie a hug. "See you in the morning, girl."

They walked me back to the front door. I turned

to say goodbye to Shirley and stopped. Something shining in her eyes behind her dark-rimmed glasses made me blurt, "Is everything okay, Shirley?"

"With me," she replied. But her glance remained narrowed. "But with you—Kendra, you know Carl was my friend."

I nodded. Oh, shit. Had she changed her mind and thought now I'd murdered him? Surely not. She'd never let me tend to her even dearer friend, Rosie.

"I know you were friends, too. And that's why I don't think you harmed him." Thank heavens! "But I watch the news, hoping to hear of a break in the case." She hesitated. Would she accuse me after all? My defenses reached out and began hastily to construct a flimsy brick wall around my emotions.

"Kendra, who do you think killed Carl?"

Conrad Taylor, my mind shouted. I visualized my written list. Or Carl's son-in-law Waylon Shinnick. Or his VP, Eve Adolph. Or a neighbor. Or . . .

Anyone but me!

But I'd learned a valuable lesson from the accusations hurled at me.

"The jury's still out," I told Shirley. "But you can be sure I'm not going to let myself get railroaded."

"You're conducting your own investigation?"

"Damn straight."

She smiled. "I figured. Good for you. But, Kendra, be careful."

"No worries," I told her. "I've developed the proverbial eyes in the back of my head. And they're getting really good at watching my butt."

Laughing, she said, "What an image. I think I'll use it in one of my press releases."

CHAPTER 21

"You guys stay out here." I was about to go feed the defrosted mouse to Py. That was bad enough. Though I'd brought Lexie and Odin that day, I didn't want any doggy distractions.

Inside Milt Abadim's North Hollywood home, I headed first to the fridge, where I retrieved the rodent. I'd kept it in plastic, which I removed, but damned if I was going to actually touch the deceased python-dinner, finger to fur. With a paper towel, I stuck it into the microwave for a few warming seconds and made sure it wasn't too hot. Then I transported it into the living room and prepared to put it in with Py.

The snake was again curled into a ball at one end of the tank. No, *still* curled up. As far as I could tell he hadn't moved from where I'd left him yesterday. His eyes were open, staring. His mouth was closed. No forked tongue darted out.

My heart started to pound. "Pythagoras!" I tried not to panic. Was he dead?

He didn't respond. I knew what should get him excited. "Here you are," I gushed, carefully placing the damp, dead mouse carcass right before those unblinking eyes.

He still didn't move. That wasn't good. He hadn't eaten in a week. He had to be hungry.

What would I do if he really were dead?

Leaving the mouse where it was, I went into the kitchen for Milt's emergency numbers. I was tankside again when I called. I held my breath as the phone rang and even after Milt answered.

"Hi, Kendra. Is something wrong?"

"I'm not sure. You know Py's the first snake I've ever sat for. He doesn't seem to have moved since yesterday. He didn't even get excited when I put his mouse in with him."

"The poor baby," Milt said with a sigh. Was he mourning his dead pet? "He misses me."

So much he died of grief? "I'm sure he does," I soothed. But what was I supposed to do now?

"I was afraid of that," Milt said. "He may not eat if he's upset. Is he curled into a little ball?"

"Yes."

"That shows he's in distress. Here's what you'll need to do, Kendra, so he'll feel better. What are you wearing?"

It was okay for Jeff to play that game, but was Milt a telephone pervert?

When I didn't respond, he said, "Go to the closet in my bedroom and get my safari vest, the one with a bunch of pockets."

Uh-oh. I knew where this was leading. "But, Milt, I—"

"Please, Kendra. He needs to be near a person's warmth to feel better. Otherwise, he might die."

Bad enough I had to deal with a dead mouse. But if its predator kicked the bucket, too. . . . No, kicking anything was impossible for snakes. Still . . .

"Do you have the vest yet?" Milt demanded in my ear.

I thought about turning the cell phone off. Giving the expensive thing back to the company I got it from. Too many times lately, I hadn't liked what the person on the other end was saying.

With a sigh, I headed down the hall to Milt's bedroom. No problem figuring out the vest he meant. I pulled it over my blue T-shirt and glanced in the mirror. Not a combination I'd have chosen, but at least the vest was unisex. It was a little large, like Milt, but the length worked thanks to his truncated height.

"I've got it on," I told him.

"See the deep pocket on the right side? That's where I put Py when I can't let him ride around my neck the way he likes."

"And you want me to stick him in there?"

"Of course."

Back in the living room, I headed for the huge tank on the table in its middle. I looked in at Py. He'd raised his head a little. He was alive! I told Milt.

"Has he swallowed the mouse?" he asked.

"No."

"If he was happy, he'd have eaten it by now. Please put him in the pocket, Kendra."

I sighed. Py unfurled as I lifted him. I was afraid he'd whip his long length and somehow swing himself across the room. He surely didn't want me to stick him in that little pocket. That little pocket so close to me . . .

Apparently, that was exactly what he wanted. I held my breath once I'd placed him in, tail first, and waited as the pocket bulged and danced till he found a position he liked. And then he was still. Except that he stuck his head out and looked around. Apparently satisfied, he ducked back inside.

"How is he?" Milt asked.

"Settling down," I told him. "And I have to carry him like this for how long?"

"An hour. Maybe two. Once he realizes he hasn't been abandoned, he'll feel better."

Yeah, but would I?

I took Lexie and Odin back to Jeff's. Though they sniffed at Py's pocket, they didn't seem particularly peeved that I had other company upon my person.

Py accompanied me on the rest of the day's rounds. Later, I even took him out of the vest pocket now and then. Let him twine around my neck like a twisted scarf, like he did with Milt. I got a charge out of watching double-takes of people I passed on the streets while dog-walking as Py kept his serpentine lookout.

Eventually, I was through. I took Py home, lowered him into his tank, and watched long enough to see him slither. I returned to the kitchen. I'd put the mouse back in the fridge before we'd left earlier. Now I warmed it a little in the microwave, tested its temperature, then took it back to Py.

This time, he was interested.

I couldn't look. "Bye, Py," I called.

As I returned to my car, I realized how much of a kick it had been having a snake as a companion. When I returned to Jeff's that night, I had a real feeling of accomplishment.

Whatever else I might have done that day, I just might, by being friendly, have saved a long, slithery life.

I called Darryl at his home to tell him about it. I sat at what had become my favorite evening phone call position: on Jeff's sofa, accompanied by Lexie and Odin.

"Good job, Kendra," Darryl said. "You're one hell of a pet-sitter."

"Yeah? You never flattered me like that when I was a hell of a lawyer."

"That went without saying. I knew you were good, since you could afford to leave Lexie with me."

I laughed, even as I wondered whether I'd ever practice law again.

"Have you heard from Shirley Dorian yet from

Las Vegas? She usually calls me a couple of times a day when Rosie's here. Drops in, too. Nice lady, but she can drive me nuts."

"I got a call from her on my cell a while back," I said. "Second time in so many hours. I was feeding some yowling cats and feeling nervous about it. Pythagoras Python was pretending to be my necklace, and the cats were eyeing him as their lunch."

"I'll bet Py reciprocated," Darryl said.

"Exactly, though they were a lot larger than mouse-size. Anyway, I told Shirley I'd talk to her tonight. She made me swear that Rosie was fine and promise to call her back. She was easier to deal with in the lawsuit I handled for her. I was on her case then, but she never got on mine."

"That's Shirley," Darryl acknowledged. "And you gave her good news, that Rosie's all right?"

"Yep, she's great. Shirley'll be home late tomorrow, but I'll still drop in a couple times first to see Rosie."

"To make sure she gives her owner a glowing report, so she'll hire you again next time?"

"You got it."

Jeff called later that night. He'd be home earlier than expected—most likely tomorrow, too.

"Any other trips planned soon?" I asked hopefully.

"Probably, though nothing's scheduled now."

My sigh must have been audible.

"Hey, that hurts," Jeff said.

I laughed.

"We might even enjoy being in the same city at the same time for a while," he said. What kind of fun did he have in mind? "I may even be able to investigate the Cuthbertson matter for you."

"That'd be great." I'd be delighted to let him deal with his undeclared enemy, Noralles.

"We might consider a sleepover or two to discuss it." I heard the leer in his voice and laughed again.

"We might. Then again, I can't wait to get back to my attic over the garage so I can eavesdrop on my tenants' latest parties. Bask vicariously in the lives of jet-setting reality TV stars."

"Sure. See you tomorrow, Kendra. We'll talk then about how to clear your name in Carl's murder."

How sweet that sounded.

But late the next day, before Jeff's return, I became certain I'd never clear my name again.

When I got to Shirley's for the third and last visit of the day, I turned off the alarm and unlocked the door. Rosie wasn't there to greet me.

"Rosie?" I called, and heard a shrill bark from upstairs.

Shades of déjà vu made me shiver. Cheesie had greeted me that way the day I'd found Carl dead.

Nah, I told myself. One dead pet-sitting customer was more than enough for any career.

"Rosie?" I called again. A scrabbling of claws on the hardwood floor was the first response, followed by another yap.

Could she have locked herself in one of the rooms?

"Where are you?" I cried as I mounted the stairs.

My heart thumped nastily in my chest, causing it to tighten so much I wondered if I'd ever breathe again.

Of course I was just imagining things. There was nothing to worry about. Nothing here should remind me of finding Carl.

Except when I got to Shirley's bedroom and opened the door, Rosie launched herself at me. I grabbed her and held on.

Unlike Cheesie, she hadn't been standing watch over her mistress. But as with Carl, Shirley lay on the floor. Still. Not breathing.

With blood all over her chest.

Her petite, fluffy, yappy pet wriggled in my arms, whining, trying immediately to get down.

I didn't let her.

And I was certain no thorns of Rosie's had stabbed Shirley so viciously.

CHAPTER 22

Second verse, much too similar to the first.

Oh, lord, I thought as I sat on a low brick wall in Shirley's backyard, staring nearly unseeing at the breeze-blown wildflowers in her compact garden. What if there were more . . . ?

I nearly laughed aloud. Bitterly. There'd be no more murders of my pet-sitting clients—at least not, allegedly, by me. Not if the frighteningly cordial cop facing me had anything to say about it. I had no doubt that Detective Ned Noralles was merrily mapping out my tardy—in his estimation—arrest.

The detective leaned on the garden wall. We'd had to leave the house while others photographed and scoured it for clues. As always, Noralles wore a suit—charcoal today. His necktie was striped and flat and not nearly as flashy as Py the python.

As much as I loved to decipher things from legal briefs to thriller novels, I found Noralles's dark, blank features utterly illegible. It didn't help that he'd been nearly silent since ushering me out here. Didn't even glance at the notebook in his hands. Did he expect I'd get so nervous I'd blurt out a confession?

I could demand to call my lawyer. At this time of day, Esther was likely to be in court, but once I'd asked for my attorney, I couldn't be interrogated without one.

But if I did that, I'd look guilty.

Who the hell was I kidding? To Noralles, I *was* guilty.

But I was also a lawyer. I had to act like one now. On my own behalf. That meant keeping my emotions to myself. And I was full of emotion. Mostly grief. Shirley had been a nice lady. We'd had a history together. She had stuck up for me, not believed the stuff that led to my suspension from law.

After introducing her to Darryl, I'd seen her around his place often. She had been determined to make sure Rosie's days were a bed of roses, as she'd really cared about her yappy little poodle. She'd had a loving heart. Until someone had apparently stabbed her through it.

I didn't dare cry. Instead, glaring, I took the offensive. "What's my motive supposed to be this time, Detective?"

His black eyebrows rose. "You tell me."

"Why don't I tell you, instead, what happened. If you start acting accusatory, I'll stop and ask for my lawyer. Got it?"

"Sure," he said, his smile much too friendly. I figured the drill. He wanted me off guard. I'd gathered, during the investigation into Carl's killing, that the LAPD took its time before making accusations to ensure they'd stick. Unless Noralles simply wanted to toy with me before coming in for the proverbial kill, the better, he might imagine, to jab at Jeff. The reality was probably a pinch of both. But in any event, despite Noralles's professional, mild demeanor, I'd caught a glint in his gaze. He was too damned sure of himself.

But once more, he hadn't read me my Miranda rights. He was fishing again. And I wasn't about to be caught. I hoped.

"I'd like a glass of water first," I said. My throat was so dry that I felt as if a Mojave wind had swept through it. Which would explain why my voice sounded so gritty.

"Sure," the detective said. "Hey, Wherlon, come here."

The short detective with bushy brows and a receding hairline stood nearby, talking on a cell phone. Or pretending to. More likely he was eavesdropping. Or making sure I didn't stab his boss, though I'd been searched for weapons. It wouldn't have been easy to hide something like the knife that killed Shirley under a T-shirt and jeans. Nearly as big as the one that killed Carl, it had been left on the floor beside Shirley, same as at the Cuthbertson crime scene. I suspected, though, that it had come from Shirley's well-equipped kitchen.

Noralles didn't press me until Wherlon brought a bottle of water, presumably from one of the cop cars. I took a few sips. It was warm, but it wet my throat.

"Tell us what happened this time, Ms. Ballantyne." Detective Noralles's tone remained dispassionate. But I knew he wouldn't believe a shred of what I said, short of a confession. He turned on his tape recorder and started making notes.

Looking beyond his shoulder toward a neighbor's house, I inhaled warm afternoon air and described my day, from when I'd awakened at Jeff's, walked and fed Lexie and Odin, through my earliest morning rounds and the first visit to Shirley's.

"She wasn't here then?" He leaned forward as if prepared to pounce at the tiniest discrepancies in my discourse.

If there were any, they'd come from tension, not terminal guilt. And I intended to wear my litigator's mantle like a suit of armor. To stay cool . . . Hell, that wouldn't work. Those heavy metal outfits had to be damned hot. Anyway, I wouldn't sweat about it. I'd tell my story, then walk away. "Ms. Dorian wasn't expected home till this evening," I told Noralles. "Could be she got home early and surprised someone burgling her home."

"Like Carl Cuthbertson did." The words were a bland statement but dripped with silent sarcasm.

"Maybe. Anyhow, I took Rosie for a walk, fed her, made sure she had enough water for the rest of the day. Then I went to the next place on my schedule."

"Can I have a copy of that schedule?"

"Sure. We'll do it the same way as last time." Lord! We were developing a course of conduct on what to do after a murder. My chest constricted, so I forced my lungs to expand. *Breathe!*

I spoke automatically, though I forced myself to listen to my own words as if they were someone else's. Fortunately, I said nothing I'd object to if I were a lawyer representing myself. I continued through my pet-sitting visits.

Then I came to the day's second visit to Shirley's. I continued my narration, including getting out of the car, tackling her security alarm, opening the large oak door to find that Rosie wasn't waiting, hearing the dog's whines from upstairs, following the sound . . . finding Shirley.

"I called 911," I said. "I . . . I touched Shirley to see if she had a pulse, but I didn't feel any. She wasn't breathing." Neither was I. And despite my best intentions, I noticed that my cheeks were wet. I wiped the tears with the back of my hand, then glared defiantly at Noralles. Despite my very first impression of the man, I was now well aware that sympathy wasn't his strong suit. Neither was anything else that might have smacked of emotion, except for cocksureness. "That's it," I said.

"You'd known Ms. Dorian before you started watching her dog?" Noralles asked.

"Yes, she'd been a law client of mine."

"Mmm-hmm. Another one. Tell me about *that* case."

There wasn't much to hide about it. Most was public record. But I'd promised myself I wouldn't answer questions without Esther's presence. I doubted Noralles could trip me up, but it would be better for Esther to know what he'd asked and how I'd replied when she defended me on a homicide indictment. Or two.

"Sure. We'll do it again like last time. We'll set up a time, and I'll come to the station with my lawyer."

Crap. Another course of conduct established.

But at least our appointment would be in the future. In the meantime, I would be free.

For now.

I hadn't been aware that Shirley Dorian had a significant other, but Noralles introduced me to Burt Edgars in the house's entryway.

Burt was tall, thin, lugubrious, and clad in brown. He clutched a shaking Rosie while darting me the evil eye. Noralles wasn't the only one who figured he knew who'd stabbed Shirley.

I, on the other hand, was happy there'd been a man in Shirley's life. That meant another possible suspect.

Until . . . "We got back from Las Vegas a few hours ago," Burt said stiffly. "We went straight to my office for a meeting. Got there just in time. Everyone was waiting. Shirley was tired, so she talked first, got on my computer for a minute, then left."

He, apparently, didn't. Sighing inside, I moved his name down on my suspect list. He'd been in plain sight of others when Shirley was stabbed.

"We were planning to meet for dinner," he continued, "but . . ." He cleared his throat three times, each stronger than the last. When he could speak again, he asked, "How could this have happened?" He glared as if waiting for me to explain how Shirley and I suddenly developed an overwhelming hatred for one another and why I'd decided to end it the most final way.

Instead, I told the glowering man, "I'm glad you've got Rosie. After I found Shirley, I was worried her dog wouldn't have anyone to care for her." He looked ready to swing Rosie far from my grasp when I took a step toward them, but I managed to rub the silver poodle's fuzzy topknot. "Be a good girl, Rosie." My voice broke. I didn't look at Burt. He'd probably figure I was as skilled an actress as I was a slasher.

Rosie licked my fingers. Like Cheesie, she didn't act accusatory. Both were witnesses to their masters' murders. If only they could speak English! Or even if Lexie did, and could translate . . . *Now you're really losing it, Kendra.*

News vans were everywhere when I left Shirley's. Mikes were thrust into my face as reporters recognized me again. "Ms. Ballantyne, what happened in there?" "Ms. Ballantyne, is it true another of your clients was murdered?" "Kendra, talk to us."

Like hell. I kept a grim smile on my face and

kept walking toward the blessed haven of my car.

The cell phone calls I made as I headed toward Jeff's should have felt as rote as finding another dead body. First, I called Esther. For a change, I caught her in her office.

"You won't believe this," I said.

She didn't. Not at first. Worse, I suspected she didn't believe in my innocence, either, though she was too good an attorney to say so. But I could almost hear the scrambling inside her mind to figure out how to present a defense to a jury.

Two murders? Not that Carl's was relevant to Shirley's. A prosecutor couldn't bring it up as evidence of my guilt. But any prosecutor worth his crowded government caseload would find a way to get it in. Even if he didn't, juries don't spring from the womb of assembly rooms newly born, without an inkling of what's been in the news during the months it takes to get to trial.

"Let's get together and talk, Kendra." Esther spoke so calmly I could almost imagine she *wasn't* already sweating an anticipated loss on her spectacular record of trial triumphs. "I want to hear exactly what happened."

"Sure." We set a time for me to come to her office. When I hung up, I realized I'd pulled over and parked the car—a good thing. I'd talked myself into breathing before, but now it was too fast. I forced myself to slow it. It'd be a hell of a mistake to drive while hyperventilating.

Next, I called Darryl. "Hey, guess what," I said when he got on the phone. "You know how much I enjoy being the subject of news stories? Well, watch the news. I'm back."

"I've seen it. Kendra, what happened?"

"I know as much as I did when Carl was killed."

"Zilch?"

"Yep. Except that I'm prime suspect number one again."

"So I gathered." He paused so slightly that I wouldn't have noticed if I hadn't been overly sensitive just then. Being a multiple murder suspect did that to me. "Kendra, you didn't—"

"Kill Shirley?" I finished for him. I heard him try to talk but didn't let him. "Sure I did. Carl, too. And if I check the papers, I'll bet there've been some recent drive-by shootings I could be implicated in. Oh, wait, my m.o. is to stab people. Well, there've got to have been more of those, too." As I spoke, my heart pounded harder as my tone grew more shrill.

"Hey," Darryl said. "That's not where I was going. Kendra, where are you? Can I come and get you?"

"No!" I shouted. Then, ratcheting my mood down several notches so fast that I deflated like a pinpricked balloon, I said more softly, "No, I'm fine."

"Come by, please?" I hadn't heard Darryl plead before. "We'll talk. I know you're not a killer."

"Of course." Yet if I was in his position with a

friend who just happened to be present multiple times when bloody murder victims turned up, I'd have a suspicion or two myself.

And maybe that was the whole idea.

CHAPTER 23

Jeff Hubbard was already home.

I'd expected his return later that night. I had planned to give a full report on how well Odin behaved. And how well I had treated his pet. Then, thrilled or not, I had intended to take Lexie and go to our garage apartment. And pray Jeff's next trip wasn't far in the future.

But when I pulled into his driveway, my Beamer had company—his black Escalade. I'd already figured Jeff must do well in his security business. His high-end SUV proved either that he had money, or that he wanted his clients to believe in his success. Probably both.

I considered knocking before entering, but why bother? He knew I had the code to disarm his security system and a key to get in. He also knew I'd be back that evening, if for no other reason than to retrieve my spaniel.

Inside, I saw a large backpack and a wheeled suitcase in the entry. No pups greeted me, which suggested they were distracted.

"Jeff?" I called. "Hi. It's Kendra."

Dogs barked from the direction of the kitchen.

I headed that way. Before I got there, Odin barreled down the hall toward me, followed by the smaller Lexie. Both leapt on me, and I laughed at the enthusiastic greeting. "Hi, you two."

"Hi to you," responded a deep, decidedly human voice. I looked up from the furry heads I stroked to see Jeff in the kitchen doorway. His arms were folded, his posture tall and forbidding. I couldn't see the expression on his face, for he was backlit, standing in shadows.

"Welcome home," I said in a tone a heck of a lot brighter than the hall.

He gestured toward the room behind him. "Need a drink? I do."

"Amen," I said fervently.

A short while later we sat holding Scotch-and-sodas, dogs at our feet, my big purse on the pillows beside me. If the sunkenness of Jeff's blue eyes and the lines at their corners were any indication, he was beat.

Poor chap. He didn't need to hear my problems and strange speculations. Not yet, at least. After a good night's sleep—assuming I could snooze instead of stewing into the wee hours—I would sit down, puzzle out what pieces of information I could beg him and his best computer geek to find for me, then call and lay on him my latest tribulations and the notions they'd solidified.

But my druthers were quickly disbursed by his first remark. "So, are you really into stabbing your pet-sitting customers? I hope not. I'm usually a good street-fighter, but I'm probably too tired to fend you off tonight."

I glared into his face. Exhaustion seemed to set the cragginess of his cheeks and brows and chin into even sharper angles. Sexy? Oh, yes. And why the hell was I noticing this now?

Maybe it was because, if I weren't lucky, I'd be swearing off sex for the next twenty-five years to life. Or longer.

Jeff's mouth crooked up on one side. "Can I assume from that gesture that you've decided not to take me on for now?"

"For now." Not in either way, for my common sense remained stronger than my sex drive, thank heavens. I think.

"So tell me about your day," he said.

"You don't want to hear."

"Actually," he said, "I do. You're the lawyer, but I've worked beside the legal system long enough to know you're innocent till proven guilty. And though we've mostly been the proverbial ships passing in the night, I don't figure you for a murderer. Or if you were, I'd guess you'd be more genteel about it—fast-acting poison, maybe. At worst, a small pistol. Not something with all that blood."

"You've got me pegged."

His dark blond brows lifted. "Is that an invitation?"

I felt a flush creep up my face but didn't move my gaze. "Could be. But you've got to earn it."

"Yeah?"

"Yeah. I need a little help here. There are a couple

of people who know I'm innocent—me, and the real murderer, who's been busy framing me. Maybe it's even the same person who set me up before, for the ethics violation, or maybe the murderer figures I'm a prime patsy since I was already mired in that muck, way over my head. I know the legal end of things, though criminal defense isn't my specialty. But I don't know investigative stuff. If I did, I'd have figured out by now who killed Carl, proved it, and put everything except mourning my dead client behind me. And if I'd accomplished that, maybe Shirley would still be alive."

"Interesting theory."

"But you don't buy it?"

"I didn't say that. In fact, it makes some sense. But there are other possibilities, too."

"Yeah, so, let's brainstorm."

"Sure." Although I had to wonder what condition his brain was in, given how exhausted he looked.

Not to worry. Jeff Hubbard was one cool dude. He got to the crux of the situation without blinking. "So you knew both Carl Cuthbertson and Shirley Dorian. And I'll assume since you've told me you didn't murder them, that you didn't. I'll also assume, at least for now, that Shirley's murder, under such similar circumstances as Carl's, wasn't a copycat killing. That means we need a connection between Carl and Shirley. Maybe it's you, and maybe something else. Do you know of any other friends or acquaintances they had in common?"

"Well . . ." I'd been mulling that over. "Yes, but

no one who had reason to kill either of them. And since I'm smack in the middle, that adds another dimension. Whoever it is knows about me and the fact I'm now pet-sitting. Maybe even knows *me*."

Jeff nodded. I hadn't noticed his notebook, but now that we were into details, he jotted on the tiny loose-leaf binder.

"The victims worked in the same industry, more or less," I continued. "Shirley was in PR and Carl in production. There could be a cast of thousands with connections to both that I don't know of. But those whom I know are Darryl Nestler, plus some attorneys in my firm, including those who helped with the litigation I handled for each of them. There was some overlap in the timing of their cases."

"Darryl," he repeated.

"But we both know it couldn't be him."

I didn't grasp the reason behind Jeff's abrupt glower. "You're quick to defend him."

"Were you accusing him?" That was another instance Jeff had said something strange about the sweet guy who'd referred him to me. Why? "You don't think Darryl—"

Before I could conclude, Jeff interjected, "And the lawyers at your firm are . . . ?"

Better to leave contemplation of Darryl as the bad guy far behind. "There's Royal Marden," I responded. "He's the top name partner, and I admit I wanted him to be guilty of killing Carl after my last conversation with him. And he wears a suit."

I grinned at Jeff's look of puzzlement. "Carl's neighbor Isabelle said she saw someone in a suit peer in Carl's window while he was away, then get in a snit because he wasn't home."

"Any reason for Marden to be angry with Carl?"

"He's a transactional type. He was handling the paperwork in the sale of Carl's production company, the deal brokered by Carl's former sworn enemy Conrad Taylor. The transaction was falling apart, though all Marden would be out was legal fees. Even if he got stiffed, I can't imagine him killing for it, though maybe he was getting a cut of the action. Not kosher, but it's done sometimes." And I'd savor pointing a finger at the righteous Royal and screaming "unethical" right back at him.

Jeff's back straightened, and his exhaustion seemed to evanesce before my eyes. "I'll have it checked. Now, this Taylor. Explain how he might have known Shirley."

"I wish I knew. But since he was driving the deal for Carl, maybe he approached Shirley's company as a possible buyer, along with Millipede FilmAmericam. That's only speculation, though. I doubt a PR outfit like hers would scoop up a production company, even one with creative properties she wanted."

"Worth checking." He made more notes. I noticed how he held his black ballpoint pen. Nice, strong hands. Lithe fingers that might have the magic touch to drive a woman wild . . .

211

Lord, I was losing it. I took a quick swig of Scotch, wishing it contained a lot less soda. Then again, my inhibitions would be easier to ignore if I imbibed straight alcohol.

Not necessarily a bad idea.

"What other lawyers might have known both of them? And you, for that matter."

"I was a junior partner when I handled their cases, so I still reported to the head litigation partner, William Sergement."

"Any others?" he asked.

"An associate, Avalyne Milton, assisted me. But I really can't think why either Bill or Avvie might have wanted to kill either Carl or Shirley, let alone both. Though both would know enough about me to set me up as a suspect."

"And how about Darryl?" he asked.

"Are you kidding? You know him. He's as much of a big puppy dog as any of his charges." At Jeff's skeptical sneer, I said, "Do you have a problem with Darryl, of all people?"

"Not at this moment," he said without explanation.

After we'd exhausted everyone I knew who were acquaintances of both victims and me, we discussed the matters I'd handled for them. I described again Carl's suit against Conrad Taylor for stealing a film script. I told Jeff how Carl had referred his friend Shirley to me when her entertainment industry PR firm was sued for defaming a client by damning him with faint praise.

"So if they were friends, it was probable that some of their employees knew one another."

Agreeing, I mentioned Carl's assistant, Eve Adolph. "But she hadn't been with Carl long, and the stuff you already found on her didn't set off any alarms. Plus, I only just met her. I can't think she's setting me up. Same thing with Burt Edgars, Shirley's significant other. He's got custody of her orphaned poodle. And he had what appears to be an iron-clad alibi for the time Shirley was killed. He seemed pretty broken up about her death, and even if he knew Carl I have no idea why Burt would have had it in for him."

"Were Carl and Shirley lovers?" Jeff's voice caressed the last word as if he were licking candy. His baby blue eyes, no longer sleepy or sneering, were on mine, igniting something inside me that got my blood pumping. My body responded without even the tiniest touch. The guy was sex personified. And unlike others I knew who came on much too strong, he—

Hey! My thoughts suddenly turned to someone who used sex to strong-arm. "I just remembered. There was one other person involved with both Carl's and Shirley's cases. Someone I know well, too."

"And that is . . . ?"

"His Honor, and I use the term loosely, Judge Baird Roehmann."

"You're not fond of the good judge?"

213

"If he were as good a person outside the court-room as he is a judge inside it, I might be. He uses his office to seduce female attorneys."

"Including you?"

"He tried."

"The way Bill Sergement did at your old firm?"

I stared. I hadn't mentioned Drill Sergeant's penchant for coming on to new associates.

"Don't look so surprised. When I say I'm investigating a case, I investigate it. I already have dossiers on most members of your old law firm. And Mr. Sergement has quite a reputation. I didn't know about Judge Roehmann, but you can be sure I'll know about him soon."

I had mixed emotions about that. I appreciated Jeff's efforts, since they were ostensibly on my behalf. On the other hand . . . "And I suppose you have a dossier on me, too?"

His wide grin was all the response I needed.

I was on my feet so fast that Odin barked. Lexie rose, too, and looked at me with wide, wondering eyes. "Time to go, Lexie."

"Murder suspects don't have the luxury of being sensitive, Kendra. Besides, I haven't found anything you should be ashamed of."

He was right. Coming from a dysfunctional family and agreeing to a suspension of my law license for something I didn't do weren't shameful. And those were the only things I could think of that I didn't want people knowing.

But the idea of losing my privacy rankled.

"Did your search turn up how my high school boyfriend and I were caught by the cops playing strip poker in the Disneyland parking lot at three A.M.? Or how about how I nearly married a guy I met in law school till he dumped me for the daughter of a state senator? He had delusions of political grandeur that I couldn't further the way she could."

"No to the former, yes to the latter. Tell me more about this strip poker game." He leered as my glare grew more malevolent.

"You wish."

"Yeah, I do."

Suddenly aware of certain sensations down deep in my body, I just stood there. I'd never before considered lust and anger different sides of the same firebrand. But both heated the psyche. And mine was definitely aglow.

"Let's play a game," I dared him. "If I win, you bare all and turn over everything you learned about me. I'll tear up anything I don't like and you'll promise not to recreate it."

His lascivious smile was already melting the clothes off my back. I had to fight the urge to help it.

"And if I win?" he drawled.

"If you win, I bare all."

"That's all? That hardly seems fair."

"I'll pet-sit free for a month. That's the only thing I've got that you want."

We were both standing by that time. The table

was the only thing that kept us apart, and suddenly it was somewhere off to my side.

"I wouldn't say that," Jeff said.

"To hell with the game," I said softly without tearing my gaze from his.

"Amen," he said, stepping forward.

CHAPTER 24

I thought I'd learned my lesson about going to bed with men I did business with. Drill Sergeant taught me that sleeping with a senior partner led to some damn awkward moments. For me, not him of course.

When he'd moved on by seducing his next junior associate, it was a relief. Stupidly, I hadn't wondered till way into the affair how to gracefully extricate myself without jeopardizing my job. I liked my then-associateship at MSY more than I liked Sergement, and it was clear that what we had together wasn't going anywhere.

Thanks to him, I'd planned how to gracefully dance away from any new affair even as I was diving into it. Relationships weren't worth the effort of figuring out if there was something there besides sex—which, mostly, there wasn't. And settling for sex was only okay if that was all you wanted from the guy. No politics mixed up with passion. Period.

I was wondering how that software had gone snafu in the computer files of my mind as I lay in bed with Jeff Hubbard late that night.

I had to force my brain to worry, for my body had clearly taken control, and all my sated carcass wanted to do was sleep. It didn't help that Jeff's bare flesh was pressed against my back, his arm wrapped around my naked midriff, his strong hand stroking . . . never mind. I've already established that I hold personal privacy in very high esteem.

His bedroom was a lot bigger than the box-filled guest quarters Lexie and I had begun to think of as ours. Not that I could make out the functional furniture in the dark of the night. Especially with my eyes closed, my breathing deep, inhaling the incomparable incense of our sex.

There'd been guys between Drill Sergeant and Jeff, but none lasted more than a few enjoyable weeks. I had a feeling, after the amazing antics we'd engaged in first in the kitchen, then the hall, then the bedroom, that Jeff would last a lot longer.

For one thing, I needed him. In lots of ways. Sexually—oh, yeah. And I appreciated the dog-sitting gig in his house as it had evolved over the past several weeks.

Also, being framed as a multiple murder suspect, I needed whatever help his investigative expertise and resources could provide. He'd already proven that his skills in those areas were as superb as those in the more sensual ones.

Plus . . . I liked the guy.

"Damn," I murmured almost too low to hear my own voice.

Jeff stirred and nibbled at my ear. "Hmmm?"

Was he asking what I said, or whether I wanted to forget it and share another round of ecstasy?

I chose door number two.

Amazingly, the morning wasn't the least bit awkward. We rose and showered—separately, as we each had things to do that didn't involve leaping back into bed. We acknowledged what came naturally and took the dogs for a quick walk on the flat Sherman Oaks street. The canines were also treated to breakfast before we ate. After all, they'd been on their best behavior the night before. They'd seen their respective masters in positions that could be mistaken for mauling, yet both instinctively forbore from attacking each other's human assailant.

I fixed coffee, Jeff fixed toast, and we sat again at the table where it had all started the night before.

"So I guess you don't stab all your pet-sitting clients," he said. "Though if I kept up last night's pace I might reach an early grave anyway."

"I dare you to try," I taunted. "The pace, I mean. Not the grave. I don't need another dead client."

He grinned and sipped his coffee. "Are you as good at lawyering as you are at . . . gamesmanship?"

"Games*woman*ship. Hell, yes. I won my first major case nearly all by my lonesome, and it's been an easy climb ever since—except for my recent detour." Damn. I was in too good a mood to think about detours now, especially the one that might have no exit back onto the high road of my legal career.

"Tell me about it. Your first case."

I knew he was just making small talk since his eyes over his coffee mug said something else altogether. Something I wanted to respond to. But I had already noticed a major niggling in the back of my mind.

Had we gone too fast? What did it bode for the future?

Not a damn thing, except maybe more fun when the mood struck us. I didn't want more. I doubted Jeff did either.

"My first case." I leapt into the subject. "Shaff v. Vanner. Bill Sergement advised me but thought it too trivial to spend much time on. He changed his tune after our incredible verdict. The damages were nearly all we asked for."

"You were on the plaintiff's side?" Still sipping, he settled back in his chair. A good thing, too, since it told me he was listening instead of leaving his libido in control.

"Yes, the Shaffs were a working-class couple trying to move their family from their declining neighborhood. Their son, an only child, was a good kid, honor role, swim team, a job on the weekends at a nearby movie theater taking tickets."

Jeff's expression said he saw where I was headed. "The victim?"

"Yeah. Killed at a doughnut shop a few blocks from their home. Sure, the gang-banger was caught, tried, and incarcerated, but that didn't help his parents. So, to add to the meager justice my clients got, we sued the doughnut shop's owners. Asserted they were negligent in keeping long hours, maintaining inadequate security, and not ousting troublemakers from their premises. The jurors went wild to agree with us and awarded huge punitive damages. Rather than wait out the defendants' appeal, we settled for less than the award. Their insurance company paid most of the money, but we were glad the owners also had to reach into their pockets. Otherwise, no lesson learned."

"And your law firm got its share?"

"You betcha. Me, too. The bonus wasn't what I was after, though. That win was the boost that started my career."

He smiled. I smiled. That electrical spark arced between us again.

"Now, your turn," I said.

"Okay." He reached over the table toward me and pulled till he'd settled me on his lap.

During the delicious kiss, I murmured against his mouth, "This isn't what I meant." I pulled back. "I've shown you mine, now you show me yours. First case, I mean. How did you start out as an investigator?"

He murmured against my ear, "My mother."

"She wanted you to be a detective?"

"Nope. I was the one who discovered she supported our family as an exotic dancer instead of on her earnings as a waitress."

I stared at him. His eyes said everything. "You're serious."

He nodded. "I grew up in a conservative Chicago suburb. My dad's a good sort—an engineer, not a lot of ambition. To make ends meet, especially when he was between jobs, my mom worked nights. We always understood—my dad, younger brother, and me—that she waited tables at a steakhouse in the next town. As I got into my teens, I wondered why her tips seemed to be so huge, since we always had money for extras. So, one night I followed her to work. It wasn't a steakhouse, but a strip club. I looked older than my age, so I managed to slip into the audience." He shook his head. "She was on stage . . . dancing."

Wow. I wanted to know more, but could hardly ask if his mom turned tricks, too. Instead, I said, "Did you tell your dad?"

"Nope. I figured he probably suspected but didn't want to know. I told her what I'd learned years later, after the Army and college, when I started working for a P.I. She asked me, like you did, what got me interested. She seemed embarrassed, but, hey, I admired her for it. She was damned resourceful, and I told her so. And, no, before you ask, she didn't let anyone touch her but my dad."

"I wasn't going to ask," I told him.

"You didn't have to."

"I like your attitude." About some things, at least. "It takes a hell of a guy to be so nonjudgmental, especially about his mother."

"Yeah, that's me." His smile was sardonic. And sexy.

Maybe there was time . . . I looked at my watch. "Oh, geez, it's late."

"What's on your agenda today?" His tone sounded as regretful as I felt. Which made me feel better.

"The usual rounds. Plus I need to pack my stuff to move back to my place. Also, though I'm not sure how appropriate it is to call Noralles, I figure it's better to act like an interested citizen than a worried perpetrator waiting to be arrested, so—"

"Whoa. Go back a step. You're moving out?"

"That's the idea. Now that you're home, Odin doesn't need a sitter, so—"

"What if *I* need one?"

"We didn't do a lot of sitting last night," I reminded him. Besides, though I didn't do one-night stands, neither did I start living with a guy just because we'd shared one memorable night.

Of course that couldn't have been Jeff's intention. Continuing our orgy was another matter. But even that felt too much, too fast, for me. And I doubted he wanted me to stay to take up exotic dancing.

"Like I was saying, I need to check with Noralles about how his investigation into everyone but me is going. Unless you'd like to do it for me, since you and he have a history."

"Of mutual dislike," he reminded me. "But, sure, I'll see what I can get from him and let you know. Meantime, I'll set my research ace Althea on the people you and I discussed last night. But back to the living situation."

Hard to argue with a guy with come-hither blue eyes. This morning, his blond-brown hair was tousled from the way we'd run the dogs on our misnamed walk. His white cotton shirt was unbuttoned halfway down his slightly hairy chest. I figured he'd left himself undone to get me panting again. But that wasn't going to happen. Or at least I wouldn't let him know it if I had any hope of escaping.

"The deal was I'd be a live-in sitter while you're away. In exchange, I get room and board, a little cash, and a lot of investigation time. But now you're in town until . . . ?"

"What if I lied and said I'm leaving today, so you have to stay here tonight?"

"I'd see through it."

"I figured." He suddenly looked too damned serious. "You having regrets about last night?"

"Hardly. In fact, let me check out what's going on at my place today, and if no huge party is planned, what say I make Odin and you a nice dinner there? We'll talk over what we each find out about Shirley's murder today, and then, if we're not totally bushed, we'll see how the evening unfolds."

That, I hoped, made my continued interest clear.

"Yeah," he said, clearly cheerful once more. "That works. And just as a prelude . . ." He stood, bent down, and gave me a kiss that spoke of lots of promise for the night to come.

But that was before the dog shit hit the fan later that day.

I didn't know anything about it at first.

After leaving Jeff's, Lexie and I headed for our own digs. Still sitting in the Beamer, I smiled to see how peaceful my large, hilltop home looked when I'd pushed the button to open the gate. No media vans spoiling the scenery, no cars in the driveway, no parties rocking the grounds. Of course Charlotte and Yul could have parked in the garage, so the silence did not mean privacy, but at least, for now, all seemed peaceful.

As usual, Lexie insisted on exiting the car by leaping over my lap. On the driveway, she strained on her leash, barking excitedly, as if happy to be home. "Me, too," I said, though my eyes strayed toward the main house that was no longer our home.

"Hi," called a voice. I turned till I found the source. One of my neighbors, a guy who rode his ten-speed endlessly around the hills for exercise, stood by the fence. I approached, tugging Lexie gently in that direction. As always, he held the handlebars of his sleek, silvery bicycle, straddling it with one sneaker-shod foot on the ground, the other on a pedal.

"How are you?" I searched my brain for his name, something reminiscent of socks. Argyle? No, Lyle. "What's new, Lyle?"

"Your tenants," he said. "I've met them." Fortunately, he was smiling, showing large, white teeth in a round, tanned face. Because he was usually sweaty from his constant cycling, his fringe of sandy-blond hair was generally wet and plastered to his low forehead below his long, squat helmet. Today, though, he must have just been starting out, for the hair that showed rippled in the late-July breeze.

"Charlotte and Yul?"

Lyle nodded. No sign of grumpiness. Hopefully that meant he wasn't irritated by the often-tossed parties on my property. From what I could see, he ate enough to make up for his endless exercise— despite his obviously robust athletic abilities, the guy had a gut. Either that, or he tucked a beach ball beneath his colorful spandex cycling shirt and matching shorts.

"Yeah. I watched her show on TV a few months ago, thought she was a really smart lady to take the money and run instead of staying hooked up with that last guy standing."

"Right," I agreed. Was that it? Not that I watched them, but I'd heard of reality shows where the contestants played games to the bitter end, selecting a person to "love" forever while sharing a secret with the show's producers and millions of audience members: If she rejected the claimed love of her life, she'd win a generous check and the promise of more TV time. A hell of a consolation prize. Who wouldn't choose it over someone she'd barely met?

Or was Yul Charlotte's sexy but stupid selection?

She obviously had money, or she wouldn't be able to pay the rent. So—

"I haven't seen you at any of Charlotte's parties," Lyle said. "She invites the neighbors. I wondered if you sold the place, so I asked her. She said she was renting it from you."

"I still live here," I said without explaining my extended absences, "but decided to simplify my life. Lexie and I stay in an apartment on the grounds." I nodded toward the garage.

"Do you—"

Before he finished, my cell phone rang. I shrugged apologetically as I answered.

"Kendra? It's Darryl." I knew it would be him since he was programmed into my phone, but Darryl didn't sound anything like himself. I'd never had trouble recognizing my dearest friend's voice, which was usually lazy, sweet, and sometimes a bit sardonic.

Now, a little shrill, a lot clipped, it contained a hint of something I'd never heard there before.

Panic.

My pulse rate accelerated. "What's wrong?"

"I'm in trouble. Can you come here? Please?"

CHAPTER 25

"Sure, I was bitten by something bigger than a flea," Darryl said. "The Hollywood bug. How could I help it, with so many of my clients in the business? And the money I was promised . . . I couldn't resist."

We were in his office at Doggy Indulgence. Its odor suggested he'd let some of his four-legged customers into his private sanctum to take care of their business. But Darryl had always maintained a separation between the pets' playroom and *his* business. I had the sudden sense that whatever his wont was before was trumped by what had just happened to him.

His usually sweet and soulful puppydog's eyes were huge and afraid. His skinny shoulders hunched forward as if he'd been slugged in the stomach.

At the moment, I felt like following it up with a gut punch of my own. Not only had my very dear friend been keeping something from me, but it was colossal. And he'd heard from Noralles about it.

Still, this was Darryl, who'd been there for me

in my worst hours. My voice level, I said, "So you were working on a movie idea with both Carl and Shirley?"

He nodded. "TV, not feature film. I got the idea one day when Shirley was here acting her usual overprotective self with Rosie. Sat where you are now. We were discussing Rosie's behavior. That day, she'd attacked Boris, a borzoi ten times bigger than her. Fortunately, Boris is pretty laid back, and in fact that was what he did."

"What?" I asked, not getting it.

"He laid back. On Rosie. She yelped but calmed down, and after intervention from me, they romped together, then rested on the couch, side by side." He gestured beyond the window opening on the playroom toward that same threadbare sofa, now occupied by several miscellaneous mutts.

"And that led to your idea how?"

"It's not unusual for dogs to change from enemies to friends, once they get to know each other. Sometimes it's work to get them to modify angry bites to playful ones. The idea horrified Shirley till I explained my methods of persuasion."

"Like?" The response wouldn't get me answers to the rest of my questions, but it would keep Darryl talking.

"Like lying on the floor and letting them creep up on one another with my body as a buffer." He grinned and scrunched arms to his sides in a parody of the prone pose he described.

"You did that with Rosie and Boris?"

"No, actually I took them on a long walk together. Let both bark at birds, cars, and neighborhood dogs. By the time we got back, they were compatriots."

"That got you involved in a Hollywood deal with Shirley?"

"Yes. She found it fascinating. Said it would make a great screenplay. Better yet, a TV sitcom with dogs as stars. The ideas poured out, and we were still talking when Carl came for Cheesie. Shirley called him in, and we brainstormed together. A lot of excitement flew around this office. We all decided to collaborate on a pilot show." He leaned back on his desk chair, looking pretty pleased. The happy-go-lucky expression was typical Darryl—except for today.

But I wasn't happy, and I certainly hadn't been feeling lucky lately. And I was considering telling Darryl where to go.

Why hadn't he told me of this sitcom scheme? And why had it somehow made Noralles consider Darryl a more exciting double murder suspect than me?

Hey, if he really thought that, then the heat would be off me. That was something I could get used to. But would it stick?

Did I want it to stick?

Darryl had kept his mouth closed about something big in his life when I thought we both exchanged important thoughts, the crux of our cherished friendship. He knew Carl and Shirley. I'd

230

introduced both to him as potential customers. I said as much to Darryl. "It's one thing for Detective Noralles to jump to the conclusion I killed Carl and Shirley, since I had keys to their houses and found them both. But why accuse you?"

That had been the impetus for Darryl's frantic phone call. Like me, he'd been "invited" to the North Hollywood Police Station to discuss what he knew about the victims.

Darryl stood and paced like a thin, tall tiger already behind cage bars. "Things weren't going well with the pilot," he muttered. Then he embellished: "They'd decided to cut me out." He stopped pacing to glare at me as angrily as if the ghost of Carl or Shirley possessed my body. His ire made me edgier, and I stood, too.

"What do you mean?"

For a second I thought he wouldn't answer. I wondered if someone or something else possessed *his* body, for the rage in his fierce frown didn't look like the Darryl I knew. Could he be the person railroading me? "Shirley discussed the project with a cable network she did promo work for. Carl's production company was part of the package. For the hell of it, I put together a script about a typical day in doggy daycare and gave them each a copy. Apparently, it stank."

So, I gathered, did his reaction to their criticism. "So they dropped the project?"

"They dropped *me*." He punctuated the last word by pounding a fist into the palm of his other hand, as if he wished it were a face. Preferably Carl's or Shirley's.

Of course that was impossible. Had he made it impossible?

I recalled now that Darryl's demeanor lately had varied from his norm now and then. He'd become more snappish, less patient. Was that because of all he hid inside?

"I don't understand," I said. "Were they intending to go forward with the dog resort TV show without you?"

"You got it. I said I'd work with a script consultant, if they wanted. Or just become a consultant on pet daycare. It was my idea, after all. But they said it was *their* idea, based on their paying dearly for their dogs to use my facilities."

I got the picture. Rather, I saw what was inside the frame as Noralles undoubtedly perceived it. A fictional doggy spa as a setting for a major sitcom: the next *Cheers* with pets instead of bar patrons, a canine or feline *Friends,* or *All in the Doggy Family.* Something possibly long-running that would earn its creators a lot of dog biscuits. Darryl was its inspiration, and Shirley and Carl had left him outside looking in, tongue hanging out as he panted for what could have been. What should have been, since he gave them that flash of an idea that would become their brilliant show.

"How did Noralles find out?" I asked. At Carl's company, VP Eve Adolph hadn't mentioned a doggy daycare sitcom. Nor had Carl's daughter

Laurie or Shirley's significant other, Burt Edgars. But, then, I hadn't asked.

Noralles had. "I gathered he quizzed Shirley's company about what she'd been working on with Carl. Someone mentioned me." His eyes suddenly sought something on the floor. "I guess I'd called in a huff one day and said some things I didn't mean."

"Like threats?"

He nodded sheepishly, then continued walking back and forth so nervously I wished I had a sedative to offer him.

I couldn't imagine Darryl threatening anyone. This big, lanky puppydog growling menacingly? Never.

But I also hadn't imagined him getting involved in a TV show. And then getting cut out of it—had he been so freaked that he'd made good on his threats, paid Carl and Shirley back? Carved out his frustration right into their bloody bodies?

But why frame me? Because I was there and vulnerable?

My questions must have appeared on my face because I didn't have to prompt Darryl to answer. "I didn't kill either of them, Kendra." His pacing brought him face to face with me. Rather, my face to his neck. I looked up. He looked down.

"Honest," he said, sounding as sincere as . . . well, Darryl.

Did I believe him?

Darryl Nestler was there for me when I was

accused of selling out my own client. Of handing over the strategy memo that spurred loony Lorraine Giles to kill my client's CEO. Of failing to represent my client competently, and worse. He'd been there when I had to agree on the suspension of my law license. I'd cried on Darryl's bony shoulders, literally and figuratively. If he ever doubted my innocence, he never let on.

Now he was in trouble. He said he didn't kill Carl or Shirley. Did I believe him?

Hell, yes. Even though, if I took his side, I'd again head the suspect short list. But it wasn't Darryl who'd stuck me there. If he said he was innocent, he was innocent.

"Of course you didn't kill them." I held his thin upper arms with trembling hands. "Now, sit your skinny butt back down." I pointed to his chair behind the desk. "We have some strategizing to do. This TV show idea opens up a whole new set of possible suspects." Who all knew how to pin things on me? "One way or another, we'll get you out of this mess."

And me, too, I hoped.

If it had been anyone less important than Darryl whom I was trying to help, I wouldn't have agreed to have lunch with His Honor, Judge Baird Roehmann.

Agreed? Hell, I'd invited him.

At least, because he'd chosen the place, he would pay. We sat across a table from one another at a busy and posh restaurant in an expensive Bunker Hill hotel, one catering to business travelers visiting downtown L.A. on unlimited expense accounts.

Though I'd spoken with Baird, I hadn't seen him in months. He belonged in these opulent surroundings, in the midst of white tablecloths, gleaming flatware, and crystal goblets. He was the consummate sophisticated jurist with patrician yet paternal features beneath smoothly styled silver hair. His nose was the tiniest bit misshapen, leaning slightly left, the result of a teenage indiscretion he'd once admitted when we'd both been a bit tipsy. Though he'd been born and bred in Beverly Hills, he'd gone slumming in the Valley in an attempt to get laid. When he got fresh with the wrong girl, she belted him, broke his nose, and, presumably, deflated his libido for that night.

Of course, his official bio stated he'd been a star boxer at his Ivy League university as an undergrad. Anyone wondering about that nose could assume it resulted from a match that the incomparable Baird Roehmann had, undoubtedly, come back to win.

"Glad you called when you did, Kendra," the judge said in a voice developed to carry clear across the vastest courtroom, though many today had microphones. A couple of businesswomen at a nearby table glanced our way, smiled, then leaned toward each other as they undoubtedly discussed their recognition of the suave, newshound judge.

Though he'd left his black robe in his courtroom, he had dressed for his role in a dark suit, crisp white shirt with diamond cufflinks, and red striped tie. He smelled of lime aftershave overlain with a hint of lust. His gray eyes hadn't stopped slipping down to my well-covered breasts.

Knowing what I faced, I'd dug inside my garage apartment's tiny closet deep enough to find a forest-green suit which I wore with a tailored blouse that revealed not a hint of skin. I'd drawn my dark brown hair back to the nape of my neck, securing it with a tortoiseshell clip. All I needed was a pair of glasses perched at the end of my nose to resemble a businesslike bluestocking from a bygone era.

"I was hearing a case that settled this morning," he continued, "and was just about to have my clerk call the lawyers on a trailing P.I. matter."

That wasn't something to worry Jeff Hubbard. It didn't mean a private investigator who'd been following someone got sued. No, a trailing case was one where litigants and their lawyers had to be ready to argue their suit at a moment's notice, but twiddled their thumbs on standby till a judge and courtroom were ready for their trial. And in the language of civil litigation, P.I. meant "personal injury."

"I appreciate your availability on short notice, Baird."

"Anytime for you, Kendra. I'd begun to think you were avoiding me." His smile suggested incredulity. Who, in her right mind, would forbear from an audience with His Honor?

"Of course not," I assured him in the most earnest, lie-obscuring tone I could dredge from my rusty litigator's repertoire. "But you know all I've been dealing with lately. I didn't want to embarrass you— someone of your stature being seen with a lawyer whose license was suspended."

Was I laying it on too thick? Not for Baird. He was used to being cosseted and complimented. He beamed magnanimously. "You're a friend, Kendra. No matter how it might look, I'd never avoid you."

"Thank you." I glanced down at the menu, dragging my eyes from his like I was flirting. Lord, if he didn't have the best resources around, I'd have gagged myself with a silver soup spoon before pretending to play Baird's sexually suggestive games.

"In fact," he said, "after hearing the latest news, I rather thought I might hear from you."

Why in hell . . . ? But before I could ask, the white-jacketed waiter came to take our orders: Cobb salad for me, prime rib for His Honor. When the guy backed away, all but bowing and scraping in deference to his august customer, I said to Baird, "You were mentioning the latest news, and how you thought I might—"

"Call me?" His Cheshire Cat grin showed gleaming white teeth. "Someone in as much trouble as you . . . Well, one uses the most powerful contacts one has in difficult situations, right?"

The pompous bastard! Yeah, I'd contacted him

before, when I'd been accused of unethical conduct, but for exactly the same reason I'd turned to him now—for a referral.

"Of course," he was saying, "when I heard of the first murder for which you were suspected, I thought you'd get in touch then. When I called, you seemed, well, shall we say, too proud to accept help. But with a second accusation—"

"I haven't been accused of anything, Baird." Though I still smiled, my teeth were gritted so hard that I wondered if they'd crack. "And the reason I wanted to meet with you was because of your expansive knowledge of the legal community. I need a referral." Yeah, I was still trying to butter him up while barely avoiding cutting him down to size. But I knew this man too well, despite working hard over the years to make sure I didn't get to know him any better. Like in the biblical sense.

"Are you dissatisfied with Esther Ickes' representation?"

"Not at all. The referral's for a friend. He's got remote ties to both murder victims, too, and I want to make sure he's well represented for any questioning."

"And that was why you wanted to have lunch?"

Shit. If I insulted him, I'd never get the referral. And Judge Baird Roehmann, one of the preeminent jurists in Southern California, knew the best criminal defense attorneys. They'd all appeared before him. I'd only done civil litigation. I knew who ruled in lawsuits where litigants sought monetary relief, but I'd never dealt with springing a criminal defendant, except with a "get out of jail free" card the last time I played Monopoly.

I'd asked Baird for a referral when I was first the subject of an ethics investigation. He sent me to the best. Esther had an excellent reputation for making even the sleaziest lawyers dragged before the State Bar seem victims of a client conspiracy. Even more, she was versatile: She also handled criminal defense and even bankruptcy—perhaps because these were also areas where her wealthy but slimeball attorney-clients needed representation.

"No, that's not why I wanted to see you," I said sincerely and without gagging. "It won't be too long before I can start practicing law again. I'm trying to put the shame behind me, and that means getting together with old friends like you. That was the main reason I called. The referral was my excuse."

Was he mollified? Maybe, because for the rest of the meal, he was utterly charming, speaking of cases he'd recently presided over, promising advice when I was ready to look for my next legal job once my suspension ended. I strung him along, chewing my impatience along with my lettuce, bacon, and bleu cheese.

When the meal was eaten and he'd called for the check, I wondered how to approach my question again gracefully—especially with his gaze fastened on my chest.

"Oh, yes, you wanted a referral to a good criminal lawyer?" he asked as he gallantly sprang from his chair to pull mine out. Of course his hand accidentally slipped so that I felt it fondle my ass.

"That's right." I smiled sweetly as I shifted the aforesaid ass out of fondling range. "Someone good, but who doesn't love media attention. Who would you recommend?"

I nearly exclaimed "Of course!" when he named his choice.

I could hardly wait to tell Darryl.

CHAPTER 26

"Can you spell that?" I heard Darryl's incredulity despite the static from my cell phone and barks from his playroom.

"Like it sounds: S-K-U-L-L. Martin Skull." I narrowly missed a big, ugly SUV that changed lanes ahead of me on the Hollywood Freeway. Good thing I didn't have a free hand or I would have laid on the horn. "I've heard of him. He's a criminal defense lawyer, low key but excellent. I checked him out on-line and in *Martindale-Hubbell*."

"Martin or Martindale?"

"*Martindale-Hubbell*'s the big legal directory. Martin Skull's your new lawyer." I gave Darryl the phone number. "I've called to prep him. He expects to hear from you."

"And you got the referral from the banging judge?"

"The wannabe banging judge," I agreed. "Baird Roehmann."

"That's supposed to make me feel good?"

"Whatever else Judge Roamin'-hands may be, he recognizes quality in counsel. He referred me to Esther."

I heard an audible sigh. Or maybe Darryl had picked up a dog with gas. "Okay. I'll call Skull. Thanks, Kendra."

"Anytime."

"No thanks. Once is a lot more than enough." He hung up.

I exited the freeway at Lankershim. As I made my left turn, my phone sang. I glanced at the number. "Hi, Avvie," I said.

"Kendra, I feel so bad. I've wanted to get together with you again, and now there's that other death of one of your clients. Are you still staying at your client's house? I'd be glad to come and keep you company for a while. We'll talk."

I grasped for a good excuse. I'd no intention of telling Avvie that I intended, if all went well, to be screwing that very client in my own bed that night. Without her company.

"Yes, he's still out of town, so I'll be at his place," I lied. "His Akita doesn't like strangers, so I can't invite guests." *Sorry for smearing your reputation, Odin.* "Maybe next week sometime, when he's home."

"Oh. All right. But are you okay, Kendra? I mean, I know better than to pay attention to the media. But I can't imagine how you must feel, with the additional accusations against you."

I couldn't imagine how I felt, either. Maybe that was why I had decided not to feel anything. If I let a shred of emotion in, I might wind up resembling that guy in that Edvard Munch painting, "The Scream." Maybe I already looked like him. I glanced in my rearview mirror. Nope, not yet.

Actually, since I'd dressed up to see Baird Roehmann, I didn't look too bad with my hair pulled back from my face. For once, I didn't miss the blond highlights.

After hanging up, I stopped at a supermarket for some seduction supplies: steak, with delectable side dishes, a nice, sexy chocolate dessert, wine.

Okay, Hubbard. Come on over.

First, though, after petting Lexie and refrigerating the perishables, I met with Esther—quickly, for we'd agreed to visit Noralles that afternoon to rehash Shirley's murder.

That interview went as usual, with the detective feigning fascination as he listened to what he perceived to be my fibs. But I did well, telling the truth and not tripping up even once. I was detained only an hour and not incarcerated. Freedom! Of course that could have been because Noralles had now aimed his stern detective's scowl at Darryl.

I still had pets to sit. I headed to Lester's. The hound looked happy to see me. I think. His sad basset eyes were hard to read. Then to a cat's place to check food, water, and litter.

Next, to Milt Abadim's, where I headed for the glass tank in the living room. Py was awake, his head up. I felt as if his tiny, blank eyes met mine when I bent to check on him. How Milt knew Pythagoras was male was a mystery to me, but I wasn't about to ask. I reached down and picked Py up. I was getting used to the snake. Maybe he was getting used to me, too. And now that he'd downed this week's defrosted mouse, I could relax and just make sure he remained the right temperature. But I recalled what Milt told me. To keep Py happy, I had to pay attention to him. Keep him close.

What the hell? Still dressed for lunch with the slimier Baird Roehmann and my afternoon interviews, I stuck Py headfirst into my suit jacket pocket. "Feel like doing rounds with me today, Py?" I pulled my pocket flap out enough to peer in. He seemed content enough in his characteristic little ball.

"Let's go," I said. There were lots of pets to tend before my anticipated evening with Jeff.

Jeff did come for supper.

He didn't stay for seduction.

He called on his way, so I pushed the button to let him through the front gate. Fortunately, Charlotte and Yul still weren't around, so I didn't have to contend with parties. No reporters crowded my curb, either. I'd already taken Py home. And I even breached my tenants' lease by sneaking my Beamer into the half-empty garage.

"Sorry," Jeff said when I let him in, "but I can't stay long. I've got a stake-out tonight for a client."

He was dressed in black, knit shirt to slacks, and looked good enough to eat. Darn it.

Odin wasn't with him, so Lexie was disappointed, too. I'd made up for leaving her alone that day by telling her she'd see her friend that evening. She wagged her fuzzy black and white tail hopefully at Jeff at first, then drooped her long ears when she realized he'd come alone.

"I've got a steak out, too," I countered, hiding my disappointment in a puny pun.

Jeff blinked his baby blues quizzically until I led him into the kitchen.

"This kind," I explained.

"My favorite."

Dinner was short but satisfying—of one kind of hunger, at least. The other expanded till I thought I'd char like the barbecue. It didn't help that Jeff and I shared long, longing gazes as we licked our lips.

As we ate, I gave Jeff a rundown of all I'd done in the twelve hours since I'd seen him. He had no comments about Noralles, but asked, "You don't think your friend Darryl was angry enough to kill his business partners when they stiffed him?"

"You must not know Darryl very well. He has a hard enough time disciplining dogs in his charge."

"That doesn't mean he wouldn't resort to disciplining people—permanently."

"Why would you say that?" Once again, Jeff seemed to be slandering Darryl for no good reason.

245

"Never mind," he said.

"I do mind. I believe in Darryl."

"Yeah, I figured. But as your investigator on this case—"

"You're my advisor, thank you, not my investigator."

"But I should be. If I were, you'd be farther ahead, and—"

"If you were, I'd be way behind. You travel too much for me to rely on you for legwork. Research, advice, those I appreciate. But I'll handle my own investigation."

And though I didn't mention it for fear of bruising his enormous male ego enough that he'd wash his hands—and Althea's computer keys—of me, I'd no intention of relying on Jeff any more than I'd rely on anyone else these days—besides myself.

"You're right for now," he acknowledged after a sip of wine, "but I'll take over when I have more time in town."

"And go after Darryl?" I accused.

"You going to protect him?"

I didn't carry the dispute further. Instead, I told Jeff my frustration about the possible suspects I'd have to add now, thanks to the info Darryl gave me about Carl and Shirley planning a sitcom together. I wouldn't know most of them. That didn't mean they didn't know of me.

Then I gave a rundown on my discussion with Baird. "The guy's a damned good judge," I finished, "but as long as I've known him, I've wanted to kick him right in the . . . er, mushrooms?" I finished, passing him the plate of portabellas I'd grilled with the steaks.

"Yeah, kicking a guy in the mushrooms can certainly be a turn-off."

I sighed. "Too bad I can't get your friend Noralles to go after Baird instead of Darryl."

"Any reason why Judge Roehmann would have killed those two people and set you up for it?"

Startled, I stared at him. "I'm kidding."

"I'm not. It's a game I play. I make up far-fetched scenarios and see how they develop. Sometimes they give insight on how something really played out. So, tell me why His Honor might have had it in for those two and you."

I laughed. And then I pondered as I sawed off a sliver of steak. "There is a connection, however tenuous. Baird was the judge in the cases I handled for Carl and Shirley."

"There you go. So did anything happen in either lawsuit to turn the judge against your clients?"

I sat up straight. "Only that they were my clients," I said slowly.

"Explain."

My hand not holding the steak knife erased the air in front of me. "Too absurd."

"Absurd is good. Tell me."

"What if he killed them because they were my clients? To get my attention."

"Why would he do that?" The intensity in Jeff's

eyes now had nothing to do with lust for me and everything to do with excitement about what I was saying.

I shrugged. "He's been trying to get me into the sack since I've known him. I've resisted, though I suspect a lot of lady lawyers don't."

"So why would his murdering your clients get you to go to bed with him?"

"You're the one who said to follow this absurd idea. You tell me." I chewed the tasty steak while awaiting a reply.

"Revenge," he said with a smile.

"That's stretching things."

"Sure, but what if he decided to get your attention by framing you and then saving your lovely little ass?"

I barely even registered his lustful leer as my mind went blank for about a minute. When it came back, it was generating ideas at warp speed. My steak sat suddenly ignored on my plate. "What if he was the one who got the strategy memo in the loony Lorraine Giles case and leaked it to her? He wouldn't know she'd shoot John Germane, but he'd know how to amass the rest of the evidence against me. He's handled enough criminal trials to figure out what to plant."

"Like what?" Jeff asked, looking interested. "What was the evidence against you?"

I barely took a breath before continuing, ticking off on my fingers the list in my mind that mirrored the written one I'd once made. "Well, there was a call to Lorraine's number from mine that I couldn't account for. Baird knew where I lived, could have broken in and phoned her. Also, once he was there, he could have found my checkbook in my desk drawer, gotten my account number, and deposited the money allegedly from Lorraine." I sighed. "Of course the worst evidence against me was something he couldn't manufacture: Lorraine herself didn't deny I'd conspired with her, but by then she acted so loony that no one gave her story complete credence. Still, when I was accused, it wasn't beyond the realm of possibility that I'd turn to Baird for advice."

"And did you?"

"Eventually, when I asked for the name of the best counsel to represent me in the ethics hearing before the State Bar."

"How did he behave then?"

"Nothing unusual. He told me what I wanted to know, then tried to get me into bed."

"And you rejected him, I gather."

"You gather very well."

Jeff grinned. "It's my job. Stay with me on this a little longer. He still didn't get what he wanted. His ego inflated, and so did his pants when he thought about how you'd rejected him, so he tried another way to attain his goal—your attention."

"By murdering my pet-sitting clients? Speaking of far-fetched . . ."

"He called after Carl's death to ask you out, didn't he?"

"Yes, and I said no. Then Shirley was murdered, and I called to ask Baird to lunch."

"So he got a date, thanks to this series of events."

"But an innocent date as a motive for multiple murders? I don't see him killing anyone just for the exciting opportunity to treat me to a salad."

Yet after Jeff left, I continued to mull over this strange scenario long into the night.

Good thing I did. I had barely dozed off into the lightest of nighttime sleeps when Lexie's growl awakened me.

Lexie wasn't a growl-in-the-night-at-a-creeping-rodent sort of spaniel. But in the faint light squeezing through mostly closed mini-blinds from the streetlight outside, I saw my Cavalier crouched on the floor, facing my bedroom door.

I heard a noise. It sounded like a footstep inside the garage, on the stairs to my apartment.

Lexie's growl grew more menacing. Still, if the nocturnal stair-stepper heard it, there'd be no doubt from its near-soprano sound that I didn't have a rottweiler protecting me.

Icy puppy paws clawed up my spine, and they weren't Lexie's. But lying there shivering wouldn't help me learn who was outside my door.

"Lexie, stay," I commanded. Not that I expected my Cavalier to obey. Like a child, she listened when it suited her.

To be sure it suited her now, I grabbed my clock radio's cord, made sure it wasn't plugged in, and used it to anchor Lexie to my dressing table chair.

I needed a weapon. The best I came up with was the long emergency flashlight kept by my bed to counter power outages in earthquakes.

I hadn't wanted to feel sexy going to bed alone after the big buildup my libido gave itself yesterday, so I'd slept in sweats. A good thing—I didn't have to hunt for a robe.

I tiptoed from the room, holding the flashlight aloft, prepared to clunk it down on an offending head.

Of course Lexie barked.

Someone swore. That gave me a location. I shrieked and ran toward it, zigzagging and ducking and doing everything I could think of to dodge a bullet, should one be fired at me.

I met up with the person just inside my outside door. Apparently, he hadn't gotten far. "Who are you?" I yelled. "What are you doing here?"

No response. Big surprise. With the door shut, the room's only illumination slipped in at the edges of the closed window blinds from the security light outside the garage downstairs. I couldn't see the intruder, only his shape as he lunged toward me. I screamed. Brought the flashlight down. Hit something. I couldn't tell if it was skull or crossed bones, though I felt a satisfying thud, followed by a grunt of pain. I grabbed, but the piece of clothing I caught yanked away as the person launched himself out the door and clattered down the steps.

I thought of following.

Then I thought how lucky I was that I hadn't been shot or stabbed.

My breath rasping in gulps, I locked the front door and leaned against it, but only for an instant. I turned on the tiny entryway's light and headed for the living room—and the nearest telephone. I called 911 and told the operator to send help.

After finding his cell phone number, I called Jeff. Fortunately, his stake-out had ended, and he promised to come, fast. "Here's what you do in the meantime." He issued me orders. Assuming I would eventually stop shaking, I figured I'd obey.

But while I tried to take in what he said, I turned back toward the now-lighted entryway and saw it.

On the floor lay a long-handled, big-bladed knife.

Just like the one I'd last seen beside the dead body of Carl Cuthbertson.

CHAPTER 27

"You didn't see who it was?" Jeff had convinced me to remove the section of the sofa I'd dragged in front of the door so he could come in.

While waiting, I'd sat in the tiny entryway, hugging Lexie, making sure neither of us was near a window where a bullet could enter and splinter my life further.

I knew better than to touch the knife. It still lay there, stark and evil-looking against the dark tile of the floor.

Had my unwelcome visitor intended to mutilate me as fatally as Carl and Shirley? I didn't want to think about that. So of course, bloodied pictures of myself zipped through my brain.

Now, in my living room, Jeff sat on the piece of sofa I'd enlisted as a blockade. He was still dressed in black and, with his focused scowl, looked ferocious. Fine with me. I needed advice and answers, not sympathy or coddling.

Especially because I'd called Noralles. He was on his way.

I looked up from Lexie and met Jeff's eyes.

They were quizzical. Oh, right, an answer was pending.

"No, I didn't see him. Not really. It was dark, and I—"

The sound of a car entering the driveway interrupted my thought. I felt my eyes go wide in fear, but they hardened fast as I stood to take a look. Lexie, lying at my feet, also leapt to attention and began to bark. I held her collar to silence her.

"Stay there," Jeff commanded. "It's probably the cops."

I wanted to disobey but didn't bother. My knees were too wobbly to hold me. Besides, I had to tend to my agitated dog.

In a moment, I heard voices and clomping on my stairway.

"Ms. Ballantyne," said a familiar, too-friendly voice. Detective Ned Noralles dominated my living room doorway. It was three in the morning, but his alert features suggested this was the prime part of his day. He even wore an unrumpled suit. It didn't look as if my call had interrupted his beauty sleep.

"Detective," I acknowledged. Feeling Lexie's rumbling growl, I lifted her into my lap. It wouldn't do for her to take out this night's frustrations by chomping on a cop.

Noralles entered without further invitation, followed by Jeff. He sat on the sectional piece where Jeff had been, beside me, and I noted by Jeff's frown that he wasn't thrilled about it. He took a matching seat across the room in my pint-sized parlor.

The detective took out a notebook and pen. "That knife on the floor . . ." He nodded toward the entryway, where I glimpsed other detectives or other crime scene types twittering in muffled tones about evidence. "Did you take that out to defend yourself?"

I saw the sly gleam in his eye. Obviously he, too, noticed the resemblance between that blade and at least one of the murder weapons. If I happened to have its match, there's no telling how much easier it would make the job of apprehending me.

Never mind that he'd supposedly found a better candidate in Darryl. Good cops kept open minds, didn't they? And how much more fun for him if he could prove that Darryl and I had formed a lethal alliance.

"No," I said. "Whoever broke in dropped it."

"I see." He sounded so blasé that I wanted to shake him. "Tell me what happened."

I did. He made notes. Jeff looked from Noralles to me and back, absorbing it all. It didn't take me long to finish.

"Now tell me again. Where did that knife come from? Do you have more like it in your kitchen?"

Give me strength. And patience. Belting an official investigator would do me no good.

"No, detective, I don't. As I said, the person who broke in dropped it."

"And you didn't just stage this whole thing?"

"Why the hell would she?" This erupted from Jeff, who otherwise had stayed sensibly silent.

"Because Ms. Ballantyne is obviously an intelligent person." Noralles's words spilled from a smile that suggested he was speaking with an idiot.

Oh, lord. Things would only get worse if these arch-enemies resumed their fray over me and this unnerving episode.

"I agree," Jeff said. "So?"

"So let me suggest a scenario. I'm not saying it's true, but what if Ms. Ballantyne decided she needed a diversion to remove suspicion from herself? Or from her friend Darryl Nestler, whom we're also considering a person of interest in the apparently related murders of Carl Cuthbertson and Shirley Dorian."

A person of interest. That meant they didn't have enough to arrest Darryl yet, either. *Hoorah.* And with Martin Skull representing him, hopefully they never would.

"So Ms. Ballantyne stages this break-in, makes sure her prints aren't on her knife, and leaves it where it appears someone dropped it in a scuffle that never took place. She could claim the murderer was after her, too. If we bought into that, some heat would be off her. She could get it off Nestler, too, if she gives a description of her alleged attacker that couldn't be her friend." He looked at me expectantly.

Weren't cops just supposed to ask questions,

not put words into a victim's mouth? Most likely, he was warning me not to try something as unbelievable as the scenario he'd suggested. Fine with me, since it wasn't true.

With a sigh, I spoke. "Like I said, I didn't really see the person. Darryl would never have attacked me. I don't think it was someone as large as either of you two . . . gentlemen." My intentional pause suggested I considered them anything but.

"Then what *did* you notice about this person?"

"It was dark, so I couldn't see him. I think I surprised him as much as he surprised me."

"So he wasn't very big. Was he small?"

I shook my head. "I don't think so."

"Perhaps you could come to the station later this morning," Noralles said, "when you've had time to think about this more. Maybe you'll think of something useful to add."

"No way, Noralles. She has no obligation to go to the station to talk with you. Not unless you arrest her."

Don't give him any ideas! my mind shrieked at Jeff. Which was absurd, because that idea was already deeply entrenched in Noralles's closed little detective mind.

"It's up to you, Ms. Ballantyne," Noralles said, his eyes assiduously blank.

"If I think of anything helpful, I'll call you," I said. I'd gotten away relatively painlessly in my last two treks to his home territory, but I didn't want to push my luck.

He hung out with the other investigating detectives for what seemed like an eternity. I sat with Jeff and Lexie in the living room, pretending to ignore their inescapable presence. I was so exhausted both physically and mentally that after they finally left, I didn't even have an urge to see Jeff naked.

And I had to get up in only a few hours to take care of my charges.

Jeff insisted on hanging out at my place while I tried to sleep for the short time before I had to start my rounds.

I should have been grateful for his big, brave, masculine, protective presence. And for the way he demanded that I move back to his fortress that evening, the better to take care of Lexie and me.

Bullpucky. I didn't need to be taken care of. I didn't want to be taken care of. I just wanted all the nightmares of the last months to end, so I could wake up and have my life back.

Only . . . what *was* my life wasn't my life anymore. And neither would the nightmare end merely because I told it to.

On top of it all, although I felt sure Jeff accepted my side of all stories, he wasn't sure about Darryl. He was sage enough not to say so right now, but when I tried to suggest other suspects, he made it unequivocally clear that Darryl still topped his short list, damn him. Why was he dumping on Darryl these days? I suddenly craved a nice, long hiatus from Jeff Hubbard—the better to cast away my free-sailing sexual urges, too.

As Lexie and I got into the Beamer bright and early that morning, I didn't dare think about how little I'd slept.

"See you later," Jeff called as he entered his Escalade. He still wore his black outfit of presumed invisibility, only he was pretty obviously there in the San Fernando Valley morning sun.

"Right," I lied. Maybe I *would* cave in and see him later—for advice only. I pulled onto the street and headed for the day's first doggy customer.

Would I dare to come back?

Where were my demon tenants when I needed them?

Who'd dared to break into the sanctity of my humble abode? And why?

Go with the absurd, Jeff had suggested as we'd brainstormed before.

We'd already come up with Judge Baird Roehmann committing murder in revenge for my having rejected him. If Baird *had* been the bad guy, he'd gotten part of what he'd wanted yesterday: I'd called and dined with him. But I hadn't gone to bed with him.

Had he sneaked over at night to rectify that by dropping the knife, increasing suspicions that I was a murderer? But why?

Unless he thought I'd call again for advice . . .

That seemed so extreme, yet Baird *had* worn a suit to lunch yesterday.

I glanced around. I was in a residential neighborhood, not unlike Carl Cuthbertson's.

I nearly screeched the Beamer to a halt along the curb and dug into the lists I'd made. I had a phone call to make.

"Hello?" said an aging female voice.

"Hi, Isabelle, this is Kendra Ballantyne. Remember me? I was Carl Cuthbertson's pet-sitter, and—"

"Oh, my, yes," she said. "Do you believe in ESP? I was just trying to find the card with your phone number. Could you come over? I'd like to hire you."

I hadn't been to Carl's Toluca Lake neighborhood for a week. It didn't look different, in spite of the gruesome murder committed there.

Isabelle Lane's little green bungalow was around the corner and a few houses down from Carl's. A white picket fence surrounded it. I opened the gate and walked up the path that meandered around rose bushes to the front door.

It opened before I rang the bell. A round woman in a flowered housedress stood there. I didn't recognize her until I recalled that the only time I'd seen her, she'd had a scarf around her head. That was why I hadn't noticed her huge golden curls. But the damp blue eyes told me it was her.

"Come in, dear." She glanced around. "I didn't tell anyone I invited you, or the whole neighborhood would have barged in. For my protection, you see."

My heart constricted as tight as if Py had wrapped around it. "They still think I killed Carl."

"Some do," she said, looking downcast.

I didn't mention that one of her neighbors had reported my last foray here to my nemesis Noralles. What good would it do?

Isabelle's house was homey, with lacy doilies decorating everything from overstuffed chairs to the top of her big-screen TV. It smelled of cleaning agents, which told me she'd unsuccessfully tried to mask some pet odor, though my current means of earning dollars kept me used to such scents.

She showed me to a seat in the living room, on a fluffy beige couch behind a long wooden coffee table. A wood-and-wire mesh cage squatted on three legs in a corner. Two multicolor bunnies hopped around inside. My mission was clear. I was to bunny-sit.

Good thing I'd parked Lexie in the car, in the shade of a tree. Windows partway down, of course, and plenty of lapping water in a bowl. She was a spaniel. She might think it her sworn duty to hunt bunnies.

But then, from a back room, I heard a dog bark. No, not one. Several, and a few sounded young. Another reason Lexie was better off where she was. It was a good idea to check out the friendliness of new canines before introducing them to my own.

I didn't have long to wait. "Just a second, dear," Isabelle called as she headed through the door. She

261

returned with a pretty Siberian husky trailed by four others a fraction of her size. Puppies. Young ones, all fuzzy fur and blunt baby muzzles. They pushed past the adult and, yelping, rough-housed around the room, even knocking into the rabbit hutch.

"That's Helga," Isabelle yelled over puppy-din. "I haven't named her babies. That's up to their owners when I sell them. They're seven weeks old, almost ready for new homes."

Uh-oh. How would I deal with a houseful of puppies with the other pets I had to tend?

"They're adorable, Isabelle," I said, "but—"

"My sister's scheduled for surgery tomorrow in Sylmar." That was a town just north of the Valley. "She wants me with her for a couple of days. I need someone competent to keep an eye on Helga and the pups while I'm gone." Which eye would Helga keep on her babies and her sitter—her blue one or her brown one? As beautiful as the mama dog was, her eyes didn't match.

The little ones were leaping around the living room, much too active for me to figure out their eye colors.

How could I say this tactfully? "Isabelle, bunnies aren't a problem, and I'm honored you'd trust me with Helga and her litter, but I'm not sure it's a good idea. I'm caring for a lot of other dogs, and I can't be here all the time. And—"

"That's okay. I mostly confine them in the kitchen. But I don't want them alone all the time. Can you stay overnight for the next couple of days?"

Hey. A serendipitous solution. I'd already decided that staying in my apartment alone after last night's attack wasn't the smartest idea, but I didn't want to stay at Jeff's, either.

"Yes," I said with a smile that she reflected back with big, yellow-stained teeth. "I can."

I made friends with Helga, who had the temperament of a canine Madonna. I got down on the floor and laughed as four lively furballs leapt onto me, licking and emitting puppy growls. Only one had mama's mismatched eyes. When I extracted myself and rose, I even got to pat the bunnies.

And then I got to the reason I'd called Isabelle in the first place. "About the man in a suit you saw hanging around Carl's . . ." But Isabelle still didn't remember much about the guy, except that he had hair. A lot of it.

That eliminated bald men, though I had none as suspects.

It didn't eliminate His Honor, Judge Roehmann.

I headed for Darryl's after my morning rounds, to see how he was getting along. His doggy playroom was crowded with canines, but I didn't see him among the caretakers. I let Lexie loose for the few minutes I intended to stay.

"He's not here," Kiki, the bleached blond fashion plate, said when I asked after him. She held a panting pug. "I think he's seeing his lawyer." She glared at me as if I was contagious, the reason her boss needed an attorney.

I had no reason to stay without Darryl there, but before I got to the door, Fran Korwald entered. "Hi, Kendra." She watched me expectantly. Though her hair was still permed into a youthful cloud and her slim midriff showed beneath her tight knit top, she'd started to look her age since I'd last seen her.

A blunt-tipped bullet of guilt ricocheted through me. I hadn't had time to do further legal research on her problem.

"How are things with Piglet?" I ventured. "Any resolution yet on the custody matter?"

Her long face grew longer. "No," she rasped. "I guess you haven't come up with any answers, either."

"I'm still working on it. Meantime, maybe you can get someone here to testify for you as an expert on dog psychology that Piglet's best interests would not be served by shipping him endlessly from to Alaska and back." As I'd told Darryl, I explained to her that the growing body of law said pets' best interests were being considered, the same way kids' were.

"That's what I thought. You've done some research?"

"A little. But—"

She hugged me. "Wait a minute." She dashed past me and retrieved the pug from Kiki's arms. That had to be Piglet, a pup so ugly she was adorable. Sure enough, Fran introduced me to her homely baby. She looked so proud of her pet that I had a renewed burst of good intentions. I would keep on hunting for a way to resolve her custody dispute.

I could only keep my fingers crossed I'd find one.

I still had a key to Jeff's, so I called to make sure he wasn't there before dropping Lexie off to keep Odin company, and vice versa. Then I headed downtown.

It wasn't hard to learn His Honor's tentative schedule. All I had to do was check the calendar posted near the courtroom door. I had to pass through the usual courthouse security, but as a lawyer, I knew tricks about getting around public corridors to a judge's chambers. I waited for Baird outside his door.

He did a double-take when he saw me. "Kendra." He drew my name out as wide as his wolfish smile. "What brings you here?"

"You do, Baird." I grinned back. "Have a minute?"

"For you, sure."

Was this a man who could have attacked me last night and further implicated me in a murder or two, just to get me to visit him? Unlikely. I mean, how could he know I'd show up at the courthouse today?

Or was his plan to commit other similar nasty acts until I somehow got the picture?

I followed him into his chambers. As with many in this aging downtown L.A. courthouse, his walls were lined with floor-to-ceiling wooden bookshelves, all filled with official-looking federal and state reporters and specialized treatises. His desk chair resembled a leather throne, and the uncomfortable-looking chairs facing it made it clear who ruled in these chambers.

Black robes hung from a clothes rack beside the door.

I sat on a chair and leaned over his neat desk. "So, Kendra, what can I do for you?"

"Did you come to visit me last night, Baird?"

His gray eyes narrowed from welcoming to wishing I'd go away. "I gather by your tone that you don't mean for a social call. If it was a friendly visit, there'd be no uncertainty about it. So what's the reason for such an odd inquiry?"

I was asking the questions, so I sidestepped his with another. "Did you know Carl Cuthbertson? Outside the courtroom, I mean. You were the judge on the case in which I represented him."

"I never saw the man, once his matter was resolved."

"Shirley Dorian either?"

Baird's elegantly handsome features froze in a parody of themselves. In fact, His Honor looked downright ugly. And old. "What's this about, Kendra?" he asked coldly.

"You were seen peeking into Carl's house, you know, around the time he died."

He was on his feet and towering over me almost before I realized he'd moved. "If you think you'll eliminate yourself as chief suspect in those murders by attempting to implicate me—"

"Who told you I'm the chief suspect?" I interrupted.

"It's obvious," he blustered. "From your interaction with those victims. From what the media says. From—"

"From your imaginative mind and into Detective Noralles's ears?" I asked sweetly. "Not anymore, Baird. Tell me, did you kill Carl and Shirley?"

"Bailiff!" he hollered.

"No need to get huffy. I'm going. But I'm not through, Baird." With that, I stalked from Judge Roehmann's chambers.

CHAPTER 28

I had a lot of time to think on my long walk to my car—once again parked far away to save on expensive lot fees.

I barely glanced at the suited lawyers accompanying scared-looking clients around the government end of downtown. I passed courthouses and City Hall, all within spitting distance of several renowned and redoubtable entertainment complexes. Homeless people held out their hand to well-heeled professionals, and cars spewed smelly emissions because there was too much traffic to get anywhere fast. Above it all, a brilliant blue, cloudless Los Angeles sky mocked the mayhem below.

Including the mayhem in my mind.

Did I really think Baird did everything I'd all but accused him of? Hell, I *had* accused him.

He hadn't denied murdering Carl and Shirley. A guilty person would have denied it to obfuscate the truth; an innocent person would have denied it as a lie.

Which was it?

My cell phone rang. I pulled it from my purse

and glanced at the number. It was Jeff. "You okay?" he demanded.

"Fine," I fibbed. I was one big raw nerve-ending. Someone had tried to knife me last night, maybe the man I'd just confronted.

"Where are you?"

"Downtown." Hell, I might be mad at Jeff, but that didn't mean I couldn't tap into his expertise. "Have a few minutes? I'd like to brainstorm with you."

"I'm off to a meeting about a security system, but we can talk later. When you come to my place for the night."

This wasn't the time to tell him he'd be on his own.

"I just met with Judge Roehmann," I said. "I wanted to find out if he was the one who broke in last night."

Silence. What did I expect, applause? An accusation of utter foolishness for tipping my hand? Jeff's howl of laughter at my folly, since he clearly thought Darryl was the bad guy?

And then, "Was he?"

"I don't know. He didn't deny it, though."

"Kendra, look. My meeting should last a couple of hours. We need to talk, so don't you—"

"What? Sorry, my cell phone's cutting out." I hung up before he told me what I shouldn't do and stuffed my cell phone back in my bag.

Did I really think Baird was guilty? Right now, I doubted I could think at all. But one idea really stuck out in the mess that was my mush-filled mind. Someone was mounding murder victims on my pet-sitting path so I'd trip over them. Someone had slipped loony Lorraine the strategy memo and stuck me with that charge, too. The same someone?

I drove back toward the Valley and checked on Helga and the pups. Everyone was fine, even the bunnies. Then I went to the Doggy Indulgence Day Resort. No Darryl. The poor guy was probably still involved in his tête-à-tête for three with Noralles and his own counsel, Martin Skull.

On to my usual rounds, including checking Py. Good thing I didn't try to get all my clients in one spot, as I suspected that my new bunny charges might entice Py's erratic appetite.

I intended to drive by my home, glance at the garage, and make sure no one lurked in shadows— where were the media vans when I needed them?— but at the last minute I decided that no one would be dumb enough to do anything in broad daylight. So I checked my mail.

Good thing that I did, for I'd forgotten all about that night's scheduled litigation Bar Association meeting.

His Honor, Judge Baird Roehmann, was the speaker.

The bar meeting was in a posh downtown hotel. Dressing hurriedly at Isabelle's, I arrived too late for dinner, a good thing, since I couldn't afford it. As I entered, I scanned the sea of tables to see who I recognized in the crowd. A few faces looked familiar from my days of representing clients adverse to these other lawyers. The loud hum of conversation was punctuated by the chime of silverware meeting dessert plates.

I spotted the MSY table. Marden sat there, and so did Bill Sergement, Avvie, and others. Transactional whiz Marden at a litigation lecture? Who would have guessed? I headed that way, glad there was a spare chair. Had it been saved for Borden Yurick? I hadn't seen the third senior partner in ages, not since his rumored breakdown. No wonder, working with that group . . .

"Hi." I sat down beside Bill Sergement. Avvie was at his other side.

"Kendra, hi," she said with a smile. Her suit jacket was over the back of her chair, and the neckline of her silk blouse had been lowered for evening wear. Her short dark hair, too, had been primped to look dressy. She was the only one who seemed pleased to see me. And since she clearly wasn't going to eat the profiterole in front of her, I picked up a clean fork, scooted the plate past Bill Sergement, and dug in.

Bill hadn't changed from his usual office attire, and his hair looked as if it hadn't been combed since last Christmas. Maybe that was by design, for it was clearly stampeding from his forehead in droves, more now than I'd ever seen it. Couldn't call him bald, though, I thought, considering Isabelle's mystery man in a suit.

He leaned toward me as I nibbled. "Good?"

"You should know. You ate yours." I nodded toward his empty plate.

"Yeah, and I shouldn't have. I'm putting on weight."

I glanced at his waistline and noted the bulge above the belt. Still, I was in a magnanimous mood. "Just adding a little muscle." Wasn't that the way men always deluded themselves?

"Well, you look great, Kendra." There was a note in his voice I'd never heard before—sincerity. Startled, I looked at him. He was looking back, with what appeared to be wistfulness. "Your new life obviously agrees with you."

"Yeah," I agreed, tearing my eyes away. I'd intended my gaze to land on my dessert, but first, beyond Bill, I noticed Avvie's neatly manicured fist grab a wine glass from the table.

I leaned past Bill toward her. She was smiling. Sort of.

"Has Bill told you we're both going to a bar conference in Tahoe next month? We'll be earning all our remaining continuing legal education credits."

Figuring that wasn't all they'd be doing there, I was glad I didn't have time to respond, for the lights dimmed, the crowd hushed, and Baird rose to the podium. His poised and powerful demeanor under his formal black suit made him a vibrant speaker, even though what he talked about was a bit of a bore: how to ease court congestion. He didn't speak long. When he was done, I thanked my former associates for allowing me to share their table, then I headed toward the front of the room.

When Baird saw me, his complexion turned nearly as pale as his well-combed hair. He turned away, immersed in conversation with a lovely lady lawyer who'd undoubtedly come to fawn over the powerful jurist's prose.

I could have made a show of getting to speak with him, but why bother? He knew I was there.

Still, for the heck of it, I called his private cell phone number later, as I pulled into Isabelle's driveway. He answered, probably not recognizing the incoming number. "Excellent speech, Baird," I told him.

"Kendra, is that you? What were you doing there?"

"Watching you. Have a good night, Judge. See you soon."

"I don't know what you want, but keep away from me, Kendra."

"You wish. I'll be after you as long as it takes to get the truth." I hung up. Was I coming on too strong? Not if he really had framed me. And if he hadn't? Well, if he thought I'd lost it, maybe he'd think twice next time before singling me out for attempted seduction.

I went inside to see how Helga, Lexie, puppies, and bunnies were faring.

I didn't want Jeff to worry, so I called. "I have

this new client," I told him. "She's got rabbits, a Siberian husky, and four lively puppies. I promised to keep a close eye on them. You understand." Sure he did.

"Where are you? I'll stay the night there, just in case."

In case last night's intruder was on my trail? Unlikely. No one besides Isabelle knew I was here—one big reason I'd accepted this assignment.

But just in case, I was prepared. And alert. I'd even checked out Isabelle's kitchen knife situation, ready to run in there and grab something if I needed a weapon of self-defense.

Or did Jeff mean just in case I needed a playmate in bed? Been there, done that, had fun, but now needed room to breathe without panting. I had an investigation to conduct, to ensure that neither Darryl nor I was tied to the rails and run over by a train named Noralles.

"Thanks," I told him, "but we'll be fine. I'll talk to you tomorrow. Maybe we can get together for a strategy session."

As it turned out, I didn't have time. The next morning, after I'd made sure Helga and her babies were safely secured in their pen in the kitchen, I left Lexie with them, did my rounds, and headed for Darryl's.

He was back. "How did things go yesterday?" I asked, hurrying to where he stood with a yorkie under one arm and a schnauzer in the other.

"Fine. I'll tell you about it later. That guy Skull was something. But you have to know—"

"Kendra Ballantyne?"

I turned toward the unfamiliar squeaky male voice. No wonder the guy sounded like that: He was really short, all nose and overbite, like a mouse. He held a manila envelope before him like a shield.

"Hi," I said uncertainly. Another potential pet-sitting client? Business hadn't slacked off after Shirley's death as it had with Carl's, so I wasn't sure I had time to take anyone else on, especially with the time I had to devote to Helga and kids.

"Kendra Ballantyne?" he asked again.

"Yes, but who—"

"I'm serving this subpoena on you." He thrust the envelope into one of my hands despite the fact it remained at my side.

"What!" I tore the envelope open. And gasped.

I was ordered to appear in court that afternoon. It was an order to show cause why a temporary restraining order shouldn't be issued against me.

To stop me from stalking His Honor, Judge Baird Roehmann.

I dragged Esther along but didn't contest it. I would leave the judge alone.

Was this a ploy to keep me from unearthing clues he left while framing me? I didn't think so. For a man who'd been so eager to get me into bed, he now seemed terrified of me.

Not exactly the demeanor of a brutal murderer.

After my appearance, I felt so angry that I rivaled an ill-trained rottweiler for bad temper. I was mad at Baird for taking me to court, and at myself, since this time I'd actually done what I was accused of, at least colorably. I'd gotten in His Honor's debonair face too many times, the better to coerce a confession. Instead, I got a slap on my already bruised wrist.

"Are you all right, Kendra?" Esther asked as we stood in the hall outside the courtroom. Her gray-haired little-old-lady look seemed natural as she touched the slumped shoulder of my navy suit jacket maternally.

"Sure," I said. I saw Baird come out from the court-room with his own attorney, as suave as his client, and I turned away. I didn't want to be accused of stalking His Honor by sending him the evil eye.

After saying my thanks to Esther at the court-house entry, I headed farther downtown.

Cathy, the MSY receptionist, barely spared me a sneer. "Are you here to see Avvie?"

"Yes, thanks." I was determined to be on my best behavior, oozing etiquette if it killed me.

In a few minutes Cathy gestured me into the hallowed MSY hallway. "Go ahead to her office."

I took the long way around, so I passed Royal Marden's office. I peeked in, but he wasn't there.

"I didn't know you were coming," said a voice behind me.

"Susan. Hi." My former secretary hadn't been in her cubicle across the open corridor a minute ago. "This was a spur-of-the-moment thing. I was in the area." *Getting my butt reamed on behalf of Baird Roehmann,* I finished in my head. My main reason for coming was to learn if that particular part of my reputation had already spread.

"No new messages for you," Susan said, sounding almost sorry. Maybe because her inability to take messages for me sheared away what was left of any tie between us.

I didn't want her to feel bad. She'd been a damned good secretary, even if we hadn't developed touchy-feely feelings between us.

"That's okay. I didn't really want most of the last ones anyway, since they were from reporters. 'No news is good news,' " I quipped, "especially now."

"Because another of your pet-sitting customers got killed?" She sure didn't like the idea that I'd gone down in the world that far. At least that was the impression she gave by the nasty spin she put on the phrase "pet-sitter."

I nodded. "At least this time the police are looking into other possible suspects." I didn't mention that their new main suspect, Darryl, had definitely not done it.

"Hi, Kendra." Avvie came down the corridor from the direction of the ladies' room. Her conservative attire and smooth hair were back to office-appropriate.

As she passed Bill Sergement's office, he came out and said hello to me. "Did you recuperate from Judge Roehmann's talk last night?" he asked.

"More or less." Did his question suggest he'd heard of my most recent ordeal? Or was he just making small talk?

The latter, I figured, for he'd have revealed the ugly incident to Avvie if he knew it. And all she said was, "I wished we'd had more time to talk. Want to come into my office for a cup of coffee?"

"I'll take a rain check. I've got to do pet-sitting rounds. Would you believe I'm hanging out at a house full of puppies?"

"You sound as if you really enjoy your new . . ." Drill Sergeant fumbled for the word. Obviously he didn't consider tending pets much of a career.

"Lifestyle," I supplied. "And, yeah, I actually love it. My law license will be restored soon, and I'm not sure what I'll do with it, but I want to keep up what I'm doing, at least for a while."

"You're serious?" Bill sounded astounded.

"If I say no, will you give me my partnership back?" I countered. Of course, there was no way in hell that I'd rejoin MSY—for I'd learned, in leaving, that it *was* hell.

"Well, you did resign, Kendra," he said sternly, with only the slightest uneasiness in his voice. "And I don't think—"

I glanced pointedly at my watch. "Sorry, gotta run," I said, turning with a wave. "We'll talk again soon."

I hid my guffaw until I'd gotten through the office doors.

And I kept laughing until I reached Isabelle's—and found the puppies had pulled a prison break from their pen in the kitchen and were right, smack in the middle of raiding the pantry.

CHAPTER 29

The room was a mess. I'd never seen such a chaos of clutter, punctuated by an effusion of smells. White stuff spewed from chewed containers. Gnawed boxes disgorged a conglomeration of cereals, pastas, and unidentified gooey glop.

Four husky puppies had rolled in all of it.

In the middle of it all sat Lexie, her lively Cavalier head cocked as if chiding me for allowing this to happen.

"I locked the pen," I cried. But she just glanced at her calm companion Helga, whose mismatched eyes were upon me.

I maneuvered the scruffy puppies back to the pen. The gate was still locked but the fencing had been bumped away from the wall. The pups regarded me as if I were a grinch who'd just stolen their favorite toys. "What I don't know, guys, is whether what you ate will make you sick." Tears surged to my eyes. I thought I'd been cautious with my charges but . . .

Heck, no time to flog myself now.

I called and explained the situation to Isabelle's

emergency vet, listing the litter on the floor. "No chocolate," I said in answer to one of her questions. A good thing. Dogs might fancy themselves chocoholics, but chocolate's caffeine was poison to them.

"It doesn't sound as if they ate anything harmful," the vet said, "but I should take a look."

How on earth would I handle that? Four frisky, filthy puppies in my Beamer?

I yanked my cell phone from my purse, praying I didn't get stickiness from my fingers on it. When the mechanical voice asked who I wanted to call, I wailed, "Darryl!"

Darryl wasn't the only one who came to save my bacon. Jeff called while Darryl all but rolled on the grubby floor with laughter.

Darryl brought his spa's mini-van, and we transported the babies to the vet. Though I'd need to watch for signs of sickness, the pups seemed fine. I reached into my oversize bag for my credit card. No way would I palm this expense off on Isabelle, though my own balance would suffer. But I'd handle it like I did all debts these days. No more bankruptcies, ever.

Eventually, thanks to help from Darryl and Jeff, Isabelle's house was clean, as were the pups. Still damp after a healthy scrubbing, the pups lay on the paper in their pen and went to sleep. I checked on them often. They were fine. I was a wreck.

Darryl turned to leave when things were under control.

I threw my arms around his skinny body and gave him a hug. "Thanks for everything."

When he was gone, I found Jeff right behind me. "Got one of those for me?" he asked gruffly.

Jeff was anything but skinny. If I squeezed him the same way, I'd be reminded how sexy he was. Hell, I'd already been reminded. That insight always tweaked my hormones when he was around. And he'd come galloping through the night in his own SUV to rescue a damsel in distress—even though this particular damsel was damned well used to dealing with her own distresses, and liked it that way. Except for tonight. I'd called Darryl for help and hadn't insisted that Jeff hold his horses. I'd even given him Isabelle's address.

The moments of my indecision didn't deter Jeff. He took the bull by the horns and grabbed me, pulled me close, and didn't stop with a hug.

His kiss would keep me awake all night. A good thing, since I had puppies to keep an eye on.

Did Jeff want more? Probably. I did. But I backed away. Yawned. Thanked him. Told him he could go home.

"I'll hang out here tonight, Kendra. On the couch. I'll even take first shift watching the pups. Get some sleep. Oh, and by the way, after seeing Darryl in action, I think you're right. He's nearly as unlikely a murderer as you."

Great! We agreed on something. Now all we

had to do was agree on the killer's identity. And something in Jeff's tone still suggested that his internal exoneration of Darryl didn't mean he liked him again. What was that all about?

It hit me like a hellhound going for the jugular. "You aren't jealous of Darryl, are you? And my friendship with him?"

His affronted "Of course not" was anything but convincing.

"He and I—" I stopped. I owed Jeff neither apology nor explanation. In fact, *he* owed *me* a little of each.

And I'd just unearthed another aspect of Jeff Hubbard, P.I.—and one I didn't exactly admire.

The next day was Saturday. Jeff had left Odin at home and departed early to tend to his own best friend. He promised to return whenever I wanted him to look in on the puppies.

After an extra examination of the puppy fence, I started my rounds. Lexie came along. There wasn't much she could do if a pup got a tummy ache.

We visited Py the python, who seemed listless at one end of his glass-enclosed world. I checked the tank's temperature and called Milt. "I'm not sure yet when I'll be home," he said. This certainly was turning into one long wedding. Or had his mom taken sonny boy along on her honeymoon? "I'm sure Py's fine," he continued. "He spends a lot of time not moving, though I'm sure he's quieter since he's lonely." He sighed. "I miss him, too. Can you take him with you today?"

"For a while." Only on dog-walking rounds; I wouldn't bring a snake to Isabelle's. The pups were too big to look like lunch, but I'd had enough anguish over them to worry whether Py might try. Besides, there were the bunnies.

Meanwhile, to prepare for Py's next real meal, I transferred a mouse from freezer to fridge.

Avvie called while I was walking Alexander. The pit bull's owner had returned from vacation and was so pleased at how happy he was, she'd hired me to visit each day he was home alone. On weekdays she left her boy at Darryl's, but she was in show biz and often worked weekends. As a result, Alexander and I hit the streets together on this Saturday.

"Hi, Avvie," I answered her call. I watched as a couple of crows and a cat scattered upon seeing the playful pit bull stare their way. Or maybe it was the way my pocket wriggled.

"You weren't upset about how Bill acted yesterday, were you Kendra? Either about your pet-sitting or about your not coming back to the firm? He and I talked about it afterward, and I kind of wondered . . ."

"Not at all," I said truthfully.

"Can we get together for coffee this afternoon?"

"Another time." I explained the Helga-and-offspring situation.

"Oh, how fun. Can I come see them?"

What the heck? Where I was hanging out was hardly a secret any longer. And I figured Avvie's visit would be all right as long as she didn't bring fleas or rabies, so I gave her Isabelle's address and the time I anticipated being back.

After taking Py home, I met her there right on time. She'd taken to heart my long-ago admonishments to look professional even off duty, for her skirt was a neat gray, her blouse subdued and silky. She backed off as the exuberant—and, thank heavens, healthy—pups gave their greetings. Avvie was obviously more concerned about snagged stockings than making friends. Her smile was similar to one she gave to particularly obstreperous judges.

Jeff popped over, and Avvie seemed more interested in him than the small canines. She didn't stay long, for though Jeff was friendly enough, he seemed impressed by neither her legal mind nor her once-overs of him.

Soon there I was, alone again with Helga, five youngsters, some bunnies, Lexie, and the man who'd made me remember I had a libido. Relaxed at last, I dared a glance at Jeff. His return grin made me uneasily aware—again—of how attractive he was and how much I wanted to jump his muscle-clad bones. Again. That very moment.

Which seemed beyond the realm of the moment's possibilities, though I read between the lines at the edges of his sexy blue eyes that he was interested that way, too.

"So," I said to make conversation, "there've been developments you don't know about."

"Like Judge Baird Roehmann hauling you into court yesterday to get a temporary restraining order against you?"

I stared. That latest fiasco had somehow eluded the media, and I hadn't mentioned it during our puppy preservation efforts. "How did you know?"

"My techy guru Althea taps into all local court records and scans them daily. Totally legally, of course."

"Of course."

"So what was it about?"

I told him I'd been trying to get Baird to admit he'd set me up to avenge himself on me for not leaping into bed with him. Or maybe for a different reason I hadn't figured out, since even egotistical Baird must be rejected by other women without attempting to avenge himself on them in such an extreme manner. "My suspicions against him may have been unwarranted," I admitted. "But the more I think about it, the more certain I am that, with all the stuff that's happened to me lately, *someone's* orchestrating it—someone with a grudge against me." Maybe I'd developed that theory simply to avoid digging into the common connections between Carl and Shirley, but I didn't think so. I glared at Jeff defiantly, waiting for him to propose that I was paranoid. He didn't.

He also didn't stay the night, which was the way I wanted it. Wasn't it?

The next day, Sunday, I did my pet visits early with Lexie.

The puppies were fine, but I still kept close watch over them. Isabelle paid her babies a short visit midday. I told her what had happened, and the chubby, blond senior citizen beamed at me, brightening my day even more. "You've done a fantastic job with these sneaky rascals, Kendra. Thanks so much. I feel more comfortable leaving you here with them for an extra couple of days. My sister's surgery . . ." She trailed off.

Sympathetic, I asked, "Complications?"

"Yeah, in her mind. It's not like a woman her age . . . I mean, she wouldn't have had more kids anyhow, but she's crying about it. I'll stick around as long as I can stand her, now that I know you're doing so well."

Darryl came by while I was between pet-tending rounds. Avvie called and gushed about how much she loved the babies. Jeff visited, too, with Odin this time. He let his dog sniff Helga and her energetic crew, then shut him out of the kitchen. Lexie was glad to see the Akita, bounding into the backyard with him.

And I was glad to see his owner. So glad, in fact, that when he suggested he'd be able to spend the night, I firmly told him to head home.

"You don't want to brainstorm anymore?" he asked, his voice cool, his uncool reaction to rejection broadcast in the flash of his eyes. We were sitting around the kitchen table, ostensibly keeping two sets of eyes on the puppies. But at the commencement of this conversation, I saw his back stiffen. No wonder. Mine did the same.

"Not unless you have any ideas about who might be framing me," I said to him. "Other than Baird Roehmann, of course."

"No, but I did call Ned Noralles on your behalf."

"You didn't tell him my theory, did you?" Speaking of sticks up my back, I suddenly felt as if my T-shirt had sprouted a central broomstick. Even if Jeff hadn't accused me of paranoia, the redoubtable detective would no doubt jump on any hint of my mental instability.

"No, but I asked how his investigation was going, offered your further cooperation, that kind of thing."

"Thanks for asking me first."

"You're welcome. The suggestion made him soften up a bit, thank us both, and tell me that though it's none of my damned business, he wasn't seeking a warrant for either your arrest or your friend Nestler's. Yet. When I asked about other suspects, he said they were still narrowing them down. I took a few guesses, like Cuthbertson's daughter and son and some players at both of their companies, and got a Geiger-counter reading of how hot and cold each possibility was. None got beyond moderate, so I gather that my former co-workers are stymied, too."

"That's not a good thing."

"No, but it could give more credence to your theory. Assuming you're not just p—"

"Piddling!" I exclaimed, preempting him from saying the word I didn't want to hear and jumping up from my seat.

He blinked, confused.

"That puppy." I pointed toward the young, furry culprit making my move toward the offending piddler.

"Oh. Yeah."

We shared a pizza that night, and nothing else. Except the promise to talk again tomorrow.

Another day passed peacefully. I was itching to investigate on my own sometime Monday, but hadn't yet decided where to turn. Toward standard suspects, like those who did business with both Carl and Shirley? Or should I try to find someone to satisfy my fantasy that I was the center of a conspiracy?

Jeff offered no more suggestions. And Isabelle had decided to stay where she was until Wednesday.

Though Shirley would be interred privately, I went to her memorial that afternoon, since no one had invited me not to. I ignored the pointed stares, mourning Shirley silently. *She* knew how much I'd liked her.

At least the day's pet-sitting went well. Lexie seemed content. Helga and her husky kids were fine.

I knew I shouldn't relax, not until dear Detective Noralles had collared someone else for the killings. But with everything going as it was, it was hard to focus on worrying.

Until Tuesday morning, that is, when I walked out Isabelle's front door to discover that my Beamer had disappeared.

And almost before I'd grabbed my phone to call 911, a familiar-looking dark sedan stopped at the curb. The detective I'd been trying not to think about got out. As usual, he wore a suit that enhanced his own dark-complected good looks. But his smile looked so bland that I cringed. Here it came—whatever *it* was.

"Ms. Ballantyne, I got a call on my way to work. A vehicle registered to you was involved in a hit-and-run situation a few blocks from here. Fortunately, a witness got the license number. You ready to talk?"

CHAPTER 30

And just where had my missing Beamer committed such a nasty deed? I guessed it straight off.

We sat in the familiar interview room at the North Hollywood station. Esther was on her way, but I figured I'd answer all I could without incriminating myself. The room was small and occupied only, for now, by Detective Noralles and me.

Tall, dark, and stonily handsome, Detective Noralles was at the far end. I could virtually smell his excitement about closing a big, visible case.

Three big, visible cases. Or at least two killings and a little bitty hit-and-run that tied them both together with a big, red bow that said *Kendra Ballantyne, erstwhile Attorney at Law, murderer, and more.*

"So what did the thief hit with my car, Detective?" I tried to stay suave and cool. Inside, my heart played a staccato beat that suggested it might ricochet up my windpipe and out my mouth. "If I were to guess, I'd figure it had something to do with

Judge Roehmann, since I've been ordered by a court to stay away from him. Right?"

"That's more than a guess, isn't it, Ms. Ballantyne?" His smooth voice could have been spread on soft bread with a butter knife.

"No, it's not. So . . . was Baird hurt?" I might have been fuming at His Righteous, Two-faced Honor, but I didn't wish him that kind of harm.

"No. Fortunately, he wasn't in his Jaguar when *someone* plowed your car into it inside his garage and sped off."

My poor, stolen car. At least I'd brought all my client keys and info inside with me last night. Sometimes I left them locked inside to keep from forgetting them the next morning. Thank heavens my pet-sitting wouldn't have to wait today for their retrieval.

"I don't suppose you were out driving last night, were you?"

"No," I said, "and before you ask, the only witnesses to my whereabouts are dogs."

"Too bad the judge wasn't injured, isn't it?" The solemn detective studied my face, presumably for any sign of anger or admission. Happily, I must have showed none.

That irritated him, for his coolness slipped. "I'm going to read you your Miranda rights, Ms. Ballantyne. I think it's time you told me what's really been going on."

"Soon as I figure it out, I'll let you in on it, Detective," I said with a sigh. Shoot. I wasn't ready to be taken into custody. I had murders to solve. "Obviously you and your resources are stuck in the same old uncreative rut, chasing me. I'm not an investigation expert, but it looks like I'll have to solve everything myself. But right now, what I really want is to know the condition of my poor car."

Good thing there was a knock on the door right then, or the uncharacteristically furious expression on the detective's face might have manifested itself further in the fists at his sides. Right into my face.

I sprang to my feet in relief as Esther joined us. I went over what I'd said, which wasn't much. My adroit little-old-lady lawyer, wearing a magenta suit, looked at me, shook her head, and allowed the "interview" to continue.

When it was over, Detective Noralles thanked me through gritted teeth and promised he'd be in touch.

But, thank God and Esther, I remained free.

My car, however, was under arrest pending further investigation.

My mind wasn't free, either. Esther and I had a quick cup of coffee, during which she bawled me out for not waiting for her and for baiting the cop who obviously itched to incarcerate me. I did my damnedest to focus on her warnings, but my thoughts were off on their own damned track.

Darryl had, as always, been a lifesaver. I'd had to borrow him and his van to rush through my pet-tending rounds before heading for the police station that morning. Noralles had sent along a uniform to shadow me to make sure I wasn't using my work as an excuse to elude his interrogation.

Darryl had left me at the station. Now, Esther promised to drop me at Darryl's.

But first . . . "Kendra, are you listening?" she demanded.

"Not entirely." I figured my abashedness showed in the way I slid my lips together.

"Come on. Let's get in the car, and on the way we'll go over it all again."

She made me repeat things like a school kid learning by rote. Lawyer or not, I wasn't to give interviews without my counsel present. Most of all, I wasn't to intimidate, stalk, smash into, or murder anyone.

Else? Esther didn't say the word, but I felt a sinking sureness that my own lawyer now actually doubted my innocence. Not that she wasn't a pro. She knew that, in our legal system, even the guilty deserved a defense.

"I didn't do any of it," I assured her quietly when she pulled her red Mercedes into the parking lot outside Darryl's doggy spa. "Not even to get a ride in your car."

"This isn't funny," she said.

"Do you see me laughing?"

Darryl and I talked some more. "Someone is doing this to me," I said. "Someone who knows I've been staying at Isabelle's."

"Don't look at me." He put his long, skinny hands out to ward off any accusations I might send his way.

"I've already decided it can't be you," I assured him. "So don't prove me an ass, okay?"

"No sweat. So who else could it be?"

"Jeff Hubbard knew I was there, but I'd barely met him when Carl was killed. I can't figure out any motive he'd have unless someone hired him to take care of me."

"I'd guess by the way the two of you look at each other that he's taking care of you, all right."

I glared. I also felt my face go scarlet. "We only slept together once," I mumbled.

"So far. But spare me the erogenous details, especially why you haven't just stayed in bed together while everyone else you know gets run over or knifed."

Too bad Jeff wasn't here to hear this. Not a hint of envy from Darryl as he glossed over the games I'd played with the P.I. As I'd said, we were just good friends. *Get it, Jeff? Now, get off my case.* About Darryl, that is, not the multiple murder investigation.

"Who else could be doing it?" Darryl continued.

"Isabelle knows I'm at her house, of course, and she knew Carl. I have no idea if she knew Shirley. Or if she's told her neighbors I've been dog-sitting."

"What about Avvie? You let her come see the pups. Carl and Shirley were your clients, and she obviously knows the judge."

I nodded dumbly. I'd thought of Avvie. And if not her, it could be Bill Sergement, via pillow talk. She could hate me because I once screwed her current lover, Bill, though I wasn't sure why she'd wait years to exact her revenge. Bill could hate me because I *wasn't* screwing him now. Though ditto, the question about the delay. Plus, Bill and I had ended it mutually, and that had been before Avvie had even come onto the scene. No, if it was either of them, there had to be another reason. One I hadn't figured out yet.

They had both been around when that damned strategy memo that started my problems had been leaked in the first place. They'd have had better access to it than Judge Roehmann. They'd also have better ability to plant the other evidence against me.

But again, having been on the receiving end, I wouldn't start shouting additional accusations without a shred of proof.

I had an idea, though. Probably a very bad one. For even if I learned what I hoped to, it wouldn't do me a hell of a lot of good in a court of law. Plus, it was a long shot.

But I made calls that afternoon after leaving Darryl's, and I gave a big sigh of relief and remorse when I managed to set up an appointment for midday tomorrow.

I didn't tell Jeff what I was up to, even when he insisted that he and Odin would camp out on

Isabelle's couch again so he could testify on my behalf if further mischief occurred that night.

I was exhausted after spending extra time with all my charges that afternoon to make up for rushed visits in the morning. Too tired to argue. Too relieved—though I hesitated to admit it to myself, let alone Jeff—that I wouldn't be alone.

Before bed, over wine for us, petrified pigs' ears for Odin and Lexie, nutritious dogfood for Helga and her kids, I told Jeff in more detail than I had earlier about what had transpired that day, as well as my unconfirmed suspicions.

We sat on the couch he'd promised to sleep on. I kept an ear tuned to the kitchen in case a puppy yelped some complaint.

"So you think a couple of attorneys you used to work with are behind all of this because of some grudge about your sleeping habits?" Leaning into the opposite corner of the sofa from me, Jeff sounded incredulous.

"It's not how I sleep, it's who I do or don't sleep with. And you're right. I can't believe that would be the reason. But so far, until I figure out something better, it's the only thing I've come up with as a motive Avvie or Bill."

His sexy straight brows lifted, and he leered suggestively. "Tell them it's none of their damn business, it's in the past, and you and I now have something going."

"Do we?"

Shit. I hadn't meant to ask, and I didn't want

an answer. There wasn't a good one. I didn't want us to have something going. He was officious and jealous, and I just didn't do well with men when it went beyond casual. But because we'd slept together once and were still obviously attracted to each other, we *did* have something going.

"Do you want to?" He raised one of those brows dubiously, suggesting he knew my answer.

"You know I'm really attracted to you, Jeff. And I do want you. After the night we spent together, that has to be evident."

"So explain the 'but' you haven't added yet, the one that's kept us at arm's length."

I squirmed into the sofa. "Well, first of all, I don't like your attitude toward Darryl. If it's jealousy, you're fighting your own fiction. As I've said, he and I are just friends."

"Old habits die hard," he muttered. "But I'll break that one. You're friends. Got it."

Old habits? "Who else have you been jealous of?" He didn't respond. Then it hit me. "Your mother? But I thought you kind of admired how she danced her way to your family's financial security."

"Right," he said. "Anything else?"

I wasn't satisfied with his affirmative yet abrupt reply, but I moved on anyway. "Yeah," I replied. "There's more. I've been in relationships, Jeff, and I've seen a lot of others, too. I'm not naïve enough to believe in 'happily ever after.' Not even happily till next week. So, what I believe in is living for the moment, seeing what comes, keeping one's freedom. And I have to admit, since my own freedom is hanging by a hair right now, that part's particularly dear to my heart."

His angular features quirked unevenly around his wry smile. "That sounds like a guy's list of platitudes. In any case, it works for me. I'm on the road too much to please a lady who wants a lively lover on a short string. So we'll play things by ear, or maybe other body parts, when the mood strikes us."

I nodded. "I'm glad we've cleared the air. And now, I'm tired. I'm going to bed."

I stood. Jeff did, too. We walked into each other's arms. His kiss was the nightcap I needed, and our understanding was what I required to throw aside my inhibitions.

Apparently, the mood had struck us both. We headed for Isabelle's guest bedroom, Lexie and Odin at our heels.

The next morning, everything between us felt just as fun as it had after our first sex-filled night together. But we had to get moving, as Isabelle was due home that day.

"I'll talk to her later," I told Helga. "If she's not back by noon, I'll pop in to see how you and the youngsters are."

Those same youngsters were enmeshed in puppy pugilistics on the kitchen floor. Helga gave me a long-suffering maternal look as I waved goodbye, and Jeff and I headed back to his house to drop off Lexie and Odin for the day.

Jeff gave me a hot-blooded, mood-bending, every-carnal-part-of-the-body-stimulating kiss before we left the privacy of his place after getting the dogs settled in. At my request, he dropped me at a place on Lankershim Boulevard where I could rent a junker of a car.

At the rental place, Jeff and I exchanged the most cursory of kisses, like we'd been together for a long time instead of a couple of incomparable nights. He was leaving town again soon, and tomorrow looked like the day. Fine by me—having him in the same city was making my libido need a constant cold shower when I wasn't letting it have its way.

He wanted my commitment to appear at his house early that night for my next Odin-sitting mission.

I, on the other hand, needed space again after so many close encounters with him the night before.

His acknowledging my need for freedom apparently hadn't really sunk into his enormous masculine ego. My intention wasn't to deflate it anymore than I wanted to deflate any other part of him—except temporarily. As a result, I told him I'd call him later. I'd need to spend some time at my place if I was going to desert it again so soon.

Morning pet-sitting rounds went well. That left

me ready for my early afternoon meeting at the new Desert State Hospital in Palmdale, north of L.A. I'd called the attorney who'd represented Lorraine Giles many months ago when she'd sued my client company, GerLaDex, and gotten the lawyer's okay to see Lorraine on my own, since I no longer represented the opposition.

I checked with her doctors, too. One said she'd meet with me first and might stay in the room when I visited Lorraine. That was fine by me.

I checked in at the front desk. An assistant came to get me—a woman whose sweet demeanor and petite stature chipped away at my preconceived picture of an attendant at a facility for the criminally insane. Her nametag simply said "Bevvie." Beaming beatifically, she sent me through a metal detector and watched as a uniformed guard checked my purse. Then she walked me to an elevator, and we went up a few levels.

We strolled through locked doors and into what looked like any patient lounge at any hospital—colorful chairs along the periphery, a magazine-laden table in the middle. Then there was the two-way mirror in the wall that Bevvie pointed out. She told me that, although we'd have some privacy, she would watch so she could come to my assistance or Lorraine's, if either of us needed it. The doctor had decided Lorraine was okay with just this extra level of caution.

The idea of such a protective measure should have relieved me. Instead, it forced to the forefront of my mind exactly who Lorraine was and what she'd done.

She never snuck around like whoever murdered Carl and Shirley. Lorraine was upfront from the beginning. Via the strategy memo, she'd learned how GerLaDex, the pharmaceuticals company she'd sued for wrongful termination, planned to prove she'd messed up, been rude to customers, sent letters in wrong envelopes, continuously came to work late, and generally made a joke of her job, perhaps due to mental instability.

Her counter had been that she was a whistle-blower, uncovering their failure to disclose the dangers of a particular drug to the FDA. Messed up? Not she. The claims in her file had all been manufactured. And once she'd learned that her ex-boss, CEO John Germane, had cared enough about her case to cast such terrible aspersions on her, she'd gotten mad and decided to get even.

Mental instability? She'd show them mental instability. And she had: She'd blown Germane away.

And then she claimed it was all because she'd learned of GerLaDex's trial strategy. And it sent her over the edge.

And that strategy memo? Well, she never revealed exactly how it came to be in her possession. But she always implied, and never denied, that it came from me.

The door to the lounge opened. A tall, thin

woman with short hair and a big smile walked in. She wore gray slacks and a black, lacy smock. A woman in a nurse's uniform followed, urged her into a stiff-backed chair beside the table, and said she'd wait outside.

"Ms. Ballantyne?" said the newly seated woman.

I didn't recognize Lorraine at all. The last time I saw her, she'd been heavier, and her hair had been as wild as her brown eyes and several shades darker. Her now-subdued voice had been shrill and piercing.

But though her eyes were calmer now, they were still the same shade and just as sly. This was definitely the woman who'd helped to turn my career into chaff.

"Hi, Lorraine," I said. "Thanks for agreeing to see me."

"You're not a lawyer anymore, are you?" She'd been blunt during depositions. Apparently that wasn't something that medications or therapy had dulled.

"Temporarily."

"My lawyer told me. She said I didn't have to see you, but it was okay if I agreed, since you weren't representing anyone adverse to my interests right now. In fact, you weren't representing anyone."

My teeth automatically gritted beneath my forced smile. "I appreciate your agreeing to talk to me. I know a lot has happened, but there's a loose end about your case against GerLaDex that was never tied up." No use wasting time pussyfooting around the problem. "That strategy memo. How did you really get a hold of it?"

Was that slyness in her smile? Hell, now it turned to calculating glee. "You gave it to me, remember?"

I sat on that for a second, trying to decide how to respond. "Maybe if you tell the truth, I could do something to help you. Is there something you need? I'm not sure what I'd be allowed to send to you, but I can ask about books, or clothes, or—"

"Not things. Or money. I want justice. That's what it's all about. All things, all events, all life. It's all about justice, don't you agree?"

"As a lawyer, even one who's not currently practicing, I do agree, but I don't understand—"

"You don't need to understand. I never thought you needed to understand. But justice equals revenge, doesn't it?"

"Well, no, but—"

"Yes!" She was suddenly on her feet, towering over me. For the first time, I felt afraid. The woman she'd been, who had shot the man who dared to prepare to contradict her case in court, was still inside, and now she erupted to the surface.

I pushed my chair back and stood. "I'm sorry if I've upset you." I hoped my appeasing tone didn't sound too terrified.

Lorraine breathed fast, her fists clenching and unclenching at her side. Most horrible of all was the little laugh burbling in spurts from her throat.

"The thing is," I blundered on, "some things have

304

happened that could be related to what occurred before. I think someone is setting me up again, maybe the same person who set you up. Maybe together we can get justice, Lorraine. Will you help me?"

That laugh exploded. Then, just as suddenly as she seemed to go off the deep end, she calmed. She sat back in her chair. No laughs, not even any smiles, and her hands folded demurely in her lap. She watched as her fingers wiggled.

"I have no answers for you, Ms. Ballantyne. You asked me questions in depositions when my case was going on. I answered the best I could. Not good enough. You were going to hurt me. Mr. Germane was going to hurt me. I got the memo, thanks to you." She looked up calmly. "Justice. That's everything."

She wasn't going to tell me more.

The woman could know the name of the person or people who had wreaked such havoc in my life. Paranoid or not, I couldn't help thinking that what had happened revolved around me. If nothing else, the vortex had grabbed me, threatened to sink me, and this mad woman, this murderess, refused to throw me a lifeline.

"Tell me, Lorraine," I insisted, this time rising spontaneously to stand above her. "Tell me how you really got that memo."

The door opened and the nurse and Bevvie burst in. Where were they when Lorraine had acted so menacing a few minutes ago?

Right now, the roles were reversed.

What they saw was the inmate of this facility for the criminally insane, acting calm, cool, collected, and civil.

And her visitor? Well, I was the one suddenly in crisis.

CHAPTER 31

I calmed down quickly, since I didn't want the staff at Desert State to figure that the visitor was the biggest fruitcake in the room. They might have authority to detain those they considered borderline bananas. Who knew?

I thanked everyone, including Lorraine, who simply smiled placidly, as if her medication had finally kicked in.

Then I got in one last glance at her eyes. Their shifty smirk nearly got me going again. But I was the sane one.

I got back on the road. Fast.

To avoid distractions, I'd had my cell phone turned off. A couple of messages were waiting.

One was from Isabelle. She was home and busy adoring her babies. I was an absolute dear and could stop in anytime that afternoon to bring back her keys and pick up a check.

First, I had to go see Py.

My favorite python's master had called yet again to say his visit to his mother's had been protracted. Something about an impending annulment already, and his mom was a mess.

I'd slipped Py his weekly mouse yesterday. Considering all the other miserable stuff I'd handled that day, a thawed rodent hadn't been too bad. But it still lay in Py's cage. He hadn't eaten it. Didn't stick his forked tongue out when I stroked his back. Just stayed curled in his little blue-and-pink ball.

I didn't call Milt this time. I knew the drill.

On my way to Isabelle's, I got a call from Jeff. He sounded rushed, and I could hardly hear him over background noise. "Got an emergency call," he said. "I'm at the airport. You're in charge of Odin, your place or mine, it doesn't matter. I'll call you."

As in, *See you around sometime?* or, *It's been real?*

I slammed on the brakes. Not the car's. My mind's. For an astute woman who'd shunned the entire idea of starting a relationship, I was thinking a lot like someone who felt dumped.

The guy was a businessman. He was off on business, which was a good thing. It would give me time to get my head on straight. And right now, that orb on top of my neck very clearly needed an attitude adjustment.

A short while later, I said goodbye to Helga's frolicsome offspring and hello to a nice, sizeable check. Isabelle had been generous. A good thing, considering I'd also checked in with my buddy Noralles, who said that the good news was that my Beamer could be sprung tomorrow, though his tone suggested I wasn't clear of future claims—if not criminal, then at least civil.

The worse news was that the collision with Baird Roehmann's prized Jag left my aging auto undriveable. I'd not only have car rental costs, but repair expenses, too, presuming that the car could be healed at all. And though I had liability insurance, collision coverage had long since become a luxury I couldn't afford.

I felt as if the final straw had not only been broken; it had been twisted, stomped on, mangled, and maimed. Like my own fractured psyche.

I stuck Isabelle's check into an empty pocket of my suit jacket. Good thing I did, for I remembered then who was curled inside another one: Py. He hadn't moved much, but according to Milt he was happy that way.

I took time from my rounds for a little R and R: rumpus and rhubarb. To take my mind off my troubles, even temporarily, I headed for Darryl's.

The Doggy Indulgence Day Resort was as chaotic as usual. The staff was engaged in a spirited game of doggy catch. I grinned as Kiki missed the ball and landed butt first on the slick floor.

No sign of Darryl until I glanced into his office. Fran Korwald was there. She stood up when she saw me. "Hi, Kendra. Any ideas for me? Rubin is leaving next week for Alaska, though he'll be back for Piglet's custody hearing in a few weeks."

A pang of guilt shot through me. I caught Darryl's eye. He regarded me without reproach but knew I'd done no more research. I'd have told him if I learned anything helpful. Or even if I'd tried and figured that Rubin would wind up the winner paws down.

On the other hand, surely a court would figure that Alaska wasn't in the best interests of a short-haired mini-dog. Poor Piglet could wind up as lunch for a stray wolf or eagle or—

A flash of inspiration streaked before my eyes. It grabbed my dormant legal mind and shook it loose.

Practicing law wasn't all taking precedents and reshaping their holdings into arguments to suit a client's side of things. It also consisted of a huge quantity of creativity.

"I've got an idea," I said. "There's risk involved, and you'll have to tell me if the psychology of it is likely to move your ex, but how about this?" I outlined my proposal, watching Fran's sad stoicism segue to smiling excitement.

Darryl laughed. "I've met Rubin. It's gotta work. You've done it again, Kendra."

I could only hope. And since it took some planning before being put into effect, I'd have to wait and see.

When I left Darryl's, my mood was back to my long-lost ebullience. I'd conquered a problem, or at least taken a good stab at it.

But the blades of my own dilemma still hung over me like sharp swords, ready to slice my tenuous peace of mind to pieces.

Still, I'd come away with renewed resolve. I'd

take matters into my own hands once more. Not that I'd been simply twiddling my thumbs when shit happened around—and to—me, but now my determination kicked into overdrive. I'd solve the murders and figure out who'd been messing with my life, with all due speed.

Yeah, and wouldn't Detective Ned Noralles love to know his job was toast? I would solve everything without his input. What else could I do? Thanks to his snide demeanor, I felt certain of his certainty that I was not only the murderer, but also the one who'd run my own vehicle into Judge Roehmann's Jag. He would prove it one day—whether or not it was true.

I stopped at a mall and parked outside. I used the back of a client's instruction sheet to create one of my handy-dandy, catch-all, forget-nothing lists. This one looked more like a chart: I posted along the left side all the people I'd imagined could have been involved with my original ethics dilemma, then the suspects in Carl's and Shirley's murders. I had to leave blank spaces for the show biz contacts Darryl mentioned who'd been involved with his TV series idea.

Along the top I stuck headings of means, opportunity, and then the mother of them all: motive. Of course I still wanted all my heaviest checkmarks to line up after Conrad Taylor, but they didn't, partly thanks to my paranoid theory of my own pivotal part in all this. Some of my old cronies, though . . .

Still, no solution struck me in the face. I still had investigating to do.

Pulling out of the lot again, I called Avvie. "I hope Bill and you can join me for dinner tonight," I said. "I've got some ideas about my future plans, and you enter into them." I hoped that would spark their curiosity enough. And indirectly, it was true.

If they were the ones who'd turned my life into chaos, I wanted to know it immediately, so I could deal with it.

And if they weren't? Well, I hadn't eliminated Baird Roehmann, but my suspicions against him were waning. He'd actually seemed scared of my alleged stalking of him. He had to be a good actor to get on the bench, but he wasn't *that* good.

That meant I'd have to change my way of thinking, for I had no absolute proof as to which of my suspects was framing me.

And if I was in the middle of everything for no reason but coincidence?

Yeah. And I was a python's grandmother.

Avvie and Bill were available. They were also both ready to leave the office to have an early dinner in Beverly Hills.

I mentioned to Avvie where I'd gone that afternoon—and not just on my pet-sitting rounds. If one of them had slipped the strategy memo to Lorraine, they might be a little on edge knowing I'd gone to see the murdering lunatic that day.

Good thing I still wore my suit jacket—we ate at a fancy place. But I'd hardly have removed the jacket. Speaking of pythons, I'd all but forgotten I still had company. An occasional shift in my deepest pocket reminded me, but Py's continued lethargy kept my life simpler just then. I'd take him home after dinner.

I was glad when Bill suggested that the firm pick up the tab. "Want to talk business?" he asked. "Then it'll be legit."

"What business?"

"You tell us." He took an inelegant swig of chianti from his elegant crystal wine glass. His hair looked as frazzled as his nerves—in other words, normal. I had no doubt Avvie had told him of my visit to Lorraine. Was that grating on him?

I could only hope.

We had salads, gourmet grilled fish, and gossip. But nothing came out that had a bearing on what I wanted to know.

I'd learned as a lawyer that hedging only got one farther into the bushes. Directness was the way to go.

"So," I said, "I'm glad we could get together tonight, since I have stuff I'm eager to run by you."

"What?" Bill's relaxed dinnertime attitude switched into Drill Sergeant mode. His near-set eyes narrowed and regarded me as if I'd caused the halibut on his plate to swim onto his lap.

I took a bracing sip of wine. "It's no secret that

I've seen my share of troubles lately, starting with Lorraine Giles' murder of John Germane."

Avvie nodded. "Is that what you talked with her about today?"

"Indirectly. I asked point blank who really leaked the strategy memo to her."

"You saw Lorraine Giles?" Bill said, apparently playing dumb. "Did she tell you?" Did Bill look more nervous than usual?

"No, or I wouldn't need this brainstorming session. The thing is . . ." I paused dramatically for effect. "I think the same person not only leaked that memo and set me up then, but also killed Carl Cuthbertson and Shirley Dorian to frame me."

Avvie's hazel eyes went expressionless.

Bill's brown ones shifted to the height of skepticism. "Why?" he asked. "And who?"

"I don't know. Have any ideas?" I forbore from staring point blank at Avvie for answers. Bill reacted the way I expected from anyone who figured I'd started to see little green men pursuing me. Avvie, on the other hand, wasn't reacting.

"No, I don't," Bill said. "And why would anyone?"

"Exactly." I slid another sidelong look toward Avvie.

She finally spoke. "I thought you wanted to talk about whether MSY would hire you back if—when—you put this all behind you, not make ridiculous accusations—"

"I haven't accused anyone," I pointed out. "But

make a suggestion, tell me a motive, and I just might."

My mind had been churning over the questions. Maybe they hadn't been in it together. Avvie now had my vote. Because she was still jealous that I'd slept with Bill? Nah, that didn't make any more sense now than it had before. And despite my request, she was hardly likely to hand me a motive over dinner.

"Were you following Baird Roehmann," Avvie said, "because, as the judge in all three cases, he could have connected you to the problems?"

"I figured *he* was the connection. Then."

"I talked with him," Avvie said. "Before, he got the TRO against you, he was concerned he'd be your next victim." Pushing her empty fish plate away, she leaned on the table toward me. "I tried to convince him that that was ridiculous. I didn't know what was going on, but I knew you were innocent." She shook her head, and the highlights in her short hair glimmered in the restaurant's dim light. "Or at least I thought you were. But I should have considered Carl Cuthbertson."

"What about him?" I asked. Was she implying now that she considered me guilty? If so, why?

"I thought one of your defenses for the day he was killed was that you didn't even know he was in town."

"Right."

"Well, he'd left you a message that he was coming back early."

"Really?" I felt my gut turn to lead. If anyone could prove that . . . And if Carl had left me that message, no wonder Avvie's trust was wavering. "I never saw it. How did you know about it?"

"I talked to him. He was transferred to me, but I couldn't find your new cell phone number." Avvie's eyes widened, and she shared a look with her lover. I might not have known Carl was coming home early, but *she* did. Maybe Bill, too. I kept my face as noncommittal as Noralles's.

She must have known what I was thinking, for she continued on the offensive, "Don't look at me that way, like you think I killed Carl just because I knew he was in town. You could have gotten the message but denied it. And now you've gone to see Lorraine. Your car rammed Baird's. Were you hinting before, when you asked for suggestions and motives, that one of us did it? If so, I'll bet you're trying to hide your own guilt by accusing us."

"No, but I am trying to find out if either of you is hiding your guilt by framing me." I looked from one to the other. No shock at my suggestion marred their practiced lawyerly composure. They shared a serious glance, then turned back to me.

And then, in unison, both shook their heads. Cute move. But it didn't do me a damned bit of good.

Bill cleared his throat. "Actually, till tonight I really thought you were guilty of everything."

"And now?" I had to ask.

"Now, after hearing all you've said in this conversation, I may be wrong, but I think you're innocent."

Hallelujah! Or . . . was he just humoring me?

Unlikely. Drill Sergeant wasn't known for any kind of humor. And trying to keep someone from feeling bad simply wasn't in this single-minded litigator's makeup.

"I know it wasn't Avvie or me," he continued, "and probably not the judge. Any other ideas?"

I shook my head mournfully.

"I know you had a meeting with Royal Marden," Avvie said. "He's not happy that our firm has been in the papers for things other than winning mega-million-dollar cases, but in a way, that lets him off the hook, too: He wouldn't have done all those things that gave the firm a negative image."

"What about Borden Yurick?" I asked. "Where is he? I haven't seen him in weeks."

Avvie looked away. Bill suddenly discovered that his wine glass was empty and signaled to a passing waiter to rectify that horrible state of affairs.

Both were very obviously avoiding the issue.

"I've heard rumors he had some kind of breakdown," I said. "I know it's a long-shot, but I've been considering again who leaked that strategy memo in the first place and let me take the blame. I have to believe it's someone from the firm. Could it have been Borden?"

"Why?" Avvie asked. "Did you ever do anything to harm him?"

"No, though I used to think there was something wrong with the way he practiced law. Especially when I was in the middle of a big, important case, spending long hours and watching him come in late and leave early. He made it look too easy and spent more time socializing with clients than handling their cases. But I never said anything to him about it. And now I even admire it. If that was somehow the harbinger of a breakdown, though—"

"He did go off the deep end," Bill muttered.

"Yeah." Avvie's tone turned suddenly as dry as the wine, and I looked at her. She didn't look at Bill, but aimed a teensy smile at me. "He's leaving the partnership. That's a sign of madness in itself. But what's really bothering everyone is the number of clients going with him. He brought most of the larger ones in."

"No kidding?" I really admired the guy now. Except— "How will he handle their cases without all of you to back him up?"

"He's not worried, and neither are the clients." Bill practically inhaled the glimmering liquid from his new glass of wine. *Someone* obviously was worried . . .

We finished the meal by kicking around other ideas. I was grateful that, for argument's sake, they seemed to accept the possibility that I was innocent, not paranoid.

But even pooling our three skilled legal minds, none of us came up with an obvious solution.

I remained roasting over the rotating spit of Detective Noralles's suspicions. And one of these days he was likely to turn it till that ol' goose of mine was trussed, cooked, and devoured.

CHAPTER 32

When I left the restaurant, I felt as down as I ever had during this whole ordeal. Even though there was nothing particularly exciting or erotic about the restaurant, Bill and Avvie apparently needed no stimulation but each other's company. They had begun making eyes at each other, which told me not only that our evening was ended, but also how much of a third wheel I was. Worse, I couldn't hang onto my certainty that one or both were my nemesis. And if neither was . . .

Reaching my rental car made my mood even worse. I aimed its ugly nose toward the Valley. At a light, I remembered I'd turned my cell phone off, in keeping with the restaurant's sophisticated ambiance. I turned it back on, and it beeped. I had a message.

"Hello, Kendra, this is Susan Feeney," it said. "Sorry I didn't call earlier, but I was copying a brief with a lot of attachments that has to be filed tomorrow, so . . . never mind. I was here late and didn't get around to calling you." She sounded her usual brisk, grumpy self. "I wanted to tell you about some new phone messages for you. A few were from people who didn't ID themselves. Reporters, probably. Some might be important, though. Call in the morning and I'll read them to you. I also had a question about the files on the GerLaDex matter. Before they're destroyed tomorrow, I wasn't sure if you want me to pull out your personal notes for your own ethics matter, or if you've kept a separate record. Tell me first thing." *Click.* Dead air. But not dead enough to keep my mind from swirling in it.

The GerLaDex files were being destroyed tomorrow? The firm's records retention period was much longer than a couple of years, unless the client wanted the files back.

Bill and Avvie had been my backup on the case. Why hadn't they mentioned this little matter at dinner? To make sure the wool was pulled over my eyes so tight that I'd never see the light of day again?

The Valley? Hell. I was heading downtown.

At night, the parking lots in downtown office buildings gouged less, with flat rates that were only painful, not fatal. I pulled into MSY's lot. I needed to get into the offices that night, go through the GerLaDex files, and figure out who was so eager to hide whatever evidence was about to be destroyed.

That presupposed I could get by the building guards. I used to know the night shift by name.

It had been simple to share camaraderie when I left work so often in the wee hours of the A.M.

The old guys would know I was persona non grata. If I couldn't get in now, though, I'd be stuck with bulldozing my way in tomorrow and demanding that my former cohorts give me access to files I no longer had any business seeing.

Better to try now. And I just happened to still have one of my former security access cards, a duplicate issued once when I'd misplaced my old one. It had been languishing at the bottom of my usual huge purse. At first, I figured I'd turn it in one day when visiting. The thought kept slipping my mind until I realized that the slip had been intentional. Not that I ever really anticipated a need to break into my old digs. Did I?

Anyway, I concocted my story on the short trip in the elevator from underground parking to the lobby.

Was I brazen enough to pull this off?

Hell, yes.

I walked up to the uniformed guards behind the chest-high security desk. They were both strangers, thank heavens.

"Hi," I said. "Wouldn't you know it? I went to a dinner meeting and left my briefcase upstairs. Another meeting first thing in the morning." I stuck my card in the scanner and held my breath. I wasn't sure how these things worked, but if this dinged people by name and not just magnetic strip, I was damned.

"Go right on up," said the older guard with a tired smile.

The same card unlocked the firm's doors. It had only been a few months, and apparently the code wasn't changed here either. I went in, glad to see the lights were on.

I'd go first to Susan's desk and pick up my messages. That way, in case my unauthorized presence was discovered, I could stick to a version of the truth: I'd had word from my former secretary about messages, and some might be important. A good reason to break into my old employer's offices in the middle of the night, right?

Only, as I headed through the door into the main office suite and down the corridor, something clicked in my head.

It didn't make sense, but . . . Had an answer finally come to me now, when it might be too late? One I hadn't even considered sticking onto my list.

Maybe I should leave, think things over, and come back in the morning.

Only—the click I heard wasn't the truth finally falling into place in my mind.

"Hello, Kendra," said my former secretary, Susan Feeney. She had slipped from the doorway of what had once been my office. The big son-of-a-gun semiautomatic in her latex-gloved hand was aimed right at my chest.

She wore slacks again. What had happened to

her earlier formality? She'd been a dedicated, old-school legal secretary. Hard-working. Quick to anticipate my every need.

And for the last couple of years, I realized a few minutes too late, she had been wreaking utter havoc on my life. Not to mention those lives she'd been responsible for ending.

"Ah, it *was* you." I tried to sound triumphant, as if I'd figured all this out long before.

"None other." Her voice was its usual cool monotone, her hands steady, her brown eyes unwavering.

And my heart accelerated like I'd just jumped off this building and forgotten my bungee cord.

"You know," I said, quite coolly, "the one thing I couldn't figure out was why you've been killing people and getting me blamed for the murders. Please explain."

I was interested. And maybe my life would be prolonged for a few meager seconds if I got her talking. After all, I had to believe she hadn't pulled a gun just for the fun of watching me wet my pants. Which I hadn't. Yet.

"I thought you'd never ask." Her smile made me shudder even more than the gun did.

I reached surreptitiously into my purse. My fingers tightened around something that might help, but Susan shook her head. I brought my hand out, showed her it was empty.

"I've made coffee," she said. "I want to tell you everything . . . first."

Before killing me. But coffee? How could I be sure that she hadn't—

"The coffee's safe to drink," she told me as I preceded her down the corridor to the break room. "I didn't drug it. I want you awake and aware of everything. I want you to understand. But . . ." Her tone turned so hard behind me that I stumbled, and she shoved me. "I'll shoot you if I get even a little nervous. Better that you die ignorant than that you don't die at all."

Hell. This was my life she was talking about. I might not be on the same career course now, but it wasn't a bad life—except for all the unexpected deaths that had littered it lately. And that was undoubtedly about to stop. After my own.

She motioned with the gun for me to sit at the table in the center of the small room. "I'll get the coffee. I just brewed it, so it's hot, but don't think you can distract me by throwing some on me."

Perish the thought . . . but I obediently sat.

In a minute, she was across from me, both of us with steaming mugs before us. Hers was by her left hand. She still held the gun on me with her glove-clad right hand.

"So," I said conversationally, "what's this all about?"

"Revenge." Her smile, between the parenthetical grooves in her cheeks, was as big as I'd ever seen it.

That was what Lorraine had said. She'd given

me a huge clue, even answered my question. If only I'd understood it then.

If only I understood it now.

"Revenge for what?"

"My parents. My life. Do you remember the Vanners?"

The name bonged a big bell in my memory. "Defendants in a case a long time ago?" My very first case. Nine years back. They were Susan's parents?

"They were just the ma-and-pa owners of a corner doughnut shop," Susan continued conversationally. "They'd have been in big trouble with their customers if they'd tried to keep out gang members in that neighborhood. They were horrified when that Shaff kid got killed. And then you added insult to injury by suing them over it. Of course they kept long hours, to make a living. They couldn't afford security, and they certainly couldn't kick out customers because they didn't like their looks. But that was what you claimed in court. And do you know what that horrible wrongful-death verdict did to them?"

I figured she wanted to tell me, so I simply shook my head.

"They didn't have enough insurance. They had to pay part of the judgment themselves, so they lost their shop. Their home, too, since they couldn't make mortgage payments. I was married then, tried to help, but it wasn't enough." The gun waved in Susan's grip. She put down the mug and used both hands to try to steady it. Tears streamed down her face, washing trails in her makeup. "Dad killed himself. Mom willed herself to die."

"I'm really sorry," I said.

"Sure you are, now." She sniffled bitterly. "My husband told me to let it go. But how could I? You'd killed my parents, and for what? Money. I couldn't let you get away with it."

I didn't bother trying to contradict her. I simply listened. And waited. And hoped for help. *Guards, I'm not really allowed here anymore. Come kick me out!*

Her tale made my blood turn to bright red ice, and she seemed to go colder as she told it.

Susan, soon after divorced and her family name far behind her, was already an administrative assistant. She'd rarely come to court with her folks during the trial. It hadn't been hard to change her appearance, become a legal secretary, and use that credential to get a job with the Marden firm. There, she'd waited for years until the right opportunity for revenge against me.

She'd tried in small ways to sabotage some of my cases, but I'd been damned good—though she didn't look at it that way. I'd won most despite her efforts.

And then Susan met loony Lorraine and was able to hatch her glorious payback scheme, designed to drive me to leave town in disgrace. Better yet, to commit suicide.

It hadn't been hard for her to duplicate my

house and car keys or even my gate opener, plus steal my security code info, when I worked for MSY. She had clumsily planted the obviously manufactured evidence of the break-in that I'd claimed was how someone had got a copy of the strategy memo. Therefore, it appeared as if I'd staged it. She also planted the stickier stuff that pointed to me: phone calls from my house to Lorraine, money inexplicably deposited into my bank account. Of course she'd gotten into my purse to copy my account number.

The ethics thing went as she'd hoped. Susan was ecstatic when I lost everything I'd worked for, at least temporarily—my beloved legal career, my means of making a living. And I'd even been forced to agree to it. Then, I'd had to take on something menial. But I wasn't supposed to like it. And certainly not seem thrilled about it. So she decided to do more.

But merely sabotaging my new pet-sitting business wouldn't have been enough. She'd decided to do it with a bang—though not with a gun, but a knife: She killed poor Carl.

She knew he was coming home early thanks to his attempt to get my phone number from Avvie.

"Know why I chose him?" she asked in a confidential tone that made my neck hairs stand and shimmy. "He'd been around the office lately on some business deal. Must have figured I was still in touch and gave a damn about you, so he kept talking about you. He'd hired you to pet-sit, said he'd refer legal business your way when you got your license back. With his help, you'd get to make some other defendants suffer like my poor parents did. So, it was both poetic and actual justice for me to kill him and make it look like you did it. And of course he knew me. When I showed up at his place and said you'd sent me, he so graciously let me in."

But I wasn't arrested. I didn't give up and get out. Susan had to kill another customer, Shirley, and make it appear that I was the dastardly culprit. She'd started a pseudonymous e-mail correspondence with Shirley on the pretext of being a potential PR client and had used it that fateful day to get info on Shirley's early return. Like Carl, Shirley had met Susan at the MSY office, knew she'd been my assistant, and let her into her house as my erstwhile emissary.

Hadn't a fleeting thought of Carl's murder in his own home crossed Shirley's mind and suggested that letting *anyone* in might be a mistake? If so, it had slipped right on through in the presence of mild-looking, middle-aged Susan.

Not only that, Susan somehow convinced Shirley to go ahead and unpack while the surrogate pet-sitter saw to Rosie in the kitchen. Good time to grab the knife and sneak up on her victim in the bedroom. Susan had even found the extra set of instructions I insisted on keeping in the kitchen, so she knew how to reset Shirley's security system when she left.

On top of it all, Susan had tried to make it look like I was railroading my staunchest supporter, Darryl. But even that didn't work. Susan worried that my doggedness might lead me to the truth. Trying to nip that in the bud, she came to my apartment in the dead of night on a day she'd heard from Avvie that I was sleeping at a client's. Of course she still had the key. I'd nearly caught her in my garage, apparently, but she still managed to plant a knife from Carl Cuthbertson's stolen set. And still I survived.

She tried to drag in Judge Baird Roehmann as either the murderer or next victim, but both fell apart. She'd been delighted to hear about the TRO and only too happy to make sure it looked as if I'd breached it. She "borrowed" my Beamer and drove it to Baird's, to do the damage to his pricey Jaguar.

"Even then you weren't arrested," she growled. But then she brightened. She'd taken short-term leases in both Carl's—and Isabelle's—neighborhood and my own. "Did you know that as a neighbor by rental, I've gone to parties at your house when you weren't invited?" She smirked. "I've become buddies with your tenant, Charlotte. She's very nice. But now I've gotten tired of the games. I have to kill you. That's the only way."

"Are you ready to give up your freedom or more, just to pay me back for a . . . lapse in judgment?" Not that my case against the Vanners had been anything like that, but I had to say something to appease Susan. She was the one with the gun.

"I won't have to. Know where I got this?" She waved the weapon in a manner that made me worry that the damned thing would go off.

"Can't say that I do."

"From Avvie's desk. In a locked drawer, but I'm her secretary. I know where the keys are. And I know the two of you have been angry with one another lately."

"Not as of tonight," I told her, wondering why Avvie had a gun in her desk. Hopefully I'd live to worry about that another time. "We kissed and made up. Right in front of Bill."

"Don't get smart with me. I'll make everyone believe Avvie killed you. I eavesdropped before, heard that she and Mr. Sergement were meeting you for dinner, so I knew this was my opportunity. You'd have been seen together. I even called the guards downstairs, said I was Avvie and that you were coming up for a late meeting tonight, so they should let you in."

And I'd been worried about getting caught for having a duplicate card key. Damn. I was getting even more perturbed with this obviously disturbed woman. If only I could disarm her. With a smile. Better yet, with a weapon of my own.

"I even made sure that your . . . friend, Jeff Hubbard, is away. He's got a website for his security business, you know. I found the name of one of his out-of-town clients there, made up a disaster in a building where he installed a system, and gave him a call. Said I was that client's assistant and sounded all frantic. What is he to you, anyway?"

"My pet-sitting customer."

"Right."

"He is!" I protested her sarcastic tone. If he were more, I couldn't put a label on it. Other than "good in bed." Better than good. And if I wanted the chance to try him out anymore . . . "Susan, look. You have me where you want me. My life is in shambles thanks to you. Even if I tell anyone what you've said, they'll never believe me." Not exactly true, but she didn't need to know otherwise. "But if you fire that gun, think of the mess you'll create for yourself." And me.

"Don't worry." Yikes, was her grin malevolent. It gave me goosebumps. But better bumps than holes . . . "I know about gun residue and finger-prints and things like that. They won't find any evidence to link me with your murder. I'm not even still in the building, according to computer records. I figured out long ago how to double back and confuse things."

I recalled her versatility with all things techno-logical and believed she'd undoubtedly outsmarted the building's security.

Damn it.

"Okay, let's get this over with," she said, standing, motioning for me to do likewise.

"You've done an excellent job planning," I said, still sitting and stalling. I had an idea, but would it work?

"Of course I did." She sounded impatient. "Get up, or I'll shoot you where you are."

"All right. One last sip." I reached for my coffee mug. It probably had cooled some, but—

She laughed. "I *knew* you'd consider burning me with a cup of hot coffee, but don't even try it."

"I wouldn't think of it." I lifted the mug anyway, moving it slowly to where I wanted it—and not to my mouth. "So what are you going to do next?" I asked casually, to buy a little time. "I mean once Avvie's arrested for my murder. Do you plan to stay with the firm? Or now that you're experienced, have you thought of becoming a hit-woman? Now, that's an interesting idea."

It was then I felt the movement I'd anticipated.

Almost immediately, Susan screamed. And fired.

CHAPTER 33

I ducked. The motion was enough to propel Pythagoras, whose head was already waving in the air, from my pocket. Confused, the poor serpent slithered in Susan's direction before I could grab him.

She still had the gun in her hands, and it waved madly. I had to do something.

The only thing I could figure was something stupid. Like a self-defense maneuver Jeff had demonstrated for me after he claimed to have bought into my assertion that I was being railroaded. I hadn't tried it before, but hey, who needed to rehearse when her life was at stake?

I shrieked a sound similar to what I'd heard martial arts gurus do in movies, propelled myself into a roll on the floor, and when I stopped revolving, used my legs to pull Susan's out from under her. At the same time, I grabbed upward for the gun.

To my amazement, I got it.

She was still screaming when I realized how close I was to flopping onto poor, scared Py. I pointed the gun at her, hoping I knew how to use it.

"Cool it, Susan," I directed, my eardrums chiming like xylophones. Could I hold the weapon and dial a phone at the same time? How hard could it be? Not as bad as rubbing your stomach while patting your head. And I'd mastered that as a kid.

As it turned out, I didn't have to. I heard a noise from the hall, and suddenly the small kitchen was surrounded by a bunch of those uniformed security guys. They had guns, too. And all of them were pointed right into the room.

It didn't take long for Detective Ned Noralles to arrive, once I'd suggested to the guards his interest in matters concerning me, his favorite suspect.

Downtown wasn't his jurisdiction, but he came anyway.

Considering his usually gleeful demeanor, his brown eyes looked awfully irritable. Or maybe he was simply sleepy. His swarthy skin had a sheen, as if he were sweating. Or maybe he'd rushed straight from his shower.

He and I remained in the kitchen. Other cops, probably those supposed to work downtown, had taken Susan to a conference room. I could imagine what she was saying.

The detective kept eyeing my suit jacket. I'd managed to maneuver around Py and recapture him before he found his way into the building's infrastructure. Otherwise, I could just imagine how the management's disclosures to tenants of phantom pythons in the walls would go over.

Py was back in my pocket now, a calm little coil once more.

"And you just happened to have a snake with you this evening?" Noralles demanded.

"He was lonely today," I explained. "His owner has been out of town longer than expected, and poor Py was so crushed that he wouldn't eat his mouse this morning. I figured he'd feel better if I kept him with me."

Of course I'd meant to bring him home before, but in my rush downtown to save the files, I'd downright forgotten the little ball python was even balled up in my pocket.

"Now tell me exactly how the snake happened to jump from your pocket and distract Ms. Feeney." Skepticism oozed from the detective. But I had become inured to dealing with his doubt.

"He didn't just happen to jump at the right time. I got him to move."

"You issue commands to a snake?"

"In a manner of speaking." I smiled.

"Then speak about it, Ms. Ballantyne." He didn't sound amused.

I explained how Milt, Py's owner, had said that ball pythons reacted to heat. They hibernate lethargically in coolness, but get them close to a source of warmth and they're all energy.

A source of warmth like a hot coffee mug pressed against my pocket.

"I see." The cynical tone wavered, thank heavens. "And you maintain that Ms. Feeney tricked you here so she could kill you." Not a question but a statement, one the speaker clearly didn't buy.

"That's right."

"Exactly why did she do that?"

"I don't need to tell you, Detective." At his glare, I reached into my purse and pulled out the item I'd been able to turn on just in time, before Susan really started talking.

The little voice-activated tape recorder that, like my card key to the Marden firm office, I'd never quite gotten around to removing from my big, beautiful, bulky purse.

CHAPTER 34

I was only too eager to give a statement to the police this time. I didn't even bother waking Esther from her beauty sleep to be by my side as guardian angel and advocate.

I did insist that Noralles provide an instant copy of the tape from my recorder. Those things can be doctored, though I doubted that would happen. I might not always agree with Noralles's assumptions and accusations, but I'd no reason to doubt his integrity.

He sure treated me with a whole lot more respect during this interview than ever before.

And unlike the outcomes of my prior interviews, this one resulted in an incarceration.

Susan Feeney's, not mine.

It was almost dawn when I headed back toward the Valley.

First stop, Milt Abadim's. It was long past time to put poor Py back into familiar surroundings. I only wished I knew what to give him as a special treat. A freshly defrosted mouse, rather than the one I'd stuck back in the fridge? A live one too sedated to attack him? But how could I drug a rodent, let alone find one?

In Milt's living room, I gently extracted the balled-up blue-and-pink Py from my pocket and let him unravel in his glass enclosure. "See you soon, my slithery friend," I told him in heartfelt gratitude. This small, brilliant-colored serpent had saved my life.

I would call Milt later that morning to thank him.

Now, though, it was time to head for Jeff's. Good thing Lexie was there with Odin. At least she wouldn't be lonesome. Though I expected both solid and liquid presents from the pups when I arrived.

To my surprise, all was clean and they weren't alone. Jeff was there, waiting.

"You've had quite a night," he said. As if he had to tell me. But how did he know?

"I've got my sources," he responded when I asked.

"You've talked to Noralles?"

"A few minutes ago. After I got the word."

"From the redoubtable Althea's Internet research?"

"You got it."

"What I don't get," I said, "was how something like last night's events could be on the World Wide Web so soon. Isn't it confidential?"

"Let's just say that the report is already partway into police records . . . and leave it at that."

Ah, so the extraordinary Althea wasn't just any

high-tech guru. If I had to guess, I'd say she had a habit of hacking.

"Tell me everything," Jeff said. "I've got coffee brewing."

"Ah, coffee. It plays a major role in my tale."

"Your tail?" He gave a great suggestive grin as he guided me toward the kitchen by means of his hand on that particular part of my anatomy.

"Give it a rest, Hubbard," I said, although, despite my exhaustion, my body did manage to give a heated reaction to his groping hand. "Tell me how you happen to be back here. I thought Susan sent you off on a wild goose chase."

"She did. Worst part was, the first time I got through to my client, I was already on the plane, frantic to find the system's flaw that allowed his building to be burgled. Turned out everything was copasetic. No burglaries. No problems. And no phone calls to me from him or any of his administrators for the last week. I headed right home, figuring someone wanted me gone. I just didn't know who or why. Now I do, though I'm not sure I'd have been much help unless you'd stopped back here to enlist a security consultant before deciding to sneak into your old building. That's what you did, I gather, from the sketchy details I've gotten. So let's hear it."

I told him everything, and when I was through I was gratified by his big smile. "Hey, Ballantyne, you done good. Want a job?"

"You're hiring lawyers now?"

"No, but you'd make a good investigator."

"The thing is, Hubbard, now that I expect to be exonerated, I should be able to practice law again soon."

"And you want to?"

"Absolutely." I was a damned good lawyer, ethics and all.

The odd thing was, though, as angry as I was about Susan's sabotage of everything I once held sacrosanct, the idea of going back to my old life—despite my devastation at losing it—didn't sound as inviting as I expected.

But if not that, then what the hell would I do with the rest of my life?

Pet-sitting was fun, but I didn't see it as my ultimate career. At least not without more.

But more *what*?

Good thing Lexie leapt on my lap just then to distract the dizzying cartwheels of my cogitation. And at least I was finally taking control of my life once more.

It was later that same day. I'd taken a shower and a nice, long nap after my morning's pet-sitting rounds. I awakened around noon and found a note from Jeff. He had a different trip planned that afternoon, the one for which he'd already recruited me to tend to Odin.

His note said he'd postponed it. Could we get together that night?

I'd think about it before calling him, though at

341

that moment I couldn't come up with a reason why not.

Until I thought about my conversation with Susan Feeney—the part when she'd asked me what was between us.

Damned if I knew, even after our discussion on relationships a couple of days back. Maybe I'd take some time and find out.

I made some calls, did some rounds. And then I sat in my usual spot in Darryl's office while Lexie romped in the playroom with a passel of pups.

I'd been telling a grinning Darryl all about the events of the night before when Fran Korwald threw open the door.

"You're a genius! Kendra, I don't know how to thank you." She dashed over to give me a hug. It nearly squeezed my breath away before I recalled that this middle-aged woman in teenage clothes was a personal trainer. She had muscles.

"So what's going on?" I asked once she'd released me.

"It worked just as you said. I bought one of Isabelle's puppies—they're adorable, by the way. I brought him home while Rubin was still packing. Piglet was horrified when I brought in the puppy. I sat Rubin down in the kitchen while the two dogs got acquainted, though of course they won't spend more than a short while together. I let Rubin know he'd won. I'd decided it wasn't in Piglet's best interests for us to fight over him, and it wasn't in my best interests to be dog-less, so I'd bought myself another pup. Rubin could have Piglet to take to Alaska."

"Is that how things turned out?" I waited breathlessly. What I'd advised had involved reverse psychology—and I was a temporarily defrocked litigator, not a shrink. But those mischievous puppies of Helga's had certainly gotten my attention.

"Of course not!" Fran giggled. "It was just as you said. Rubin looked at sweet, roly-poly Piglet, then he looked at the cute, shaggy, manly Siberian husky. All of a sudden, he decided it was time we put this all behind us. He'd make the sacrifice, for me, and for old times' sake. He'd take the puppy to the wilds of Alaska and let Piglet stay with me. Oh, Kendra, you should have heard me hemming and hawing and acting disappointed that I wouldn't have the brand-new puppy I'd just picked out. But I didn't carry on too long, for fear he'd change his mind. And I certainly didn't mention that the husky would go much better with the image of a man heading toward the wilderness. My lawyer is drawing up the papers today. Thank you, thank you."

"You're welcome." I laughed. It could have had a very different result, of course. She hugged me again, then left. I sat there, sharing a smile with Darryl.

"Hey, Kendra," my thin-faced friend said. "Things are looking up for you."

"You bet." My mind was doing the same kind of somersaults I'd done to get the gun from Susan, awkward flipflops that seemed right, but that I hadn't practiced before.

Ideas were flitting through it.

Ideas about my future.

See, part of litigating is negotiating mutually acceptable settlements, and what I'd helped to do with Fran Korwald was even more critical to today's court system: a form of intervention to avoid down-and-dirty court appearances.

Plus, the legal research I'd done had uncovered an area I'd never looked into before: pet law.

One day soon I'd be able to practice law again. Where, how, with whom—those all were yet to be seen. But wherever I landed, I had a feeling I had just added a new twist to it: doggy dispute resolution. Animal arbitration. Mediation of the unhuman kind. As an adjunct to my pet-sitting, protracting the pleasure of it forever, it was a combo that couldn't lose.

"You thinking about your future?" Darryl was once again attuned to my thoughts. He stood and straightened his green logo shirt.

"Yes, the law. And negotiations."

"Speaking of negotiations, any idea what's happening with Carl Cuthbertson's company?"

I grinned at him. "You still thinking about breaking into show biz?"

He shrugged.

"Actually, I spoke with Conrad Taylor about it today," I admitted. "I talked again with Isabelle to alleviate her concerns about the good home

Helga's puppy was going to have, either here or in Alaska. Afterward, she finally gave me a good enough description of the guy in the suit that I thought I could ID him. Sure enough, Taylor admitted he'd been at Carl's around the time his new buddy was killed but had been afraid to say so. Now that there's good suspect in custody, he figured he could tell the truth. He happened to have seen a car resembling Susan Feeney's parked on the street. He noticed it because it nearly ran into him when it left in a hurry."

"Good deal."

"No, bad deal, actually. After I told him to 'fess up to Noralles, he told me that Laurie Shinnick, Cuthbertson's daughter, put the kibosh on the sale of the company to Millipede." Which didn't bring a single tear to my eye. Not when it meant that Conrad lost his finder's fee. Buddies with Carl or not, after what he'd pulled in the past, I didn't think he deserved a cent from Carl's company.

"What a shame."

I didn't bother to contradict Darryl. He wasn't looking at me anyway, but through the glass into his beloved doggy day spa. A couple of people had just walked in. I didn't recognize either of them.

"Have you met Cheryl Sallar?" he asked, nodding toward the women. "The one with the Bedlington terrier named Lamb Chop."

I shook my head.

"She's a new client," he said. "Lamb Chop's a champion, retired from the show ring but not from stud service. Cheryl mentioned to me yesterday that she's involved in a dispute with the owner of a Bedlington bitch over a stud fee. I'll introduce you to her."

"Good idea, Darryl," I said with a smile. Who knew? Maybe Cheryl needed a pet-sitter. Better yet . . .

Cute little Lamb Chop and his studly service might just give me a leg up on a whole different direction for my legal career.

ACKNOWLEDGMENTS

Kendra and Lexie would like especially to thank Paige Wheeler of Creative Media Agency, Inc., Linda O. Johnston's wonderful agent, without whom their stories would not be told. They would also like to thank their excellent editors at Berkley Prime Crime, Cindy Hwang and Susan McCarty, for their discrimination in selecting the Kendra Ballantyne, Esq., Pet-Sitter mysteries for publication.

And, yes, they acknowledge Fred Johnston, Linda's husband, to whom she dedicates all her books. Lexie in particular thinks he's an okay guy—he's always surreptitiously treating her real, live counterpart. Kendra, not trusting her taste in men, reserves judgment.